GOTTA B

GOTTA B

Claire Carmichael

RANDOM HOUSE AUSTRALIA

A Random House book
Published by Random House Australia Pty Ltd
Level 3, 100 Pacific Highway, North Sydney NSW 2060
www.randomhouse.com.au

First published by Random House Australia in 2009

Addresses for companies within the Random House Group can be found at
www.randomhouse.com.au/offices.

National Library of Australia
Cataloguing-in-Publication Entry

Author: Carmichael, Claire.
Title: Gotta B / Claire Carmichael.
ISBN: 978 1 74166 298 6 (pbk.)
Target Audience: For secondary school age.
Dewey Number: A823.3

Cover photograph courtesy Getty Images
Cover design by Ellie Exarchos
Internal design by Midland Typesetters
Typeset in 12/15pt Adobe Garamond by Midland Typesetters, Australia
Printed and bound by Griffin Press, South Australia

Random House Australia uses papers that are natural, renewable and recyclable
products and made from wood grown in sustainable forests. The logging
and manufacturing processes are expected to conform to the environmental
regulations of the country of origin.

10 9 8 7 6 5 4 3 2 1

For Sheila

ONE

Tal stifled a yawn. So far Monday at Braidworth High had been typical – interesting one minute, dull the next. Science was promising to be particularly mind-numbing.

'Did you hear?' said Rick, joining Tal in the corridor. 'They reckon Carter Renfrew's coming to the school next week.'

Tal looked up from texting on his iZod. 'Who?'

'You know, the scientist guy who says kids are evolving into a new digital race.'

'Oh, *that* Carter Renfrew,' said Tal, going back to his texting. 'There are always rumours about him.'

'Word is, he's going to ask for volunteers for some new research project.' Rick grinned. 'I'll be first in line. You get paid, and maybe get excused from some classes. Couldn't be better.'

Tal's iZod buzzed: U GUYS HVE GR8 TIME W/PEAS

AS IF, he sent back to Petra.

Beside him, Rick was peering at the little screen of his own iZod and smiling as he tapped in SOOOO BOOORRING.

Back came a reply from Jennie. B NICE TO VEGGIE.

'It's not fair,' Rick said as they filed into the science room. 'Petra and Jennie have all the luck, while we're stuck with the Cabbage raving on about experiments with peas.'

'If you were into sport,' Tal pointed out, 'you could get out of class too.'

'Sport? No way. Not even if I could be a hot super-jock babe magnet like you, *Talbot*.'

Tal laughed. 'This too could be your life. Why not join me for an early morning run tomorrow?'

Rick's derisive reply was drowned by the gravel voice of Mr Babbage, the head science teacher. 'Blair, Lawrence, turn those communicators off, right now, or you're on detention.'

Rick sketched a salute. 'Yes, sir! Quick smart, sir!'

'Watch it, Lawrence,' Babbage growled, but there was a slight smile on his face.

Tal glanced at Rick, amused that even someone as gross as the science teacher had a soft spot for his friend. Rick was slightly built, with floppy dark hair and a mischievous smile. But there was a sad, vulnerable side to him that brought out a protective streak in the most unlikely people.

'Just made it,' David gasped as he skidded to a halt beside them.

Babbage scowled. 'Another moment, Segal, and

you'd be looking at detention.' His frown deepened. 'The other two – Petra and Jennie – where are they?'

'On the basketball team playing Hawthorne High.'

The teacher grunted. 'Waste of time.'

The Five, as they'd been called since kindergarten, were Tal, Rick, Petra, David and Jennie. They'd been grouped together on their first day of primary school, and for some reason hit it off from the beginning. A teacher had jokingly called them the Five, and it had stuck. There was an element of self-mockery to the name now, but their allegiance to each other had endured.

'How's your grandfather?' Tal asked Rick as they made their way to their desks. Les Lawrence had had a bad fall from a ladder while cleaning gutters two weeks earlier and was in hospital.

Suddenly serious, Rick shook his head. 'Not good. He's still in a coma.'

'Hurry up,' Babbage bellowed as the class settled in. 'We'll begin our unit on genetics with a revision of Mendel's experiments with pea plants.'

'Can't wait,' someone said.

Tal glanced over at Allyx, who had her blonde head bent, surreptitiously texting while apparently studying the diagram displayed on her desk monitor. Tal looked at her with pleasure. They'd only recently become an item, and he had to admit he was proud to be seen with her.

Tal's iZod vibrated in his pocket. He smiled when he read Allyx's message: DONT 4GET BrawnBlasters 2NITE

Allyx and Petra had been lucky enough to get into video game design, an elective course so wildly popular that the school had to run a ballot system to select students for the class. Allyx and Petra had been the first team to complete the assignment to create an original video game. *BrawnBlasters* was to have its world premiere at Petra's house tonight.

Tal sent back GR8 QT, then, knowing Allyx would have sent the message to the Five as well, he glanced at Rick and raised his eyebrows.

Rick mouthed 'What?' Tal tapped his iZod.

Rick was frowning at his communicator when Babbage leaned over him. 'I gather, Mr Lawrence, you're not finding nineteenth-century genetics to your liking?'

Without waiting for an answer, Babbage put out a fat, freckled hand for Rick's iZod. 'Give it to me.'

'I wasn't using it,' Rick protested. 'Can't, 'cause it's not working.'

'Then you won't be needing it back.'

'But –'

It was an empty threat. Teachers couldn't confiscate communication devices because they were so vital to the school's interactions with students. Most families had stopped bothering with desktop PCs or laptops. Instead they had full-size screens and keyboards that could connect wirelessly to individuals' communicators. School timetable changes, scheduled excursions, homework, class assignments and health and security alerts were sent electronically to students' comms — as were notices to parents' devices on students' progress.

Babbage told Rick to collect his iZod at the end of the period, then lumbered to the front, swung around and surveyed the class. He pursed his lips as he looked for a fresh victim, picking a dark, shy girl who was new to the school. 'Here's your chance, Felicity, to astound us with your knowledge. Explain how Mendel's findings uncovered the basics of heredity.'

'Ummm . . .'

'That's your response?' A pause. 'Well, *is* it?'

Felicity blushed brick red.

Babbage gestured towards her. 'Behold, ladies and gentlemen: the pinnacle of evolution, *Homo sapiens*. And all she can say in reply to a simple question is "ummm".'

'You've got it wrong,' said David's mocking voice from behind Tal. 'Felicity's actually *Homo electronicus*, the next step in evolution. Sorry to have to tell you, Mr Babbage, but you're a seriously superseded model.'

Several people laughed. Babbage narrowed his piggy eyes. 'Who said that? Segal? Was it you playing the fool again?'

Tal twisted around to grin at David. He was the class clown, always eager to liven up dull lessons. Whippet-thin, his head a little too large for his body, David sat smiling cheerfully at the teacher.

'Haven't you read *Brains in Flux: Evolution and the Teen Mind*?' David asked. He added helpfully, 'I can lend you my copy if you like.'

'Segal, your insolence has won you a detention,' Babbage snapped.

Not at all put out, David said, 'Well? Have you read Dr Renfrew's book? It's a bestseller.'

'They say Renfrew's going to be at the school next week,' someone called out.

'The man's theory is absolute garbage,' Babbage declared with a contemptuous snort. 'Not to put too fine a point on it, Carter Renfrew is a charlatan.'

He stabbed a thick forefinger at Felicity, who literally shrank back in her seat. 'Here's an easy question – what's a charlatan? Well? Let's have your definition.'

Tal hated the way Babbage took pleasure in bullying. He opened his mouth to answer for Felicity, but before he could speak, Allyx said, 'A charlatan's a phony. A fake.'

'I didn't ask your opinion, Allyx.'

'Sorry, sir,' she said with a demure smile.

Babbage wasn't immune to Allyx's charm. 'It so happens you're correct,' he conceded. 'Renfrew *is* a phony and a fake. And to say you kids are evolving into superior beings –' he sneered – 'is more than ludicrous – it's totally absurd. Now to return to a *real* scientist . . .'

Tal looked over at Allyx and rolled his eyes. 'Save me,' he whispered.

Allyx laughed and put up her hand. 'Mr Babbage, before you go on, could you just briefly explain Dr Renfrew's theory?' She gave the teacher her most winning smile. 'Please? I'd like to know what all the fuss is about.'

Realising this was an excellent diversionary technique, several students made affirmative noises.

'Please?' Allyx repeated.

'Oh, very well,' said Babbage. 'I suppose it could be useful to get through your thick skulls that this is an example of pop science at its worst. In short, Renfrew's "theory" is that your generation, having lived immersed in an electronic environment from birth, show structural changes in your brains that indicate you are developing into a new species of humankind. Your children, according to his wild-eyed thesis, will carry these changes in their genes. Anyone who's studied genetics at all knows it's hogwash.'

'But we *are* different,' David declared, 'just like Dr Renfrew says. My dad's clueless about half the applications on his comm. And he can't even program his new entertainment centre. It's all way beyond him, but it couldn't be simpler for me.'

There was a murmur of agreement. 'My olds are, like, total dinosaurs,' announced Maryann Dodd, current queen bee of the school. On cue, Tiffany and Kimba, two members of her clique, giggled appreciatively. Encouraged, Maryann repeated, 'Total dinosaurs. Like, they should be extinct.'

This got a laugh. Maryann looked around, pleased with herself.

Maryann was tiny, with a pretty doll's face, pale blue eyes, and very long brown hair she wore loose so she could toss it around in a move Tal reckoned she'd practised a thousand times. She could be charming,

7

but behind her smile was a cruel streak that had made Maryann and her clique rightly feared. If they took a set against someone, they'd make that person's life a misery.

Tal suspected that Maryann was behind the recent spate of vicious cyber attacks on teachers and students at the school. Even the principal, Mr Constanza, had been mercilessly sent up in a video posted to VidYou, where he was portrayed as a bumbling idiot who had no idea what was going on under his nose.

Tal thought she was pure poison and did his best to avoid her, even though she acted as though they'd been close since early childhood. He was cynical enough to put this down to his own position in the school. Maryann wouldn't have bothered to give him the time of day if he hadn't been good at sport, and therefore popular.

There were a few people Maryann favoured. She'd always had a soft spot for Rick, though Tal had no idea why, since Rick mostly ignored her.

'Back to work!' snarled Babbage, breaking into the buzz of conversation about parents' technical shortcomings. 'You've got better things to do than discuss a ridiculous theory peddled by a man who is a virtual nonentity in the scientific world.'

'But Dr Renfrew's famous,' a student remarked.

'And you're not,' someone sniggered.

Fury turned Babbage's heavy features brick red. 'Who said that?' Unable to locate the culprit, he snapped, 'I'll be setting extra homework for the lot of you . . .'

Finally the siren signalled the end of the period. In a few moments, almost everyone in the room seemed to be instant messaging on their communicators.

Rick went to the front to collect his iZod. Tal watched his friend walk slowly back to them, peering down at the little device in his hand, his face creased with worry.

'I've run an auto-diagnostic,' Rick said, 'and there's nothing wrong – it just won't work for me.'

'No biggie,' said Allyx. 'Why don't you get a new one and have it keyed to your bio constants?'

Rick ran a hand through his hair until it stood up in dark spikes. 'Easy for you to say, but it's not just my comm. At home this morning I couldn't send tweets, or get through to MySpace or Facebook. I tried using Thelma's old PC. She's a bit clueless with computers, so she registered me as a co-user. No luck. I still couldn't connect.'

'Why didn't you say anything before?' Allyx asked.

'I thought it would be fixed, like it always is, and that it just happened to be taking longer than usual.'

Tal could see from Allyx's expression that she too realised Rick's situation could be much more serious than just the failure of his iZod. One device might fail, but if Rick couldn't connect through a PC either, it was possible his identity had dropped out of Commdat, the government's master communication database. Convicted criminals and designated enemies of the state had their names deregistered, but it was almost unheard of for an ordinary person to become a disconnect for more than a few moments.

'Don't worry, Rick, probably just some glitch,' Allyx said supportively.

Rick remained unconvinced. They all knew that outages were rectified almost immediately and that multiple redundant circuits existed to ensure there was no interruption to anyone's access to the vast electronic sea that enveloped the world.

'Maybe the problem started with Farront, and not Commdat,' Tal said.

Farront International was one of the so-called Big Three – the three huge companies providing the majority of the world's communications. Each company had developed a state-of-the-art communications device used by the majority of their customers: Farront the iZod, Tacitcomm the Cascader, and Brownbolt the BeauBrute.

'Give it another try,' Allyx suggested. 'Commdat's probably got your service up and running again.'

It was no use Allyx or Tal trying to get Rick's iZod to work. A biometric security system keyed devices such as personal communicators to an individual, so borrowing or stealing such items had become pointless. Using unique biological constants, including fingerprints, retinal markings and facial heat patterns, Rick's iZod was programmed to recognise him as the registered user, locking out anyone else.

His fingers danced over the input screen, but it remained obstinately blank. 'There's power and it's receiving a signal, but it's dead to me,' he said despairingly.

David, on his way to his next class, stopped to say with a grin, 'Any chance you've been made a disconnect on purpose? Maybe you have some secret life we know nothing about.'

Allyx shot David a cold look. 'That is so not funny. Don't even joke about being disconnected.'

David, who rarely took anything seriously, clapped Rick on the shoulder. 'Baaaad news, dude. You know you've just *gotta* be connected.'

TWO

The bus transporting the basketball team drew up at the front gate of Braidworth High just as the last bell signalled the end of the school day. Petra and Jennie met up with Tal and David as they came trooping out of class.

'How did you go?' Tal asked.

'Awesome,' said Petra, shaking her dark hair free of a ponytail. 'We thrashed the Hawthorne High team. As usual, Jennie ran them off their tiny feet.'

Tal grinned at Jennie. 'MVP again?'

Jennie shrugged modestly. She was frequently named most valuable player, but preferred not to fuss about her athletic skills. She wasn't tall – her parents were from Seoul, and Jennie had inherited the South Korean slight build and short stature, but she was a dynamite point guard, who could change direction with lightning speed and wrong-foot taller, heavier opponents with deceptive ease.

'While you girls were beating the pants off Hawthorne,' said David, 'Rick got himself disconnected.'

Petra and Jennie looked astonished. 'Omigod!' Petra exclaimed. 'Rick a DC? You've got to be kidding.'

'Would I lie to you?' David gestured towards Rick, who was approaching. 'Ask him yourself.'

Rick was shambling along with sagging shoulders and a grim expression. Tal guessed there hadn't been a quick solution to his problem.

'We heard about your disconnection,' Jennie said when Rick joined them. 'So what's new?'

Rick drooped a bit more. 'Could hardly be worse.'

'Ever the optimist,' Petra teased. 'It's not that big a deal, is it?' she asked, trying to cheer him up. 'Your iZod isn't working, that's all.'

'It's more than that,' said Rick in tones of deepest doom. 'Much more.'

Petra raised her eyebrows. 'How much more?'

'It started this morning at home. I couldn't get online. No matter what I did, I couldn't connect.'

He looked so totally woebegone that Tal wasn't surprised when Petra grinned. 'Oh, come on. It can't be that bad.'

'I tell you, I can't do *anything*!' Rick exclaimed, his face screwed up with frustration. 'I can't listen to music, I can't phone, I can't IM, I can't blog, I can't pay for anything, I can't play *TrueSim* or *Worldstrider* with you guys. I can't even do my homework.'

'No homework? That's a real blow,' said David, laughing.

Ever practical, Jennie asked, 'Did you go to the school Communications Unit for help?'

'Yeah, the school will be mad keen to get you connected again,' said David. 'You know how teachers hate it if you've got a real excuse not to do their lame assignments. And if you want an example of lame assignments, check out what Babbage expects us to do for Friday's class.'

Rick glared at him. 'Well, that's the whole point, isn't it? I *can't* check it out.'

'So did you go to the CU?' Petra asked.

'Do I look stupid?' Rick snapped with uncharacteristic anger.

'I won't answer that,' David chortled.

Rick ignored him. 'Of course I went straight to the Communications Unit, not that it did any good. Kotner – you know, the geeky guy who sweats all the time – started off saying he'd get me connected again in a couple of minutes, no worries. He tried for half an hour, and then just gave up. Said he couldn't help because the problem was with Commdat.'

'But Commdat's got so many checks and balances it's supposed to be error proof,' said Jennie. 'At least that's what Ms Ingram says.'

'Like Ingram would know,' said David with a sardonic laugh. 'She's waaay behind on anything technical. Had to explain to her how botnets worked the other day. I mean, I know she's only an English teacher, but botnets? *Everybody* knows about them.'

'Ms Ingram does too,' said Jennie. 'She was just letting you play the expert about hijacked PCs.'

'No way!' exclaimed David, highly irritated. 'I'm telling you, she didn't have a clue.'

Rick wasn't interested in the extent of Ms Ingram's technical knowledge. 'So I ask Kotner what I should do, since he was a dead loss as far as getting me connected again. He said he'd authorise me to use the school interface to contact the government's Citizen Assist site, so I could register a denial of service appeal.'

Rick added with a bitter laugh, 'And then Kotner said it'd speed things up if I got my parents involved.'

Nobody commented. Rick's parents had been dead for many years and he'd been brought up by his elderly grandparents. They weren't remotely interested in modern technology, and with Rick's grandfather in hospital, his grandmother already had plenty to worry about.

'Okay,' said Petra, 'so you logged onto Citizen Assist. What happened then?'

'The usual run-around. It took ages to register and to finally get to the Facilitation and Support section. I've been designated a Code Three, so I have to wait while more urgent Code Ones and Twos get fixed.'

'So how long?' Tal asked.

'Would you believe at least seven days? A *whole week*! I complained, of course, but the F & S service provider kept saying my problem was important to them and would be dealt with at the earliest possible time, which just happened to be seven days.' He groaned. 'I hate those simulated people. It's creepy the way the computer makes them look like you.'

Facial modelling was a recent development. As soon as a government website identified the individual logging on, it would use that person's biometrics to subtly alter the face and gender of the simulated service provider, who would appear on the screen to say in warm, helpful tones, 'In what way may I assist you?'

'Ms Ingram says the facial resemblance is to encourage you to accept what you're being told, because you're more likely to believe someone who looks like you.'

David made a face at Jennie. 'I'm telling you, don't listen to Ingram. She doesn't know what's she's talking about.'

'You're just mad at her because she gave you a failing grade in our last essay assignment,' Petra pointed out.

'You didn't do too well yourself,' David retorted. 'Anyway, it was a dumb question. "How does the world end – with a bang or a whimper?" Who cares?'

'I do, actually,' said Petra. 'No way do I want it to end while I'm still around. It's okay if it's a zillion years in the future.'

'*My* world's pretty well ended now,' said Rick mournfully.

'You're such a worrywart!' Petra slipped an arm around his waist and gave him a half hug. 'Come on – it's only a week.'

Rick refused to be comforted. 'What if it goes on forever?'

'Never happen,' said David, 'but if it does, there are things you can do about it.'

'Like what?' Tal asked.

David looked mysterious. 'There are ways of beating the system. Ask George Everett – he and his geek friends can do practically anything.'

Jennie frowned. 'We're not talking legal ways, are we?'

With a laugh, David said, 'Hell, no.'

'Don't you get an automatic lifetime disconnect if you try something like that?' Tal asked. David always had some scheme to get around things.

'Only if you're dumb enough to get caught.'

'With my luck, I *would* get caught,' said Rick despondently, 'so anything illegal is out.'

'Oh, cheer up.' Petra gave him a playful jab in the ribs. 'My guess is you'll be reconnected in no time.'

'And if I'm not? What if I'm *never* reconnected?'

Grinning, David punched Rick on the shoulder. 'Then you might as well be dead.' He added quickly, 'Only joking.'

THREE

'I hope Rick makes it tonight,' Petra said as she and Jennie turned the corner into her street. 'He has to see his grandfather in hospital first.'

Allyx had a practice session with the school band, so Jennie had volunteered to come straight from school and help Petra set up for the premiere of *Brawn-Blasters*.

'It was a bad fall, wasn't it? Have you heard how he is?'

'When I asked Rick, he said Les wasn't all that good. He's still unconscious.' The corners of Petra's mouth turned down. 'Omigod, poor Rick – it looks like his granddad's dying and on top of that, he's become a disconnect.'

'It's awful. And the disconnect bit's just *weird*.'

Petra nodded. 'It *is* weird. Have you ever known anyone to be disconnected for more than a few minutes?'

Jennie felt an unwelcome chill. Of the five of them,

Rick seemed to her the least able to cope when things went wrong. 'He's on loads of social sites,' she said. 'He's going to miss them. And did you know he's got an online girlfriend he's really serious about? Rick'll be upset he can't stay in touch with her.'

Petra looked miffed. 'How come he told you about her? He never mentioned a thing to me.'

Jennie had to smile. 'Oh, come on,' she said, 'do you blame him?'

Petra had always loved teasing Rick, even when they were little kids, and this new cyber girlfriend would be fair game for her friendly mockery.

'So what's her name?'

'Manda.'

Petra snorted. 'Rick is so easy to fool. It's probably some forty-year-old woman – or man – pretending to be a girl. Happens all the time.'

'Whatever,' said Jennie with a shrug. 'Rick really likes her, so it sucks that he can't talk with her.'

Petra didn't make a joke of it, as Jennie had expected her to. Instead she said sombrely, 'Something like this could push him into another depression like he had before.'

They walked in silence for a moment, then Petra added, 'Rick needs what my mum calls tough love. We should be telling him to stop feeling sorry for himself and to take charge of his life.'

Jennie gave her a sceptical look. 'I don't think it's as easy as that. Imagine if you were a disconnect, cut off from everyone else, except when you were face-to-face with them. Wouldn't you feel bad being on the outer like that?'

'I'd feel mad,' said Petra. 'And then I'd do something about it.'

When Petra was a toddler her parents had gone out on a limb financially to start their own business, Koslowsky Garden Stuff. By the time she was a teenager, the company had grown into a supremely successful enterprise. The downside was that it made huge demands on her parents' time; the upside was that they could afford a luxurious house in the most exclusive area of Braidworth and employ a full-time housekeeper, so there was always someone there when Petra came home. Compared to Jennie's modest family home, the Koslowskys' supersize three-storey dwelling was more a mansion than a house. It was also, in Jennie's private opinion, overwhelmingly ugly.

'What do you think of our new garden?' Petra asked as they halted at the wrought-iron entrance gate. 'Dad's just had the whole area landscaped. It's sort of an advertisement for our company.'

'Very nice,' said Jennie diplomatically, thinking that the area, previously lawn and flowerbeds, was now cluttered with far too many things: two matching marble fountains gushing water, a winding paved path lined with a variety of figures – some classical statues, others whimsical cartoon characters or animals – and an elevated sandstone platform with stone benches so you could sit and admire the display wall of decorative ceramic tiles.

Petra smiled at Jennie. 'You should see the place at night when all the lights come on. Neighbours have been complaining. I agree with them. It's all a bit over the top.'

'Well . . .'

'Mum and Dad think the garden's awesome, not that they're home much to admire it.'

Petra placed her hand in the palm reader by the double doors. 'Did you hear that Yvette Sarno is going around saying she has more than four thousand friends on MySpace?'

'Access granted,' said a cheerful female voice.

'Four thousand friends? How would you have time to get to know that many? Most of them have to be total strangers.'

'I'm friended with about two hundred,' said Petra, 'and that's plenty. But four thousand? Who has time for it?' With a mocking smile, she imitated Yvette's high, grating voice. 'Oh, it feels kinda cool to have so many people as my friends! Like, this hot guy from Germany wants to get to know me better. *Much* better. Omigod, I'm so popular!'

'What about you, Petra?' said Jennie. 'You've got to be getting lots of hits on your MyVibes video. I never knew you could sing and play the guitar that well. Have you been taking lessons on the sly? You're at least as good as that girl on MySpace who got a recording contract.'

'Thanks.' Petra, who was rarely modest, surprised Jennie by blushing. 'Truth is, I'm really not all that great. Dad insisted on spending money to get a professional sound engineer to work on the audio and a director to make it into a cool, flashy video. Dad says it's the age of the self-made celebrity.'

She added a little bitterly, 'Besides, Dad says anything that pushes the Koslowsky name is good publicity. You must have noticed the company name in the background. And my website's got the video too, with a whole lot more about Garden Stuff.'

The front door opened into a large area of blue-and-white tiles, in the centre of which was a white marble stand holding a blue vase of deep red roses.

'Is that you, Petra?' called a voice from down the hallway.

'Hi, Rosa. Jennie's here too. Tell me you've got something interesting for us to eat.'

Jennie never felt comfortable in the Koslowskys' kitchen. It was very modern – all shiny metal surfaces and space-age appliances. Rosa's plump figure, dowdy clothes and warmly welcoming manner always seemed to Jennie to be out of place in such a sterile, well-organised environment.

'Will sandwiches do?' Rosa asked. 'Or would you prefer the chocolate cake I've just taken out of the oven? It isn't iced, but you can have it with whipped cream if you'd like.'

'Rosa's chocolate cake's to die for,' said Petra, 'with or without whipped cream. My vote's for it.'

'Your mother asked if you'd call her as soon as you came in,' said Rosa, as she began to cut the cake.

'What about? Why didn't she get me on my comm?'

'I've no idea, but she did say it was urgent.'

'Mum's idea of urgent is never mine,' Petra grumbled to Jennie as she called her mother. 'Mum? It's me. What's up?'

She listened for a few moments, then said, 'Okay, I get it. No, I won't let it upset me. Yeah, all right. See you later.'

Rosa glanced up with a look of concern, but didn't speak.

The hurt, angry expression on Petra's face made Jennie ask, 'Is something wrong?'

Petra hesitated, then said, 'Everyone will know soon enough. Mum wanted to speak with me here at home in case I got upset in front of other people when she told me.'

'Told you what?'

'Oh, nothing much. Just that I've been sent a zillion messages online, all calling me a slut, or worse.'

'Petra, that's awful.'

'Yeah, it sucks.'

A thought occurred to Jennie. 'Your parents check your messages? You've never mentioned it before.'

'Well, that's why I delete so much stuff so fast, before they can see it! How embarrassing is that, being treated like a little kid who can't be trusted?'

Passing them each a slice of chocolate cake, Rosa said mildly, 'They care about you, Petra.'

'Care about me?' Petra's tone was savage. 'They're just helicopter parents, always hovering, watching everything I do. There's nothing they don't check out. You call that caring?'

Jennie thought of her own family. Her parents were very traditional, and although they took a close interest in Jennie and her sister Annie, she was sure they would never dream of invading their daughters' privacy this way.

Surveys showed that parental use of spyware programs was common, although teens' techniques for evading scrutiny often kept pace. Jennie reminded herself that if it was happening to her, she might not always know. The spyware secretly detected passwords and monitored all emails, text messages, chats, website visits and search entries.

'They keep an eye on me from the communications centre at Garden Stuff. If they want to, they can keep a record of everything I do.'

'At least you're not in the dark. You know your parents are checking you out,' Jennie said.

'Yeah, great isn't it?' said Petra scornfully. 'Mum and Dad are so busy they're hardly ever home, but they can still find time to spy on me.'

'Petra . . .' Rosa said with a note of protest.

'It *is* spying, Rosa. That's why the programs are called spyware.'

'I know you can get other programs that detect and block spyware,' Jennie said.

'What's the point? Mum would know I was blocking

it, and then she'd be totally *sure* I had something to hide.'

When Rosa moved to take something from the refrigerator, Petra took the opportunity to say softly, 'Jennie, don't tell anyone about this, okay? It's bad enough having to put up with being watched all the time, without having everyone feel sorry for me.'

'I don't think that many people would care,' said Jennie with perfect sincerity.

'*I* care,' said Petra, 'and that's enough reason, isn't it? Promise you won't mention it?'

'Promise,' said Jennie.

FOUR

Rick hated hospitals. He hated the smells and the hushed sounds. He hated the squeaking sound the nurses' shoes made on the shiny floors. But most of all he hated knowing that inside the bland walls of the building there were people who were hurt, sick, in pain, even dying.

Sometimes Rick thought dying didn't seem such a bad thing. That was probably why, after the accident that killed his parents and sister, the family doctor had referred him to a psychiatrist. Rick went along with it because he had to, not because he wanted to, and was prepared to lie stiff and silent on a couch while some guy in a white coat raved on about how he understood exactly how Rick felt – which of course he couldn't possibly.

But Dr Stein wasn't anything like Rick had expected. There was no white coat and no couch, just comfortable chairs. The psychiatrist wasn't old, he didn't have a grey beard, and he didn't speak with a foreign accent. He was, in fact, a rather rumpled, round-faced man with a soft voice and eyes of such an intense blue that when he looked at Rick closely, it almost seemed that he could burn a hole right through Rick's skull and into his brain.

Rick was just ten years old the first time he saw Dr Stein. His memory of those sessions was vague and confusing. One thing he did recall clearly was how eventually the medication Dr Stein prescribed had worked. The smothering grey fog of depression had lifted enough for Rick to function somewhat like an ordinary person, although the drugs took the edge off everything, making him feel like a human robot living in an imitation world.

Dr Stein urged him to continue with therapy, but Rick refused. He wanted to be totally normal again, and to him that meant no more sessions with Dr Stein and no more mind-numbing pills. The psychiatrist had reluctantly agreed, after seeking promises from Thelma and Les that they'd watch Rick carefully. He put Rick on a schedule to slowly wean him off the antidepressants. When he was entirely free of medication, Rick thought everything seemed more vivid – colours brighter, food more delicious, his feelings deeper.

Sure, Rick had his ups and downs, but everything had been okay. Until last year.

The dreadful grey cloud that Rick had hoped was gone forever swept in again, leaching colour from the world and eating away at hope and joy. And hidden in the greyness he sensed a dark pit yawning, waiting to swallow him up completely. He almost welcomed the idea of not existing anymore, so horrible was the despair that filled him.

He'd felt useless, pathetic. When his grandparents had realised something was very wrong, they'd arranged for him to see Dr Stein again. Apart from putting on some weight and losing a little hair, the psychiatrist looked and sounded exactly as Rick had remembered him, including his disconcerting laser-blue eyes.

Dr Stein smiled a welcome, acting as though it had been weeks, not years since Rick had last sat opposite him. At the end of the first session, Dr Stein had said, 'When you go home, I want you to write a personal journal. Start with these words: "My name is Rick Lawrence and I . . ." Then continue with anything that occurs to you. Let it flow. And if you've got questions you don't know the answers to, or particular worries, put them down.'

Rick wriggled around in his chair. 'Why am I doing this? What good is it?'

'It should help you sort things out. Whatever you come up with is just for you to read. I don't have to see a word unless you decide you want me to.'

Rick baulked at first, but once he'd written the first line, the story started to unfold almost as if someone else's hands were on the keyboard.

My name is Rick Lawrence and I'm very ordinary looking – sort of average height, average weight, average everything.

I've got straight dark-brown hair and brown eyes. I'm told I look like my dead dad. My grandparents took me in when I was ten because my mum, dad and my sister Ellen were all killed in a light plane crash – Dad was piloting and they were hit by a sudden storm. I wasn't with them on the plane because I said I had a stomach ache and wanted to stay home with my grands. I don't know now if I made this stomach ache up, or I really did feel sick. I can't remember.

What I can remember is the awful, cold loneliness I felt that day. I don't think I'll ever really get over their deaths. Thelma and Les (after the crash, my grandparents asked me to call them by their first names – I guess so I wouldn't think of them as being so old) have done everything they possibly can for me and I'm truly grateful. I love them both and wish I wasn't such a problem. It's not their fault that I screw up and get so depressed. After the accident, and again last year, I was treated by Dr Stein and given heavy-duty psychiatric drugs. They sort of fried my brain, which was horrible, but at least I didn't try to kill myself.

Dr Stein says I'm feeling 'survivor guilt' because I lived and everyone else in my immediate family died. Maybe that's true. Anyway, being one of the Five for most of my life has helped me a lot. We don't talk about it, but the other four know about the accident and about Dr Stein. Nobody else does and I want to keep it that way.

I do have one question: why was I the one to live when my family died? I can't help feeling I don't deserve to be the one who's still here.

And worries? There are so many things – doing well at school, making Thelma and Les proud of me. Also, what will I do if I'm sucked into the dark pit, and can't get out?

And what will happen if my grandparents die? They're old. I'd be all alone. I couldn't bear that.

Now, sitting by his grandfather's intensive care bed, he brooded over what he'd written in his journal. He'd been right about Les. He was an old man and had to be close to the end of his life even without the accident.

Rick had gone with Thelma to visit Les at the hospital almost every afternoon since the accident. He'd watch over his grandfather's limp body, hooked up to machines that beeped and gurgled self-importantly.

Thelma would sit quietly holding her husband's slack fingers. Then she'd lean forward and talk to him, mentioning things that had happened since she and Rick had last visited, as though at any moment he'd open his eyes and join in the conversation.

It creeped Rick out, watching Thelma having a one-sided conversation with Les, who probably couldn't hear a word. Rick would take out his iZod and log in to one of the sites where he could joke around with his friends and for a few moments push out of his mind the horrible thought that his grandfather might be slowly dying.

When that didn't work, and the insistent beeping of the hospital machines really got to him, he'd block out everything with loud music, filling his head with sound so there was no space for anything else. But the best escape of all was to lose himself in a video game.

He really envied Allyx and Petra for getting into the game design class. He had dreams of becoming a game designer and was so disappointed when he missed out on the class. It would be awesome to create fantasy worlds that people couldn't wait to enter.

Once Thelma had asked Rick what he got out of games, and he'd tried to explain. 'It's magic. Playing a great game makes me think and feel differently. It pushes me to do things faster, smarter.'

'What sort of things? Is it like an adventure story?' she'd asked.

'More than that. When I'm in the game I can be a galactic warrior, or an undersea explorer, or a hero saving the world, even the bad guy. I'm someone else and somewhere else.'

Rick could see she didn't really understand. 'You'd have to play a game to get it,' he'd said.

He didn't add, *When I'm in a game, I'm not me anymore, and that's wonderful.*

Now Rick stole a sideways look at Thelma. Since his grandfather's fall, the light had gone from her eyes. Before, she'd bustled around, laughed a lot. Now sadness filled her face and she moved and spoke without her usual sparkling energy.

She caught his glance and said, 'I know this is boring for you, Rick. But I'm sure Les senses you're here and it's a great comfort to him. But you don't have to just sit there. Play one of your games to fill in the time, or what do you call it? Twittering?'

'I can't do any of those things. I told you when I got home from school. My iZod's dead – I can't use it. I can't do anything. I've been *disconnected*, and it'll be days before I'm connected again.'

'Oh, yes,' she said vaguely, 'you did mention that. So how about one of the books on your English reading list? I'm sure you haven't got through all of them yet.'

Rick tried to smother his despairing sigh. 'They're all e-books on my iZod, so I can't read them either. Everything's *dead*.'

'Oh, heavens,' she said with a worried expression. 'I hadn't realised it was as bad as that. If there's anyone you want to get in touch with, I can send an email for you.'

'No one emails anymore.'

'I do, dear,' his grandmother protested. 'All the time. And friends email me back.'

'Okay, no one *my* age uses email anymore. It's for old people. Texting is much better and with IM you get an answer straightaway.'

Thelma shook her head. 'All this texting in the odd shorthand language you kids use – it beats me what you find to talk about.'

'Things,' Rick said.

'Things? That's vague.'

'Like what people are doing. What's cool.'

He couldn't explain why, but being able to check in with his friends was fun, even if they weren't talking about anything in particular. It felt comfortable. He liked knowing that his friends thought the same kind of things he did. Now he was cut off from them, it was like he was missing out on something important.

Talking about texting reminded Rick of Manda. She'd wonder why he was ignoring her. But what would she think if she found out he was a disconnect? Maybe he should ask Jennie or Petra to send a message that he'd be back soon. No, not Petra – she'd tease him about having a girlfriend.

He must have sighed again, because he looked up to find Thelma gazing at him with concern. 'Rick, it's quite natural to feel blue because of Les, and let little things get you down.'

'This is *not* a little thing. I'm shut out everywhere.'

She put a hand over his. 'If things get too much for you, there's Dr Stein. He's always been able to help you.'

'I don't need Dr Stein. I'm okay.' When she looked doubtful he said quickly, 'Really, I am. I'd tell you if I wasn't.'

'You sure? There's no shame in it, Rick. I often think you feel as if being depressed is somehow your fault. But of course it isn't. It's a physical thing, a chemical imbalance in your brain. It could happen to anyone. And you know from the past it can be treated.'

'I'll be fine. Once I'm connected again, I'll be fine.'

FIVE

Tal's home was in a quiet corner of Braidworth. The two-storey house was far too big for two people, but Tal's mother, Grace, refused to even consider moving. 'Matt loved this place,' she'd say when anyone suggested she might sell and move to a smaller house. 'I could never leave – I'd feel I was deserting him.'

Matt Blair had died of an unsuspected heart problem when Tal was five. Tal thought he could remember his father's thick, sandy hair, broad smile and deep voice, but it was hard to tell how much Tal really recalled and how much his memory had been influenced by the many photos that filled the house, plus family movies his mother had so often shown him.

This afternoon, Tal turned the corner to find his mother's sleek silver top-of-the-line Mercedes parked in the driveway. He was surprised. She worked long hours at her job at Farront International and usually arrived home long after him.

He found her in the kitchen, still wearing the severe navy blue suit she'd worn to work, but her hair was down, instead of being pulled back in a businesslike chignon, and she'd tied a frilly pink apron around her waist.

'Why are you home so early, Mum? Is something wrong?'

'Not a thing, it's just that I'm thinking of cooking something special tonight.' She looked up from the recipe book. 'Rob will be here for dinner.'

'Oh. I've already got plans. A bunch of us are having pizza at Petra's place. We're celebrating Allyx and Petra finishing *BrawnBlasters*.'

'Cute title,' she said with a laugh. 'Allyx was telling me they were originally going to call the game *Revenge of the Nerds*.'

'You know more than me, Mum. They've been keeping it all a big secret.'

'The girls could have picked the weekend for their party, not a school night,' she said, frowning.

'I've got my homework covered and I won't be back late, promise.'

Obviously irritated, she said, 'Don't forget you've got to be at the track at six-thirty tomorrow morning.'

Tal was training hard for an upcoming state athletics competition. 'It's okay, Mum, I'll make it.'

She slammed the recipe book shut. 'You would spring this on me at the last minute, Tal. Rob is expecting you to be here.'

He felt a silent alarm ring. Why would his mother's boyfriend want to see him? 'Tell him I'm sorry.'

'Rob was hoping to discuss some important things with you.'

This couldn't be good. Tal got on okay with Rob Anderson. Sometimes he even quite liked the guy, and it was good that he made his mother happy. But no way was Tal into discussing anything important with him. With foreboding, he asked, 'What sort of things?'

His mother made a vague gesture. 'Oh, things . . .'

'You two won't miss me, Mum. Haven't you heard? Three's a crowd.'

'Three can be a family.'

The alarm was ringing well and truly now. Tal had sensed for a while that Rob Anderson was pushing himself into Tal's life. Now Tal was going to have to shove back.

'Look, Mum, he's your boyfriend. It's got nothing to do with me.'

'It's everything to do with you.'

Tal felt a sudden surge of anger. 'You're not going to tell me the guy's moving in with us, are you?'

She hesitated, then said carefully, 'It's a possibility.'

'Do I get a say?'

'Of course you do.' She reached out to touch him, but he stepped back. 'Tal, I know this is hard. You and I have been a team for so long, but I need more in my life and Rob is someone special.'

His resentment boiling over, Tal snapped, 'He's not my father and he never will be.'

'At least give him a chance. It's hard for Rob too.

Don't you think he knows how you feel? But you were only five when Matt died and that's a long time ago.'

'Long enough for you to have forgotten Dad.'

'That's not fair.'

With a shock he realised she had tears in her eyes. His mother never cried. He said with deliberate emphasis, 'Rob Anderson is not my father.'

She rubbed her forehead with her fingertips. It was a characteristic gesture he'd seen her make a thousand times when she was puzzled or very tired. 'I don't know what to say to you.'

'Say that you get it, Mum. Say you agree he can't just walk in here and take over.'

She gave an exasperated sigh. 'Rob has no intention of taking over.'

'No? Lately he's been trying to tell me what to do. Like he has the right!'

'He takes an interest in you.'

'Yeah, great.' He grabbed an apple from the fruit bowl. 'I'm outta here.'

'I'm sorry I didn't give you more notice about tonight,' she said, obviously peacemaking, 'but you and Allyx will be here on Saturday, won't you?'

'For the barbecue? Sure.'

'It's important for my career. Vital.'

'I know that, Mum.'

For several years Grace Blair had done well in middle management at Farront International. Then she was chosen by Audrey Farront, the head of the company, to work in a new development department.

Now Grace had an opportunity for promotion to a top managerial position being created specifically to concentrate on maximising the youth market. There were several people in the running for the job, and Audrey was assessing each candidate personally.

'Don't forget to remind Allyx that Audrey insists everyone call her by her first name,' she said.

'What's *that* all about?'

'Just one of Audrey's little quirks.' She gave him a worried frown. 'Tal, I want you to make a special effort. It's imperative that every impression Audrey gets at the barbecue be a positive one.'

Tal grinned. 'I'll make a real effort not to pick my nose in public.'

She didn't smile in return. 'I can't tell you too often how important this is.'

'No worries. Everything will be fine.'

As he turned to leave the kitchen, he had a sudden thought. 'Rick's a disconnect. His iZod went dead this afternoon, and Commdat told him it'd be a whole week before the link can be restored. Because Rick uses a Farront comm, I was wondering if you could do something to get him connected sooner.'

'That's odd,' said his mother. 'I've been noticing an upswing in the number of Farront customers who've been disconnected. Young subscribers like Rick are disproportionately represented.'

'Can you help him?'

'I should be able to speed things up. Tell Rick I'm on it.'

'That's great. Thanks.'

Tal had got to the door when she said, 'About Rob – you can't stick your head in the sand. The three of us will have to discuss it sooner or later.'

Tal didn't reply.

SIX

The principal assignment for video game design was to create an original game, but the teams were also required to make a short video detailing the steps involved in developing it.

Allyx and Petra had decided that the first viewing of the video and then the downloading of *BrawnBlasters* would be restricted to the Five plus Mike, Petra's long-term boyfriend, but then Allyx had suggested inviting the other students in the class too. Petra was sorry she'd gone along with this, because the class included Maryann Dodd, who was teamed with nerdy George Everett. Maryann's smirking face was the last one Petra wanted to see this evening.

She checked the twenty or so people talking at the top of their voices as they consumed soft drinks and slices of pizza. Maryann wasn't in view. This didn't mean she wasn't coming – she liked to catch everyone's attention by making a late entrance.

Petra had been hoping no one would mention the avalanche of cyber hate messages she'd received, and so far nobody had, although she'd caught some curious looks coming her way. Perhaps they were waiting to see how she'd react, or they didn't want to spoil the evening. Petra expected no such consideration from Maryann, who was probably gloating about the success of the attack.

Much earlier, before anyone arrived, Petra and Jennie had checked out Petra's various online locations. There were vicious messages everywhere. Although she'd been furious rather than distressed to begin with, the more Petra thought about the sheer malice behind the attacks, the more upset she became.

Jennie had said, 'Did you hear about that girl who committed suicide the other day after something like this?'

'Get real! I'm not going to kill myself over a bunch of nasty messages.'

'I know you're not. You're way too tough.' Jennie's smile faded as she added, 'Thank God Rick wasn't the target. Something like this would really get to him.'

'Dodder's behind it,' said Petra, 'so Rick's safe. She'd never pick on him.'

'You haven't got any proof that Maryann's the one.'

Petra ignored that. 'You know she's in my game design class, so she'll be here tonight. I'm dying to give it to her the moment she walks through the door.'

Jennie looked alarmed. 'I don't think that's a very good idea.' When Petra's militant expression didn't change, Jennie went on. 'Why not wait and see what Mike thinks?'

Always reliable, Mike arrived early, as he'd promised. He'd winced at the malicious words on the screen, then said, 'Any idea who's behind this?'

'Petra's convinced it's Maryann Dodd,' said Jennie. 'She's thinking of fronting up to her tonight.'

'Dodder's never liked me,' Petra declared, adding, 'She's *such* a bitch.'

'So what happens if you accuse her?' Mike had asked. 'You can't prove it's Maryann and believe me, she's not going to break down and confess. Besides, you don't know for sure who's behind it.' He'd given Petra a warm hug. 'My take on it? Do your best to ignore the whole thing. If you act like nothing's happened, you win, because it looks like they haven't got to you.'

Petra glanced around the crowded room. Maryann Dodd had just swept in, creating her usual mini-commotion. Petra had to stop herself from marching over and ripping into her. Petra knew Mike's suggestion was good advice, but she wasn't sure she could follow it. *Ignore her*, she said to herself.

Her gaze rested on Mike, who was talking with Tal, Allyx and Jennie. Mike was nice. Too nice. So nice he was boring. But he was a sweet guy, considerate and dependable, and Petra didn't want to hurt him.

Inside her head a little voice said, *Hah! You'd dump him in a minute if Tal became available.*

She told herself that wasn't true, but she had to admit that Tal was special to her and had been for years. They'd been close friends all this time, with never a hint of anything romantic between them. And now he was with Allyx, who Petra liked a lot. Even if she was a blue-eyed blonde who was, if Petra had to be ruthlessly honest, both thinner and better looking than she was.

Trying to be detached, she compared Mike and Tal to each other. Tal had sandy-coloured hair, a long face and a wiry runner's body; dark-haired Mike was carrying a little extra weight, and preferred to watch sports rather than participate. Mike was shorter, but handsome. Tal was —

'Hey, Petra, it's like, wow! I mean, look at this home theatre set-up. It's got to be the best I've ever seen.'

She spun around to find Maryann smiling sweetly at her, without even a hint of a smirk on her face.

Petra reminded herself that there was a faint possibility that Dodder wasn't responsible for the attack. She resisted the temptation to extinguish the saccharine smile with a sharp slap, instead saying vaguely, 'Oh, hi, Maryann.'

'This entertainment centre must have cost a fort- une,' said Maryann in admiring tones.

She's playing nice because she wants something, Petra thought. Aloud she said, 'I suppose.'

Petra's parents had spared no expense in setting up the entertainment centre to professional standard. One half of the spacious area was for socialising, the other for viewing. All the various pieces of electronic equipment and the satellite feed, plus sound and lighting, were controlled from an elaborate touch screen console. Petra had mastered the confusion of options long before her dad and mum had, which made her wonder if there wasn't something in the idea that her generation was different.

'I'm counting on you to help me with something,' said Maryann, leaning closer and dropping her voice to a confidential whisper.

'Like what?'

Maryann looked around to check no one was close enough to overhear, then murmured, 'I heard you had smarts. I'd like to buy them from you.'

Smarts was slang for illicit drugs that improved attention and focus. They worked far more spectacularly than earlier mental enhancers, such as the legal drugs originally prescribed for attention deficit disorder.

'You heard wrong.'

'Oh, come on, Petra! I can pay you heaps.'

No way would Petra admit it to anyone, especially Maryann Dodd, but she did have access to smarts. Her dad had given her a supply, saying the pills would give her an edge academically.

'But, Dad,' she'd protested, 'I'd hate anyone to think I needed pills to do well.'

'Don't think the others aren't taking something,' he'd said. 'This is just levelling the playing field.' He'd added as a clincher, 'You know how important it is to your mother and me that you succeed.'

She'd taken smarts a couple of times before important tests, and had thought they helped a bit, but mostly her results were good anyway, plus the school punishment for being caught using smarts was severe, so Petra still had most of the supply hidden in her room.

She had to admit that there was another reason she hadn't continued to use them – it was Petra's small, private rebellion against her father's control of her life.

She realised that Maryann was smiling ingratiatingly at her. '*Please*, Petra. I know you can help me. It's really, *really* important.'

'Sorry, you're out of luck. And I haven't a clue where you'd get any.'

Maryann's smile abruptly vanished. 'I won't forget this,' she said, her pretty face suddenly mean.

'Wassup?' said Mike, appearing unexpectedly.

'Nothing,' Maryann snapped.

David joined them. 'When do we get to play this game of yours?' he asked Petra. 'Knowing you and Allyx, I'm betting it'll have babes blasting the hell out of the bad guys. Am I right?'

'We'll find out as soon as Rick gets here,' said Mike. 'He's been visiting his grandfather in hospital.'

Maryann's sullen expression lightened at the mention of Rick's name. Pointedly ignoring Petra, she said to the boys, 'I've heard Rick's a disconnect. What happened?'

David said curtly, 'A stupid computer glitch, that's all. He'll be reconnected soon.'

'I might be able to pull some strings. I know people.'

David rolled his eyes. 'Yeah? Like who?'

Maryann's long brown hair described a graceful arc as she performed her routine hair toss. 'Waste of my time telling you the names,' she said with a sneer, 'since they wouldn't mean a thing to someone like you.'

'The sooner we can get Rick reconnected the better,' said Mike. 'We need him for our *Worldstrider* team.'

Something about Maryann's hair tossing gesture had been nagging at Petra. Now that Mike had mentioned the game the Five had been playing as a team, it all clicked into place.

'Aha!' she exclaimed. 'I've got it! You're Princess Avenger in *Worldstrider III*. Your avatar keeps tossing her hair exactly the way you just did.'

David gave an incredulous laugh. 'You mean Princess Avenger in the sexy pink leather outfit? That's Maryann? Get outta here!'

'Now we know why Princess Avenger is always trying to hook up with Rick's avatar,' Petra said with a knowing smile.

Petra couldn't remember ever seeing Maryann blush before, but her cheeks were now bright red. 'Don't be so stupid,' she spluttered.

'Hey, guys,' David called over to Tal, Allyx and Jennie. 'Guess who's Princess Avenger in *Worldstrider*?' He jabbed a finger in Maryann's direction. 'Here she is. Who knew?'

'Rick's arrived,' said Mike.

Most people seemed to have heard Rick had been disconnected, because he was immediately bombarded with questions.

Now the attention was off her, Maryann shot Petra a look of pure malice. 'You'll be *so* sorry you did that,' she hissed, before stalking off to join Kimba Nash, a particularly spiteful member of her clique.

Although he looked tired, Rick seemed to Petra to be making a real effort to be cheerful as he answered his questioners. 'Why am I a disconnect? Haven't got a clue. No way did I do anything wrong, it just suddenly happened. And yes, it sucks to be shut out from everything.'

'When will you be reconnected?' someone asked.

'Commdat says it'll take a week to put me back on line.'

'A week!' exclaimed George Everett. He was pudgy and pale, as though he spent most of his time indoors. His heavy-framed specs were always sliding down his nose, so he was forever pushing them back. Tonight he wore baggy brown shorts and a purple T-shirt proclaiming that he was 'CyberJock'. In Petra's opinion, George was so totally geeky he was cool.

'Jeez!' George went on in heartfelt tones, 'I couldn't survive even a day.'

There was a murmur of agreement.

'I don't have any say in how long it takes,' said Rick, his cheery attitude fraying. 'Commdat decides who gets connected right away and who doesn't.'

'Didn't you kick up a fuss? I would've,' declared Kimba.

'I tried. It was no good.'

Seeing that Rick was starting to wilt, Petra glanced over at Allyx, who took the hint and announced loudly, 'Everyone to their seats for the first showing of our stunning video, *The Making of BrawnBlasters*.'

'When do we get to download your game?' George asked.

He already had his communicator out, a unique device he'd constructed himself using an iZod as a base. Petra suspected he was illegally connected to Farront's network, as all the communication companies had outlawed any devices that didn't conform to their technical standards.

'After you sit through our *excellent* video,' Petra said.

George looked at her suspiciously. 'How long does it run? Once you girls start hogging the camera, it could be hours.'

'You're just bitter because we finished before anyone else in the class,' said Petra. 'So what *is* happening with your *War of the Wolts*?'

George scowled. 'Do you need to ask? Have you ever tried working with Maryann? If she isn't yapping on her iZod, she's non-stop texting, leaving me to do pretty well everything. It drives me mad. She'd ace the assignment if she could be bothered trying.' Being George, he then returned like a terrier to his original question. 'How long is the video?'

'You were right,' said Petra. 'It *is* hours. How did you guess?'

Allyx laughed. 'Relax, George. It's more like ten minutes.'

Petra took her place at the central control console, dimmed the lights and projected a glowing, half-size hologram of Allyx, creating the illusion that the diminutive figure was standing on the platform beneath the video screen.

As Allyx's hologram introduced the steps required to design a video game, the screen showed images of Petra and Allyx working to accomplish each one.

Watching the video for what seemed the hundredth time, Petra was amazed she and Allyx had ever finished the project. It had been much more demanding than she'd expected. She and Allyx had had to come up with a viable concept, then devise a storyline, invent characters, write dialogue, map out the series of digital scenes in which the characters would appear, choreograph the action, select suitable background music and, with guidance from the instructor, write the software to bring their fantasy world to life.

When the lights came up, David said with a hoot, 'Thank God I didn't make it into game design! It's too much like hard work.'

Rick, who was able to watch the video because it was shown on an open screen with no requirement for audience identification, said, 'Who cares if it's hard work? Designing games is so cool. I wish I'd got into the class.'

George had his modified iZod at the ready. 'Okay, so where's *BrawnBlasters*?'

'Coming right up,' said Petra, who had set up the entertainment centre to allow everyone to wirelessly download the game to their comms.

'Remember, professional games have hundreds of people working on them. *BrawnBlasters* had only two, me and Petra.'

It was soon obvious to Petra that Rick was feeling the odd one out. While the others laughed, traded comments or were caught up in the game, peering intently into the screens of their comms, Rick shoved his hands in his pockets and leaned casually against the wall, trying to give the impression he didn't mind being excluded from all the fun.

Petra felt sorry him, and so, apparently, did Maryann. Petra overheard her say earnestly to Rick, 'It's just so unfair that you're a disconnect.'

Could it be that Dodder had a nice side Petra had never suspected existed? The answer to this unspoken question came almost immediately.

'Like, you're not missing a thing, Rick. The video was okay, I suppose, but the game –' Maryann made a face – 'is pretty much a waste of time. Oh, I'm sure Petra and Allyx did their best, but . . .' She shrugged.

'That's just your opinion,' said Rick, obviously annoyed. 'You haven't even had time to look at it properly.'

Maryann backed off immediately. 'You're right. It was just the impression I got. Maybe I didn't really give it a fair go.'

Petra grinned to herself. This was an evening of firsts as far as Dodder was concerned. Until she had been revealed as Princess Avenger, Petra had never seen Maryann mortified. And now Petra had witnessed the near impossible, Maryann admitting she could be wrong.

Petra's parents were still at Garden Stuff. Rosa, playing the role of surrogate mother, announced that it was time for everyone to go home.

Jennie and Petra looked for Rick to ask how his grandfather was. 'There he is,' said Petra, 'talking with George.'

Rick abruptly broke off his conversation when they approached.

'What did you think of *BrawnBlasters*?' Petra asked George.

'Not bad,' he said, which was high praise for him. To Rick he said, 'I'm gone. Get back to you later.'

'What's that all about?' Jennie asked once George was out of earshot.

'Nothing.'

'It must be something,' she persisted.

It was clear Rick wasn't going to elaborate, so Petra asked, 'What's the latest on your granddad?'

'No change. He's still unconscious.'

Jennie took his hand. 'Rick, if there's anything we can do, just ask.'

Looking rather embarrassed, he mumbled, 'Okay, thanks.'

Rosa had been performing her role as human sheepdog so efficiently that the room was almost empty. Maryann, accompanied by Kimba, lingered to remark to Petra, 'I didn't like to mention it before, with everyone here, but it's quite shocking what's on the web about you.'

'Real nasty,' Kimba's nasal voice chimed in. She had an ongoing sinus problem, and although she was good looking, she also sniffed constantly, which Petra found extremely irritating.

Maryann shook her head sorrowfully. 'There must be hundreds, maybe thousands of messages. And did you know there's a new site, GetPetra? It has lots about your music video.'

'Real nasty,' Kimba said again, between sniffs.

'*Must* you sniff every few seconds?'

Insulted, Kimba glared at Petra. 'I can't help it. My allergies –' She broke off to take out a tissue and blow her nose hard.

Ignoring this, Maryann stayed on subject. 'Of course they're all lies, Petra, but not everybody knows that. Awful what people will believe. You must be *so* upset.'

'It doesn't bother me,' said Petra. 'I mean, anyone who'd do that kind of thing –' she paused to give Maryann a significant look – 'has got to be a total, utter loser. *So* pathetic.'

SEVEN

Tal intended to sleep in on Saturday morning, but his mother shook him awake far too early. 'Rise and shine, kiddo. I could use some help setting up the barbecue.'

'It's the crack of dawn,' he moaned, but she'd already set off down the stairs. He pulled on jeans and a T-shirt and joined her in the kitchen.

'I've marked the things you can help me with.' Grace put down her toast and handed him a to-do list.

'This is way over the top,' Tal said, eyeing it. 'It's just a barbecue.'

She frowned at him. 'It's an opportunity for Audrey to see me in a social setting. Everything has to run smoothly. Nothing can go wrong.'

'What could go wrong? The forecast's for a perfect spring day, the backyard and the new garden furniture look great, and last weekend I checked out the barbecue and everything's working okay.'

'There's always something. Maybe the mix of people won't work. I couldn't stand it if there was an argument over something stupid.'

'You'd rather an argument over something intelligent?'

'This isn't the time to be funny,' she snapped.

'Oh, *Mum*!'

With a reluctant smile, she said, 'Maybe I am overreacting a little.'

In Tal's opinion she was overreacting big time. He mentally ran through the guest list. In the position of honour at the top was his mother's boss, Audrey Farront. She'd be accompanied by one of her senior executives at Farront International, a guy called Joe Villabona, who was new to the company.

Of course Rob Anderson would be there – that went without saying. Also invited were Tal's uncle Ian and his wife Wendy. His mother's brother was a good choice, one of those good-natured individuals who gets on well with almost everyone – even if he could drive you mad with his sudden enthusiasms for various gadgets. Aunt Wendy was extra nice too, although Tal was always amused when she gave her loud, hiccupping laugh. It was quite a surprise for people who'd never heard it before.

Apart from Tal and Allyx, the only other guest was one Audrey Farront had particularly requested – Victor O'Dell, his mother's long-time mentor at Farront. He'd been retired for many years, but had played an important role in her career. Although now an old man,

O'Dell was still highly regarded as an authority on the communications industry. His website was frequently first with breaking news and his opinion was often sought by the media.

Steven Grant dropped Allyx off in mid-afternoon. Her father was slightly built, with thick, greying brown hair and a neat, darker beard. Like Tal's mother, he was a single parent and worked in the same industry, being an executive with Brownbolt Communications, a huge company in direct competition with Farront International.

There was a friendly rivalry between the two. 'Steven,' Tal's mother said, kissing his cheek, 'got any company secrets you care to share?'

He laughed. 'Not today, Grace. Better luck next time.'

After he'd gone, Tal's mother reminded Allyx not to mention her father was with Brownbolt in front of Audrey Farront.

'I'll be careful,' said Allyx agreeably.

Tal groaned. 'Give it a rest, Mum. This must be the hundredth time you've brought this up. There's no reason for Allyx to mention her father. And even if she did, why would Audrey care?'

'I doubt she'd appreciate my son having a personal link to one of Farront's main competitors.'

'Yeah, right!'

'Look, Tal, you know how important this promotion is to me. There's no detail too small for Audrey to notice. I don't want anything negative to affect her judgement.'

'If she's that obsessive, she'll probably already know about Allyx.'

His mother sighed. 'Just for once can you do what I ask without talking it to death?'

'He'll be good,' said Allyx, taking his arm, 'won't you, Tal?'

'I'll try,' he said, thinking that Allyx could always get around him in the nicest way.

When they were alone, Allyx said, 'What did your mum say about helping Rick get reconnected?'

'She hasn't got very far. No one seems to know exactly what's going on. She's beginning to doubt there's much she can do.'

'Same with my dad. He said disconnection for more than a few minutes is very serious, because normally there are so many automatic fail-safe reconnection protocols that kick in to restore it.' She shook her head. 'Poor Rick. I was going to message him this morning, then I realised it wouldn't get through.'

'We should go see him tomorrow, but how can we let him know we're coming?'

'Actually,' said Allyx, 'Rick's grandparents don't have comms. They've still got a landline. Rick mentioned it ages ago.'

'A landline phone? Unbelievable.'

Old-fashioned instruments like this were extremely rare, although the communications companies were forced by law to provide line-connected telephones to those dwindling few who insisted on hanging on to outdated technology.

A thought struck Tal. 'Rick could have used the landline to call any one of us. It's only electronic devices like iZods that won't work for him.'

'Whatever the reason,' said Allyx, 'he hasn't called.' She pulled out her communicator – a bright pink BeauBrute, since her father worked for Brownbolt. 'How about I try Petra, Jennie and David? Maybe we can all meet at Rick's place tomorrow.'

'Jennie mightn't make it,' said Tal. 'Her family usually has church stuff on Sunday, but try her anyway.'

As he watched Allyx enter the messages, Tal wondered whether deep down she sometimes resented the closeness that existed between the Five. If he was in Allyx's place, Tal thought, he probably would.

Everything was in order by the time Rob Anderson arrived in the late afternoon. Rob, tall and lanky, towered over Tal's mother. He was in his late forties, Tal knew, but he looked younger. There was no grey in his dark hair and no extra weight on his lean body.

Tal tried to see him through his mother's eyes. Rob wasn't handsome, having a long, beaky nose and jutting chin, but he looked as pleasant as he really was.

He worked for FinagleAlert.com, an organisation run by a foundation and partly funded by public donations. FinagleAlert's purpose was to expose fraud and waste in both government and private industry, and it had an enviable reputation for fair but stringent investigative reporting.

Tal knew it was unfair to expect his mother to run her life entirely to suit him, but he couldn't help wishing they'd stay dating and not talk of marriage. In some ways he felt it would be a betrayal of his long-dead father.

'They look good together,' said Allyx, coming up behind him.

'You think so?'

'Don't you?' she asked.

'Never given it much thought.'

Allyx laughed and jabbed him in the ribs. 'Liar,' she said.

Tal and Allyx were assigned the role of welcoming committee and sent to the front of the house early, as Audrey Farront valued punctuality. As expected, his mother's boss appeared in her chauffeur-driven car before anyone else.

Audrey Farront didn't look like a supremely powerful businesswoman, Tal thought, but more like a sweet-faced grandmother. She had springy white hair, a rather stocky body and a soft, precise voice. There was, however, a hint of command in her piercing dark brown eyes and resolute mouth.

Tal had met her several times, and found she always wore a simple dress, no doubt expensive, in a muted colour. Today was no exception, even though a barbecue was a casual occasion. Her dress was olive green, her sensible shoes the same shade, her only jewellery a slim gold watch and wedding ring – she'd been a widow for many years.

'Hello, Talbot,' she said, putting out her hand to shake his.

'Hi. Nice to see you,' he replied, deliberately not using her name. Tal had never been comfortable calling her just 'Audrey', despite her protestations. It seemed easier to avoid saying her name altogether.

'And this must be Allyx,' she said, smiling.

'Ms Farront,' said Allyx politely, shaking the proffered hand.

'My dear, everyone calls me Audrey. I hope you won't be an exception.'

'Of course not . . . Audrey.'

'That wasn't so hard, was it?'

Allyx smiled. 'Not at all.'

'And how's your father?'

Taken aback, Allyx said, 'My father? Why, he's fine.'

'I haven't seen Steven for some time, but I believe he's doing very well at Brownbolt.'

Tal hid a rueful smile. So much for his mother's worries about mentioning Allyx's dad to Audrey.

As they'd been speaking, another car had driven up. A man leapt out of it and hurried to join them. 'Sorry, Audrey, I would have had to run a red light to keep up with you.'

'Well, you're here now,' she said, obviously displeased. She turned to Tal and Allyx. 'Joe Villabona, my right-hand man.'

'Call me Joe,' he said, his teeth very white against his olive skin and dark moustache. He had a slight accent

Tal couldn't place. He wasn't tall, but was powerfully built, his tight sports shirt and tailored jeans calling attention to the many hours he spent bodybuilding.

'We're the first to arrive?' Audrey asked.

'Yes, except for Rob.'

She nodded. 'Ah, yes, Rob Anderson.' Her tone was chilly.

Tal looked at her with surprise. His mother had told him that Audrey had met Rob on a number of occasions and clearly liked him.

'I can only deplore the direction he and FinagleAlert have taken lately with their investigative focus on Tacitcomm,' she said.

Along with Brownbolt, Tacitcomm constituted Farront International's main competition in global communications. FinagleAlert had been so successful in exposing deceptive marketing activities and outright fraud at Tacitcomm that an official government investigation was now underway.

Curious, Tal asked, 'Doesn't it help Farront to have a main competitor in trouble?'

Audrey's expression was grim. 'FinagleAlert's campaign against Tacitcomm unfairly shines an unwelcome light upon the communications industry as a whole. Naturally Farront adheres to the highest ethical standards and business practices, but even so, should there be any official audit of our operations, it would be a serious distraction.'

Tal was about to say he couldn't see what was wrong with exposing fraud, when Audrey effectively ended their conversation by turning her back on him and saying to Joe Villabona, 'Is the doctor on schedule?'

'I called. He's running late.'

Audrey gave an irritated click of her tongue. 'Joe, stay here until he arrives. Then point out that I value punctuality at all times.'

At that moment, Uncle Ian's ancient Toyota screeched to a halt in a cloud of exhaust fumes. Tal said to Allyx, 'Can you look after my aunt and uncle? I'll take Audrey through to Mum.'

As he ushered Audrey up the front steps, she said, 'I've taken the liberty of inviting an additional guest. I'm sure Grace won't mind.'

Tal almost said, 'Who?' but one look at Audrey's face decided him to keep his mouth shut.

Intrigued, he lingered long enough to hear Audrey tell his mother the name of the extra person she'd invited to the barbecue. Maybe there *was* something in Rick's rumour. Hurrying back to tell Allyx, he ran into his aunt and uncle.

'Uncle Ian, Aunt Wendy. Hi.'

'What do you think of this?' asked Uncle Ian, showing Tal a sleek miniature camcorder. He added, beaming, 'Just got it today. Professional standard, 3-D capacity, audio like you wouldn't believe.'

Aunt Wendy sighed. 'Tal isn't interested in your latest toy.'

A big man, Uncle Ian described himself as 'comfortably cuddly'. Others might have called him fat. His wife certainly did, but he just laughed it off.

For as long as Tal could remember, Aunt Wendy had been vainly trying to keep her husband on a diet that would help him lose weight. As if she were a living example of what he might achieve, she was very slim, with masses of frizzy light brown hair that made her head look too heavy for her thin neck.

'Took a panning shot of the big Mercedes parked in the drive and then zoomed in for a close-up of the chauffeur,' said Uncle Ian, handing Tal the camcorder. 'Take a look. Ivan, his name is. Pleasant enough bloke, but very careful what he says about his boss.'

Uncle Ian took back his tiny camcorder. 'And I reckon that other bloke hanging around the front of the house – Joe someone – is camera-shy. When I went to take a shot of him, he put up his hand and said a definite "no".'

Uncle Ian was settling in for a long chat, but Aunt Wendy took his arm. 'Come on, Ian, Tal's needed in the front.'

'Oh, right,' he said. 'Victor O'Dell was just arriving in a taxi. Your girlfriend might need a bit of help getting him up the path.'

'Allyx,' Tal heard his aunt say as the two of them continued down the hall.

'What, dear?'

'Her name is Allyx.'

'Odd name for a girl.'

Tal found Joe Villabona and Allyx on either side of a stooped old man, helping him negotiate the path from the front gate. Villabona was saying something about a motorised wheelchair.

'A wheelchair? When I'm crippled I'll have a wheelchair. I'm not crippled yet!' He caught sight of Tal and flashed his teeth in a very white smile. 'Hello, Talbot.'

'Hello, sir.'

'Sir? Respect for one's elders, eh?' He cackled a laugh. 'And there's not many elder than me.' Tal couldn't argue with that. Victor O'Dell was a frail ninety-five, but still mentally sharp as a tack.

'I'll take over,' Tal said to Villabona.

'Where's Audrey?' the old man asked. 'Holding court?'

'I guess so.'

'She's been that way since she was a girl. Queen Audrey, we used to call her. I remember that she even tried to boss her father around. Frank Farront was a hard man, but fair. He made sure she started at the bottom of the company, but he encouraged her to work her way up through the ranks.'

'I admire her,' said Allyx. 'She made it right to the top.'

'Audrey's a sharp businesswoman,' O'Dell conceded. 'If she has a weakness, it's that she trusts her own judgement too much.'

With Tal on one side and Allyx on the other, the three of them headed slowly in the direction of the backyard.

'I know who Audrey's mystery guest is,' Tal said over the old man's bent head. 'It's Carter Renfrew.'

'You're kidding me!'

'I've known Carter since he was a precocious kid,' said Victor O'Dell. 'Good brain, but he's become a bit of a fame junkie.'

'What do you think of Dr Renfrew's book?' Tal asked.

'In a word? Bulldust.'

'Our science teacher agrees. He says the whole idea is absolute garbage.'

'It's not absolute garbage,' said O'Dell. 'Instinctively people realise there's a grain of truth in the theory. You kids *are* different.'

'And are we better, too?' Allyx asked with a cheeky smile.

'Better, you ask?' Victor O'Dell's cackle turned into a coughing attack. Concerned, Allyx patted him on the back.

When he'd caught his breath, he wheezed, 'Indubitably better.'

EIGHT

The barbecue was well underway and the designated cooks, Rob and Uncle Ian, were overseeing sizzling chops, steaks and sausages, when a man came striding around the side of the house, closely followed by Joe Villabona.

'Sorry I'm late!' the man boomed in a resonant bass voice.

Tal immediately recognised him from countless publicity shots, TV interviews and online videos. Seeing Dr Carter Renfrew in reality was a little disappointing. On the screen he was a handsome, magnetic, larger-than-life personality. In the flesh, he looked older and more like an average person. He wore nondescript brown shorts and a tan sports shirt. His receding hair was cut so closely that it formed a reddish fuzz over his scalp. As if to demonstrate that his fair skin didn't tan, his sunburnt nose was red and peeling.

'He looks kind of ordinary,' Allyx whispered to Tal.

As Tal's mother stepped forward to greet the new arrival, he seized both her hands in his. 'You must be Grace Blair,' he said warmly. 'It's so very generous of you to extend hospitality to an unexpected guest. I'm absolutely delighted to be here.'

'Here at *last*,' observed Audrey with a tart smile.

Switching his attention to her, Dr Renfrew exclaimed, 'Audrey, forgive me! When I get caught up in my research, I don't notice the time flying by.'

'Well, at least you're here now,' she said, a little more agreeably.

'Believe me, I did my best to be on time –' he spread his hands contritely – 'but my best just wasn't good enough.'

For some reason this amused Tal's Aunt Wendy. She brayed a loud laugh that ended in a series of hiccupping sounds.

Audrey, who was about to say something, looked startled, then irritated. She raised her voice: 'If I may have your attention, I have an important announcement to make.'

She glanced around, daring anyone to keep talking. Oblivious, Uncle Ian continued telling one of his long, complicated jokes to Victor O'Dell, who was balanced precariously on a folding metal chair.

'Ian! Shush!' hissed Aunt Wendy.

'What? Oh, sorry.'

Audrey gave Uncle Ian a frosty look, then summoned up a tight smile as she said, 'The name Dr Carter Renfrew will be familiar to all of you. A recognised authority in the field of youth psychology, his latest book, *Brains in Flux: Evolution and the Teen Mind*, has ignited passionate debate in the scientific world.'

She paused for a moment to let this sink in, then went on, 'It is with great pleasure, therefore, that I announce that Dr Renfrew has taken a consultancy role with Farront International. Our company is seeking to enhance the totality of the communications experiences young people enjoy, and thus further grow that vital segment of our market. To that end, Farront will be fully funding Dr Renfrew's new research project to map the developing teen mind.'

His mother was so obviously surprised at Audrey's announcement that Tal realised she was hearing it for the first time.

Audrey smile grew warmer as she looked over at O'Dell. 'Victor, I'm pleased to say that an exclusive media release is being forwarded to you as I speak. You'll be the very first with this breaking news. And may I say on a personal note, how much I'll value your endorsement for this cutting-edge project.'

Her smile faded as she glanced in Rob's direction. 'FinagleAlert will also be provided with the media release, but with the proviso that you not use it until Victor has broken the news of Farront's innovative research program.'

Joe Villabona began to clap enthusiastically. After a pause, everyone else joined in, except for Victor O'Dell.

Allyx said to Tal, 'Mr O'Dell doesn't look very happy.'

'He sure doesn't.'

When the applause petered out, O'Dell, still perched on his spindly metal chair, said to Audrey, 'I'm afraid I won't be breaking the story. I'm troubled by research that submits young people to intrusive psychological probing. For this reason I'm not willing to put my seal of approval on this initiative of yours until I've fully analysed Dr Renfrew's research protocols.'

Associating Victor O'Dell's prestigious name with the project would have been a publicity coup for Farront. Tal saw his mother's anxious expression as she realised Victor wasn't going to fall in with Audrey's plan. Tal's mother had described Audrey's disconcerting rages when things didn't go her way. A glance at Audrey's expression made it clear there was a good chance they were all about to see a demonstration of her fury.

'Audrey's ready to explode,' he murmured to Allyx.

Audrey's grandmotherly face was flushed as she glared at Victor, who seemed unperturbed.

She took a deep breath, but before she could say a word, Rob broke in loudly. 'Dinner's up! Come and get it! Don't let this superbly cooked feast get cold.'

The tension broke as there was a general move towards the food.

'That was close,' said Tal to his mother.

'Look after Victor, will you? I'll try to calm Audrey down.'

'Leave it to us,' said Allyx.

Victor O'Dell was still seated when they came up to him. With a smile Allyx said, 'Let me get some food for you, Mr O'Dell. All you need to do is tell me what you want.'

'Nonsense, girl, just get me to my feet. I'm not helpless.'

'Victor! Great to see you looking so well,' boomed Carter Renfrew, 'and still full of independent spirit.'

With a hand under each elbow, Tal and Allyx assisted O'Dell to stand. He straightened to his full height, which brought him only to the doctor's shoulder. Looking up into Renfrew's face, he said, 'I look forward, Carter, to closely examining your research procedures.'

'Of course, old friend, whenever it suits you,' said Renfrew heartily. 'My work is an open book to you, Victor. An open book.'

Uncle Ian suddenly popped into view with his video camcorder. 'Smile, everyone.'

Renfrew immediately beamed into the lens. 'I'm running a video diary on my website,' he said, whipping out his communicator. 'I'd appreciate it if you transferred a copy to my iZod.'

'Will do.' Uncle Ian peered into the little screen. 'Now, if I could just work out how . . .'

While Victor and Allyx chose their food, and Uncle Ian puzzled over his camcorder, Renfrew drew Tal aside.

'I'd like to have a word later with you and your girlfriend. I've a proposition that should interest you both.'

'Is this to do with your research project?'

'That's right. I'll give you the details later.'

Rob Anderson came up to Tal after Renfrew had moved away. 'Did Renfrew ask you to volunteer to be a research subject?'

'All he said was he'd talk to me and Allyx later.'

'Did he mention how much you'd be paid for your participation?'

'No, but he should have,' said Tal, grinning. 'I'm not proud – I can be bought. Of course, it has to be a big payday.'

His flippant tone didn't lighten Rob's serious expression. 'Until today I didn't know Farront had anything to do with funding Renfrew, but over the last few weeks FinagleAlert's been picking up details of his new research project. The working title is "Got to be Connected".'

'Connected to what?'

'Connected electronically to everyone else. Renfrew is aiming to develop a three-dimensional schematic of the typical teen brain as it processes the constant stream of electronic communications bombarding it. His theory seems to be that young people must have constant stimulation for mental health.'

'I don't get what's in it for Farront.'

Rob shrugged. 'I'm not sure, but I can make an educated guess. I'd say it has something to do with the boutique communication companies nipping at the Big Three's heels.'

'You mean the ones started in someone's garage?'

'That's right. Small-scale companies with young, talented entrepreneurs who have fresh ideas, understand the youth market, and are developing innovative technology so much faster than gigantic corporations like Farront. Gander Innovations is one; Speed of Infinite Thought another. The major communication companies, particularly Farront, have all at various times tried to buy them out, with no luck.'

'But how can they compete with the Big Three?' Tal asked.

'Because they've got a lot going for them,' said Rob. 'Raw talent, original ideas, plus a willingness to take big risks, because they haven't got all that much to lose if it doesn't work out. Contrast that with Audrey's position. She has to answer to the board of directors and to the shareholders. She can't afford to gamble on a long shot and fail. For example, there are rumours flying around that Farront has spent a fortune developing some extraordinary new application for the next generation of iZods. If it doesn't take the marketplace by storm, Audrey could find herself in danger of early retirement.'

'So she must be pretty confident Dr Renfrew's research will pay off for her?'

'He and Villabona seem to have convinced her of that.' Rob hesitated, then said, 'About you and Allyx getting involved in Renfrew's research project. I doubt you'll ask me what I think, but –'

'But you've got an opinion.'

Rob half-laughed. 'I've always got an opinion, Tal.'

'Does he ever!' said Uncle Ian, overhearing. 'It's a fine exposé of Tacitcomm you're doing for FinagleAlert. Great stuff! Should be more of it.'

He indicated Audrey, deep in conversation with Tal's mother. 'Take Farront International, for example. I guarantee they have skeletons galore in their corporate closets for you to find.'

'I've a definite conflict of interest where Farront is concerned,' Rob said.

Uncle Ian seemed perplexed. Then his expression lightened. 'Of course, Grace works for Farront.' He gave Rob a sly smile. 'Speaking of Grace, do I hear wedding bells in the near future?' He gestured with his tiny camcorder. 'I'll film the entire ceremony for you with a professional soundtrack – all at no charge. So, when are you two getting hitched?'

'We've no firm plans.'

'Don't let her get away,' said Uncle Ian, slapping Rob on the back. 'If I were you, I'd put the question to Grace quick smart.' He winked at Tal. 'What do you think, Tal?'

Put on the spot, Tal felt his ears burn. 'Whatever.'

NINE

Later, as the barbecue was winding down, Carter Renfrew cornered Tal and Allyx. With warm enthusiasm, he said, 'I'm making arrangements to speak at your school next week, but in the meantime I'm delighted to offer you a personal invitation to join a team of young people I'm presently recruiting for my exciting new research project. You'll be very well recompensed for your trouble.'

'How much?' asked Allyx.

'I can't give you an exact figure, as it depends upon the level of your participation,' Renfrew said smoothly. 'All details will be spelt out in the contract you'll sign once you agree to be part of the project. Of course parental permission is required, but I don't imagine that will present a problem.'

'What are you actually researching?' Tal asked.

The doctor spread his arms wide. 'I'm offering you a truly once-in-a-lifetime opportunity to be part of a ground-breaking scientific study. What could be more exciting?'

This wasn't enough for Allyx. 'But what *exactly* is involved, Dr Renfrew? I've heard of people being harmed by scientific experiments.'

'My dear young woman, there's no danger of that at all!' He ran a hand over the red fuzz on his skull, then said with deep sincerity, 'There is nothing in the least onerous, I assure you. It's too complex to explain in a few words, but I'll give you an overview. You'll be required to take a number of physical and psychological tests, and also a series of brain scans. At no point is there any chance of harm to your minds or bodies. In fact, I fully expect everyone will find the whole experience great fun.'

'You're calling it "Got to be Connected", aren't you?'

Renfrew raised his eyebrows at Tal's question. 'Why, yes, that's the popular title I've given it – the scientific one is far more complex and dry. May I ask where you heard the name?'

Tal was deliberately vague. 'Around.' Curious to know what the doctor would say, he asked, 'Why is Farront involved in your research?'

'Involved? Farront isn't involved at all, apart from providing the funding. Businesses frequently invest in projects for largely philanthropic reasons. The company has chosen to be associated with research that will advance scientific knowledge of the unique architecture of the teen brain.'

Tal recalled that when Audrey had announced

Dr Renfrew's association with Farront, she'd mentioned that his work would help the company's marketing to young customers. He was about to point this out, when Joe Villabona, his expression grave, came hastening over to them.

'Carter, I'm sorry to interrupt, but Audrey needs to see you urgently.'

'Something's wrong?'

Villabona glanced at Tal and Allyx. Obviously not willing to reveal anything in front of them, he said, 'I'll give you all the details inside.'

'Gotcha!' exclaimed Uncle Ian, suddenly appearing with his camcorder. He pointed it at Villabona. 'Let's have one big, happy smile.'

'This is not a good time,' Villabona snarled, putting his hand up to block the lens.

'Only take a moment,' Uncle Ian protested. 'I can't see what the problem is.'

Obviously with an effort, Villabona replied in a much more moderate tone, 'Forgive me. It's a little idiosyncrasy of mine. I've never liked being photographed. Now, if you'll excuse us . . .'

Uncle Ian watched Villabona hustle Dr Renfrew into the house. 'Bit of an overreaction from that foreign fellow, don't you think?' he said to Tal and Allyx. 'No reason for him to go off the deep end like that.'

'Uncle Ian, you *can* be awfully annoying,' Tal observed with a grin.

'Wendy tells me that all the time.' He slipped his little camcorder into his shirt pocket. 'Anyway, I've got a couple of shots of him – what's his name, Villabona? I had a feeling he wouldn't cooperate, so I used the zoom to get him full face before I came over to you.'

When Uncle Ian left in search of other photographic prey, Allyx said to Tal, 'I'd love to know what's going on with Audrey and Dr Renfrew.'

'If Audrey's involved, Mum will know. Come on.'

They found her in the kitchen pouring coffee into mugs set on a tray.

'Villabona came rushing out to collect Dr Renfrew, but he wouldn't say why in front of us.'

She gave a short laugh. 'Typical! Joe likes to be mysterious, but there's no point keeping it secret – the media outlets are already on it. The Farront PR emergency team alerted Audrey to a possible public relations debacle. Two local kids made a suicide pact and left a note saying they were killing themselves because they couldn't stand being disconnected any longer. Thank God they were found in time.'

Beside him, Allyx grabbed her BeauBrute comm. 'It's out there,' she said, peering at the screen. 'Barry Lyons and Ruth Byrne. The guy's fifteen, the girl's a year younger.'

'Why's Audrey upset?' said Tal. 'Do the kids have iZods?'

His mother nodded. 'Worse than that, in their note they specifically blame Farront for driving them to take their own lives.' She gestured at the tray. 'Carry this in for me, will you, Tal? And Allyx, you might as well come too. There's nothing left to keep confidential.'

Aunt Wendy, eyes wide, came rushing into the kitchen. 'Grace! Two disconnects – mere teens – got so depressed they killed themselves with sleeping pills! Ian's just heard it on his Audio Ear.'

The Audio Ear was one of Tal's uncle's favourite gadgets, a tiny tube that was placed so it rested gently next to the eardrum. The Audio Ear could transmit a huge range of material – news items, music, educational lectures, recorded novels, bloodcurdling stories, 'how-to' advice, and so on. Uncle Ian had his Ear programmed to pick up breaking news, the more sensational the better.

'The kids didn't kill themselves,' said Tal's mother. They were found in time.'

'They were? Ian will be so disappointed.' When the three of them stared at her, Aunt Wendy hastened to add, 'Not disappointed about them being alive. That's wonderful. It's the accuracy of the Audio Ear's breaking news. Ian's been complaining about it for ages. They so often get it wrong.'

'It's not just Audio Ear,' said Grace. 'None of the media outlets take the time to check their facts thoroughly – they all want to be first with the news. And then the item's picked up and repeated, accurate or not. The problem is that when people are told something often enough, they assume it's true.'

Joe Villabona appeared in the doorway. 'Grace, where's the coffee? Audrey's waiting.'

'Coming right up. And Joe, the story's all over the internet, so don't worry about keeping it from anyone here.'

Villabona swore under his breath and disappeared back down the hallway.

Tal, followed by his mother and Allyx, carried the tray into the study. Villabona and Renfrew stood listening to Audrey. '. . . and the video will be rush-released through every possible outlet, online or off-line. Audio and print versions will also be made available.'

'But what am I supposed to say?' Renfrew looked anxious.

Audrey tapped her foot impatiently. 'It's all under control. Gus Willis, head of our PR department, is on his way with a video team. Your job is to put the best possible spin on the situation. We simply cannot have the Farront name associated with teen customers who attempt suicide and blame it all on disconnection from our network. Willis recommends you imply it's Commdat's fault. The kids became disconnects because of problems with the government databanks.'

Renfrew gave a reluctant nod. 'Okay, I suppose I can handle that.'

'In addition, you can take this excellent opportunity to publicise Farront's support for your research project. And Willis strongly suggests you also mention our new joint venture, the Farront clinics. He thinks the timing's right.'

Tal caught his mother's eye. 'Clinics?' he mouthed. She shrugged and shook her head.

'Audrey has hers black, no sugar,' said Villabona to Allyx. She handed a mug of coffee to Audrey, who took it without thanking her.

'Willis had another valuable suggestion,' Audrey continued, 'namely that we put Dr Howard Unwin on the Farront payroll. I presume you're familiar with his work?'

'Naturally I'm very familiar with my colleague's work, particularly in child psychiatry,' said Renfrew, clearly pleased to air his knowledge. 'Howard Unwin's built quite a name for himself in the area of communication deprivation. As an authority in this field – although I might mention I too have delved extensively into the topic – Unwin has named a specific syndrome –'

'Spare me the details,' interrupted Audrey. 'I'll be speaking with Dr Unwin shortly, and if he accepts our offer, you can include his name in your remarks.'

Tal saw a flash of annoyance cross Dr Renfrew's face. Like most people, he didn't appreciate being interrupted.

Eyes narrowed, Audrey was now checking out the study. 'Grace, if you clear this side of the room and put your desk in the centre – minus the clutter, of course – and move that stuff on the wall behind, so it provides a neutral background . . .'

After musing for a moment, she went on. 'Yes, I believe that will work well enough.' She gestured at Tal and Allyx. 'You two can make yourself useful and help.'

Renfrew said, 'We're making the video *here*? *Now*?'

'We haven't got time to relocate to a studio.'

'But I haven't got a script, and my clothes . . .'

Audrey's iZod delicately chimed. She glanced at its

screen. 'It's Willis with some problem. Grace, go ahead and get the room set up. Joe, calm Carter down.'

As she moved away to take the call, Villabona smiled reassuringly at Renfrew. 'Audrey's right. There's not a thing for you to worry about. The video team always turns out a polished product. A PR catastrophe specialist is writing your script, but you'll have the final say. Make-up and wardrobe people will work their usual magic. All you have to do is look and sound sincere. And we all know how well you can do that.'

'The doctor will have to reach new heights of sincerity,' said Audrey dryly, as she slipped her iZod into its discreet holster at her waist. 'Gus Willis called with disturbing news, Carter. It's spreading like wildfire that Ruth and Barry's names appear on the list of kids who've applied to take part in your research – a project with which Farront is now closely associated.'

Tal was puzzled to see Renfrew glare hotly at Joe Villabona, as though he had something to do with the issue.

'Why am I finding this out now?' Audrey demanded of Renfrew. 'I would expect you to have warned me.'

'I had no idea their names were there,' Renfrew blustered. 'Hundreds have applied. I can't be expected to remember every one of them, can I?'

Audrey began to pace up and down. 'Find out every detail of their applications.' She halted to glower at him. 'Let me make it very clear to you that Farront's financial support entirely depends on how effectively you avert a public relations disaster.'

TEN

Rick learned about the attempted suicides when his grandmother exclaimed, 'Oh, my God!' while watching television. Rick heard her from the kitchen, where he was listlessly making himself a cheese and lettuce sandwich. He wasn't hungry, but Thelma would fuss if he didn't eat something.

'What's happened?' he called out, knowing it had to be important. Thelma had strict rules about swearing and taking the Lord's name in vain. When she didn't answer, he walked from the kitchen into the living room. 'What's happened?' he said again.

She turned a shocked face to him and relayed the news. Tears filled her eyes. 'Oh, their poor families!'

'Why did they try to kill themselves?'

Thelma shook her head. 'They didn't say in the news-flash, but it's the lead story, so it'll come up next.'

On the rare occasions Rick watched live television, he usually used his iZod to view it, but that wasn't an option at the moment. Basic programming on home television sets could be used without logging in, so Rick being a disconnect wasn't a problem. He slumped into the lounge chair beside Thelma's. His grandparents didn't have the latest paper-thin giant screens – their older set took up only half the wall.

An interminable procession of ads was running, interrupted now and then with teasers for the news items to follow. The teaser for the lead story featured a photograph of a boy and girl all dressed up, perhaps for a school dance. The boy seemed awkward, as if uncomfortable in the formal suit he was wearing. The girl had a sweet, heart-shaped face. The voice-over intoned, 'A modern Romeo and Juliet death pact? Chilling details in a moment.'

'They're supposed to live locally,' Thelma said. 'Do you recognise either of them, dear?'

'No, I don't think so.'

Rick tried to imagine what it would be like to take a fatal dose of pills. You'd go to sleep and then . . . nothing. You'd simply never wake up. Or perhaps the stories of near-death experiences were true. Maybe there was a glowing tunnel of light and at the end people who had gone before would be waiting to welcome you to heaven. He'd see his parents again, and his sister Ellen.

Once he'd asked his grandfather whether he believed in heaven and hell. Les had laughed. 'Safer to, don't you think?' Then he'd become serious. 'Live the best life you possibly can here and now, Rick. If there's a heaven and a hell, you'll find out soon enough.'

Rick's throat tightened as he thought of his grandfather, lying helpless in his hospital bed, hovering in limbo between life and death.

'Rick, are you all right?'

'I'm fine.'

On the screen the ads had finally ended. An extremely thin woman with a cascade of pale blonde hair was saying in dramatic tones, 'People are already calling this a modern Romeo and Juliet tragedy. Barry Lyons and Ruth Byrne lie near death in their hospital beds, surrounded by their grieving families, who are asking *why?* Why did this happen? What drove these teens to enter a deadly suicide pact, and consume handfuls of sleeping pills, when their whole lives lay before them? And most disturbing of all, what major, household-name company may share the blame?'

The blonde woman abruptly broke into a toothy smile. 'The astonishing answer to those questions after these important messages from our valued sponsors.'

The parade of ads began again. Rick slumped further down in his chair and shoved his hands in his pockets. He became aware that his grandmother was looking at him intently. 'What?'

'Dear, I know you're a bit low because you've been cut off from all that texting and talking with your friends you're used to doing all the time. Watching this sad story can't be helping.'

'I'm okay.'

'What with Les and all, you have every reason to feel blue, but things will be better soon. This morning at the hospital, I'm sure Les moved his fingers when I was holding his hand. That's a good sign, isn't it?'

Making an effort to sound upbeat, Rick said, 'That's great. Maybe he's starting to wake up.'

On the screen, the blonde woman was back. 'For those viewers who have just joined us, we're examining the horror of teen suicide – or in this case, thankfully, a so-far failed suicide pact.' She went on to repeat almost word-for-word the information she'd given before.

'I wonder what big company's involved,' Thelma said.

The blonde woman obligingly answered the question, as an image of Farront International's head office appeared behind her. 'The young people's distressed parents blame Farront International, the largest of the Big Three communication companies, for Ruth and Barry's desperate act.'

She paused to allow a huge image of an iZod to appear on the screen. 'Both young people used Farront's communicator, the very popular iZod. Abruptly and inexplicably, both Ruth and Barry became disconnects. Ruth's father, in an exclusive interview to follow this news report, will be telling you how his daughter, driven into a deep depression by her isolation from all she held dear, begged Farront for reconnection.'

The blonde woman paused to shake her head sorrowfully. 'Amazingly, Ruth's heartbroken pleas fell on deaf ears. It's alleged that Farront did nothing to help this distraught young woman and the boy she loved reconnect to the world she could not do without.'

'Off!' commanded Thelma. The screen obediently went blank.

'Why did you turn it off?'

Her expression troubled, Thelma said, 'I don't want you watching something like that.'

'Because it's about disconnects who tried to kill themselves? Are you thinking I might do the same thing? No way!'

Still concerned, Thelma said, 'Rick, I want you to promise me that if you feel it's all getting too much for you, you'll tell me.'

He was saved from answering by the landline phone's harsh ring. Compared to his sleek comm, Rick thought the bulky instrument was ugly and awkward to use, but his grandparents insisted on keeping it.

As she always did, Thelma answered the phone with, 'Hello? This is Thelma Lawrence speaking.' She listened, then said, 'Hold on, dear. I'll put him on.' She handed Rick the clumsy receiver. 'It's Allyx calling again. She's a lovely young woman.'

Allyx had called earlier to say that she and the rest of the Five would be seeing Rick the next day, if that was okay. Delighted to hear his friends were coming around, Thelma had offered to provide lunch.

Rick made a big effort to sound in good spirits. 'Allyx? Hi. Hope you're not calling me to say there's a change in plans for tomorrow.'

'No change. It's something else. Have you heard about those kids?'

'We were just watching it on TV.'

'You're totally not going to believe this, but . . .'

When he hung up, he repeated what Allyx had told him. '. . . and right now Dr Renfrew is making a video at Tal's place that's going to be shown everywhere the moment it's finished.'

'Damage control,' said Thelma. 'No one goes to that much trouble unless the stakes are very high. Farront International must have a lot to lose.'

She grinned at Rick's surprised expression. 'I'm not entirely out of it, dear. I do know what goes in the world.'

Less than two hours later, Dr Carter Renfrew was gazing earnestly from the television screen. He was seated at a desk Rick recognised as the one in Tal's mother's study. His hands were clasped on the bare surface in front of him. He wore a dark suit, cream shirt and subdued tie.

'My name is Dr Carter Renfrew. I speak to you today as a man who has devoted his life to the study of teen psychology. My book, *Brains in Flux: Evolution and the Teen Mind*, is a bestseller and available in many formats to suit individual needs. There's even a paper edition for the more traditional reader.'

Rick's grandmother chuckled. 'Bless the man! He never misses a chance to promote himself.'

'You've seen Dr Renfrew before?'

'I watch a lot of TV. It's hardly an exaggeration to say Dr Renfrew is on one program or another most days, busily pushing his theories and his latest book. And I imagine he's all over the internet, too.'

Renfrew's television image leaned forward, deeply serious. 'I speak with you today on behalf of Farront International. Audrey Farront herself has asked me to express her personal shock and sorrow that two disturbed young people, who were part of Farront's worldwide family of iZod users, made the appalling decision that suicide was an answer to their problems.'

'Allyx said that at the barbecue Dr Renfrew asked her and Tal to be part of his new research project, but she isn't all that keen and neither is Tal,' Rick said.

'What would it involve?'

Rick shrugged. 'Something to do with looking at how your brain works.'

'Didn't you mention you were thinking of volunteering yourself when Dr Renfrew speaks at your school next week?'

'Yeah, but I've changed my mind. I don't want anyone poking around inside my head.'

On the screen Renfrew's image had assumed a stern expression. 'Because rumours and misstatements about Farront International are widely circulating, it is imperative that I set the record straight. Ruth Byrne and Barry Lyons were understandably upset when they suddenly became disconnects – that certainly is true. What is *not* true is the claim that Farront International was unresponsive when these two young people asked for help. Farront technicians did everything possible to reconnect them, but they ultimately came to the conclusion that the fault lay in the huge government databanks of Commdat. At this point in time, Commdat has not responded adequately to Farront's queries made on Ruth and Barry's behalf.'

He sat back in the chair and refolded his hands. 'Perhaps you have heard that Ruth and Barry had applied to be part of the latest Carter Renfrew research project, generously funded by Farront International as one of the company's many contributions to the community. The truth of the matter is that, although they had indeed put their names down to be part of the study, their applications were at a preliminary stage. Unhappily, parental permissions had not yet been provided, which meant that neither I nor my trained staff had yet carried out the complimentary psychological assessment that all participants are given when their applications are accepted. The pity is that perhaps this near-tragedy could have been averted had Ruth and Barry obtained the required permissions from their families.'

Renfrew shook his head sorrowfully. 'For some young people, adolescence is a time of overwhelming, tumultuous emotions and wild mood swings. A small number, temporarily unbalanced, contemplate taking their own lives. We must find ways to help them long before the situation escalates to this point.'

Now his expression changed to one of indignation. 'In my professional opinion, whole areas of adolescent psychology, most particularly the developmental stages of the young brain, have been shamefully neglected by the scientific community. Apart from my own work, and that of my colleague, Dr Howard Unwin, there are few in-depth studies of any quality being carried out. This is a disgraceful situation when the need is so great.'

He waited for a moment for this to sink in, then continued. 'It is therefore with the greatest of pleasure that I draw your attention to the two valuable initiatives that Farront International has taken in the area of youth psychology. First, as I mentioned previously, is the financial support for my research into the teen mind. Second is the establishment of the Farront Clinics, dedicated to the mental and emotional health of young people, specifically those having difficulty coping with their reactions to life-changing events, such as disconnection.'

A warm smile lit up his face. 'I'm delighted, both personally and professionally, to be entrusted with the role of director for the first of the Farront Clinics to open. My co-director is Dr Howard Unwin, who has made groundbreaking studies into CWSS – communication withdrawal stress syndrome. These vital studies examine the reactions of teens to the pressures and demands of their rapidly changing world.'

He inclined his head gravely. 'Both I and Farront International thank you for your time.'

An advertisement for the latest iZod filled the screen.

Thelma said, 'That stress syndrome Dr Renfrew mentioned could be what you've been going through since you were disconnected.'

'I guess,' Rick said offhandedly.

She gave an exasperated sigh. 'I try to understand, Rick, but it's hard for me. You and your friends are in touch with each other in ways I never experienced growing up. Your world's so filled with electronic chatter that it must be strange when you're not part of it anymore.'

'Do you want to know how I really feel?'

'Yes dear, of course I do.'

Rick said with perfect truth, 'Now that I'm disconnected, I feel like I don't exist.'

ELEVEN

Rosa always had Sundays off, so it was usually the one day Petra and her parents breakfasted together, spending time chatting about the week's activities face-to-face. This Sunday, however, Petra's father had been called to Garden Stuff because a fire sprinkler malfunction had flooded the main display area. Her mother normally would have gone too, but today she stayed at home, determined to track down whoever it was who'd initiated the cyber attack on her daughter.

On Thursday, when Petra had first experienced the sickening impact of the vicious anonymous messages, she had been all for revenge. But once she'd cooled down, Petra had decided it was wiser to let the whole thing fade away. Responding with rage would just encourage more unwelcome attention.

Her mother was, as always, immaculately dressed and groomed. This morning a tailored cream jumpsuit showed off her trim figure. Glaring into her notebook screen, she muttered, 'There's got to be some way to trace these disgusting messages back to the original senders.'

'Mum, you're not a detective. Besides, it doesn't matter who's behind it, there's nothing you can do about it.'

That got an irritated frown. 'I don't like to see such a negative attitude, Petra. You won't get far in this world if you let people get away with this kind of behaviour.'

'But you'll just make it worse. In a few days, it'll be someone else's turn, and they'll forget me.'

Ignoring this, Petra's mother announced, 'If I find I'm getting nowhere, I'm prepared to hire an expert in cyber bullying to uncover the culprit.' She added with satisfaction, 'Since both text and voice have been used to attack you, when we sue, it'll be for defamation *and* slander.'

'*Mum!*'

'What? You don't think legal action is justified? I most certainly do, and your father agrees. We can't allow the Koslowsky name to be dragged through the mud.'

Petra felt the familiar frustration welling up. It happened every time she argued with either of her parents. She knew they loved her and wished only the best for her, and they were always willing to talk about issues. The problem was, it always seemed to be what her parents wanted that prevailed. She'd often wondered if having a brother or sister would have taken some of the attention off her and made life easier.

'It's always "my way or the highway" with you two, isn't it?' she'd once said bitterly, when she'd been overruled on something she felt deeply about.

They'd both stared at her, rather hurt. Her father in particular took it to heart. 'Petra, how could you say that? We discuss everything with you and we come to a family decision.'

It was probably a waste of time to try to persuade her mother to stop playing detective, but Petra tried again. 'This sort of thing happens to people every day. It's no big deal.'

'It is a big deal when it involves my daughter.' She peered at the screen and tapped away for a few moments, then sat back with an irritated sigh. 'You mentioned it could be Maryann Dodd.'

'It probably is,' said Petra. 'She's nasty enough, but also smart enough not to get caught.'

'You know, I've never liked her mother Lois. Acts as though she's better than anyone else. And that charity she chairs for underprivileged children? It might as well have Hitler at the helm. The woman's a control freak.'

She's not the only one. 'Mum, if you turn up sure-fire proof it's Maryann, that's great. But otherwise please don't pick a fight.'

'That reminds me, Principal Constanza didn't return my call on Friday. One would think he'd show more concern about the bullying going on at his school, especially as he was a target himself earlier this year.

Clearly your father and I are going to have to schedule time away from Stuff to meet with him in person.'

It was hopeless. Petra checked the time. 'I've got to go. I told you yesterday, we're having lunch at Rick's to cheer him up.'

'How's Rick handling being a disconnect? He's always struck me as a sensitive boy.'

'Not too well,' said Petra, immediately sorry she'd not given some vague answer. Now her mother would want to know all the details on how and why Rick wasn't coping.

On cue, the questions came. 'What do you mean by not coping too well? Mind you, with his background I'd expect him to respond with some level of depression. He's not suicidal, is he?'

Petra said, 'No, of course not,' but she had the uneasy feeling that the longer he was cut off, the deeper his depression would become.

Her mother went on. 'That reminds me – did you know that Ruth Byrne's a student at Hawthorne High? I wondered if you'd run across her in some inter-school competition.'

Petra shook her head. 'I don't recognise the name.'

'It can't help Rick's state of mind that this death pact couple were disconnects, although I'm guessing it was their families' opposition to their budding romance that really put them over the edge.'

'See?' said Petra, only half-joking, 'Family inter-ference in kids' lives can be fatal.'

Her mother seemed amused by Petra's meaningful

tone, but made no comment. 'You'll be interested to know that overnight, just like magic, Ruth and Barry were reconnected.' With a cynical smile, she added, 'Farront and Commdat are both claiming credit, though they're very vague about details. Expert opinion is that neither one has any idea how or why the reconnections occurred.'

Even though her mother didn't have anything like the electronic network Petra was part of every day, Petra wasn't surprised she was so up-to-date. While her father concentrated solely on web content to do with their business, her mother was a serious news junkie who had Nuse2U delivering a constant stream of customised local, national and international stories. Because of Petra, one of the areas of interest she'd subscribed to was adolescent behaviour.

Her mother gave her a keen look. 'You've seen the kids' suicide note?'

'Of course. It's everywhere.'

'And what did you think, Petra, when you read it?'

'I don't know what you mean.'

'I'm talking about the Romeo and Juliet effect – how it's somehow terribly romantic to be willing to die for love.'

Petra *had* thought that, just for a moment, but she wasn't going to admit the frisson of dark excitement she'd felt when she first heard of the teenage death pact.

'No way,' she said.

Her mother didn't look convinced. 'One can only

hope Rick Lawrence is as sensible as you appear to be,' she said dryly.

'I'll be able to tell you after I see him. That is, if I ever manage to get there.'

'Oh, *go*,' said her mother with a dismissive wave of her hand. 'I've got plenty to occupy me here, tracking down Maryann.' With a scowl she added, 'I've a good mind to front up to Lois Dodd right now and set her straight about her noxious daughter.'

'You're not serious!' said Petra, appalled at the thought of the scene that would inevitably follow such a confrontation.

She chuckled. 'I may not be.'

Petra relaxed. Her mother's sense of humour surfaced at the oddest times. 'Mum, for a moment you really had me believing you.'

'Okay, so I was joking, but give me some hard evidence, and I'll get very serious. You cannot know how much I'd love to wipe that superior smile off Lois Dodd's face.'

Tal ran into Rob in the kitchen the next morning. He didn't expect to see his mother, as a storm of criticism against Farront had already been gathering force on the web, and Audrey had made it clear that Grace was to be in the office early on Sunday to assist with damage control.

Tal had been hoping Rob had left early too, because he didn't want to give him any opportunity to raise the subject of moving in, but no such luck.

'Morning,' Tal mumbled, thinking he'd grab something to eat and get out of there.

Rob yawned and stretched. He hadn't shaved, and was wearing ratty old shorts and a faded FinagleAlert T-shirt with the words NO STONE LEFT UNTURNED under the website's logo. 'I've made coffee. Want some?'

'No thanks.'

'How about scrambled eggs?'

'You're *cooking* for me?'

Rob grinned at his scathing tone. 'I'm not trying to offend you, Tal. Actually, I'm cooking for myself. It seemed rude not to offer you some.' His grin widened. 'I'll throw in bacon and toast if that will win you over.'

Tal's stomach rumbled. 'Okay, thanks,' he said, sounding if not friendly, at least civil.

While collecting the eggs and bacon from the fridge, Rob said over his shoulder, 'What did you think of Joe Villabona when you met him yesterday?'

'He was okay.' Tal hesitated, then said, 'I did a search on Villabona's name last night. There are lots of Villabonas, but when I narrowed it down to the Villabona working for Farront it didn't turn up much.'

Rob grinned. 'He's a man of mystery, all right. Grace is worried about the growing influence Villabona has on Audrey, because it could affect her promotion, so last week she tried his name with several search engines. Basically she got the same result as you, so she's asked me to use FinagleAlert's resources to find out more about the guy. The fascinating thing is that Villabona doesn't seem to have much of a past. He was born in

Bogotá, Colombia, into a rich family. He was educated in England. That's about it.'

Tal raised his eyebrows. 'Are you saying he's got protected status?'

'Could be. If he has, that'll make it very difficult to find out much more, but I've got access to the latest search technologies, so it's not an impossible task.'

Personal information about an individual with protected status was sealed. Most people had very little expectation of privacy because of the volume of detailed information freely shared between huge databanks, both government and private. However, in some rare circumstances – usually national security reasons were cited – someone would be granted protected status. Rumours that the very rich could buy this desirable status were rife, but government spokespeople consistently denied them.

Tal said, 'You know how Uncle Ian was videoing everything that moved at the barbecue yesterday? Villabona made a big deal about not being photographed.'

'He isn't on the personnel page of the Farront website either. I'm going to check today to see if FinagleAlert has Villabona's image stored in our databanks, so I can run a facial recognition scan. If he's ever held a licence to drive, fly a plane, or if he's appeared on a terror watch list or been found guilty of a crime, a match should come up.'

'Uncle Ian got some shots of Villabona on the sly.'

'There's no stopping that uncle of yours,' said

Rob, laughing. 'If I come up empty, I'll see if he's got anything usable.'

'What about the Biobond system? Villabona's face has to be registered, or he couldn't operate any electronic equipment. I know that the Biobond databanks are closed to the public, but what about FinagleAlert?'

'No go, I'm afraid,' said Rob, shaking his head. 'Not only is their security second-to-none, it happens to be a federal crime to even *attempt* to hack into Biobond's files.'

Cracking eggs into a basin, Rob went on. 'By the way, there's something positive you can tell your friend, Rick. FinagleAlert's web-watch system picked up that the would-be suicide kids are no longer disconnects. During the night Commdat sent automated reconnection notifications to their parents – no explanation or apology. Tell Rick it could happen to him, too.'

'Does anyone know why they were made disconnects in the first place?' Tal asked.

'Anyone who does isn't talking.'

'It seems to me,' said Tal, 'that the whole disconnect-reconnect thing is deliberate. For whatever reason, someone turns them off, then, when the shit hits the fan, turns them on again, to get rid of all that media attention.'

Rob rubbed his chin thoughtfully. 'You could be right,' he said, 'but we need the who and the why.'

'Someone who's got it in for Farront?' Tal suggested. 'The suicide note's all over cyberspace. Farront's blamed for ruining their lives.'

Raising his voice over the sizzle of the cooking

bacon, Rob said, 'Okay, let's say a master hacker gets past Farront's massive security and disconnects the young lovers. How can this hacker possibly know that Ruth and Barry will be unstable enough to attempt joint suicide, and second, be so obliging as to specifically blame Farront International?'

'So much for that theory,' said Tal. 'There has to be a reason, unless it's all a series of coincidences that just happen to make Farront look bad.'

Rob put out two plates. 'Can you handle the toast? The eggs are almost ready.'

'I'm on it.' Tal realised he was enjoying the discussion. As he got the bread, he said, 'I've been thinking Audrey's overreacting a bit. It's bad publicity for Farront right now, but how long will it last? Soon there'll be some new sensational story and people will forget about it.'

'There are any number of lawyers out there looking for clients who feel they've been wronged and want to sue to set it right. I imagine high-powered legal firms are rubbing their hands together in anticipation of the lawsuits Ruth and Barry's families will bring. They'll claim substantial damages, saying Farront contributed to their kids' attempt at suicide by disconnecting them and then doing nothing to fix the problem.'

Tal fed sliced bread to the toaster, which swallowed it up with a whirring sound.

'By the way,' Rob said as he dished out the scrambled eggs, 'Grace mentioned you had reservations about me moving in. Let's discuss that.'

TWELVE

Rick's grandparents lived in an unpretentious little house with a wide verandah and sandstone steps. Inside the picket fence the front garden was filled with beautifully kept rosebushes with blooms of different colours arranged in complementary tones. For all her protestations to her mother, Petra was the first to arrive there. Rick met her at the front door, relief replacing his woebegone expression when he saw who it was.

'Thank God you're here, Petra! I need help. Maryann Dodd turned up an hour ago, and I can't get rid of her.'

'Dodder? You're kidding me!'

He looked back over his shoulder, as though she might materialise behind him, then said in a half whisper, 'When the doorbell rang, I thought it was one of you coming early, but it was Maryann. She invited herself in before I could stop her.'

Petra felt like shaking him. Maryann wouldn't even get her nose through the door if Petra had anything to do with it. 'What were you thinking, Rick? You know she's a nightmare.'

'Maryann's always been quite nice to me,' he said defensively.

'That's because she likes you. Didn't anyone tell you she's Princess Avenger in *Worldstrider*?'

'David said she was, but I'm not sure it's true.'

'It's true. Why else do you think Princess Avenger tries to hook up with your avatar every chance she gets?'

'I thought it was you or Jennie, fooling around.'

Petra rolled her eyes. 'As if!'

'Thanks a lot.'

With the uneasy feeling that she'd thoughtlessly hurt him, Petra quickly changed the subject back to Maryann. 'So where is Dodder?'

'In the kitchen, chatting up Thelma. I think she's trying to get herself invited to lunch.'

'No way am I having lunch with Maryann Dodd!'

'But how do we get rid of her?'

Petra sighed impatiently. 'Tell her you've already got a girlfriend. Manda's her name, isn't it?'

Rick blushed. 'How do you know about Manda?'

'Jennie mentioned it. How come you never told *me*?'

'You have to ask?' Rick snapped. 'I know you'd make fun of the whole thing.'

'I would not!'

'And don't expect me to say anything to Maryann about Manda. It'd just give her ammunition.'

'You're hopeless, Rick. You know that?'

Petra brushed past him and set off for the kitchen, Rick hurrying to keep up. 'Petra, what are you going to do?'

'Get rid of her.'

The kitchen was a favourite place in Rick's house. Whenever the Five were there they usually ended up sitting around the big wooden table that was so old it was probably an antique.

Closely followed by Rick, Petra swept into the kitchen, which was filled with the delicious smell of a roast dinner cooking. Maryann was leaning against the table, chatting to Thelma as she checked the oven.

While Rick hovered anxiously, Petra gave Rick's grandmother a warm hug and Maryann a cool nod.

Maryann said sweetly, 'I had a good look at *BrawnBlasters*. Sorry to say this, Petra, but it was *so* lame.'

'Like I care what you think,' Petra snarled.

'Oh dear,' said Rick's grandmother.

Petra fixed Maryann with a hostile glare. 'Those hate messages I've been getting? You're responsible.'

Maryann gave a petulant toss of her long brown hair. 'I can't begin to imagine what you mean.'

'My mother has hired an expert in cyber bullying,' Petra lied. 'He says he can prove you're the key person in the cyber attack. My parents are considering legal action.'

'Oh, gracious,' said Thelma, her face creased with concern, 'how very unpleasant. But surely Maryann has nothing to do with it.'

Petra gave a contemptuous snort. 'Stabbing people in the back is what she does best.'

'Just try and prove it was me,' said Maryann, her pretty face made ugly with malice. 'And anyway, it's not against the law to send anonymous messages.'

'Girls, *please*,' said Thelma, uncomfortable with the direction the conversation was taking.

'Maybe you should go, Maryann,' said Rick, his tone more hopeful than commanding.

'Why should *I* go?' Maryann glowered at Petra. 'What about her?' When Rick didn't respond, Maryann exclaimed, 'Don't tell me you believe what she's saying about me!'

'Petra's been my friend forever.'

'What's that supposed to mean?'

'That I believe what she says,' said Rick firmly.

Maryann hesitated for a moment, then grabbed her things and marched in the direction of the door. 'You'll be sorry,' she tossed back over her shoulder.

'That's what little kids say,' Petra observed.

'Oh, shut up!'

As Maryann disappeared into the hallway, Thelma hurried after her, saying, 'I'll see Maryann out.'

'You were great,' said Petra.

Rick shook his head ruefully. 'Thanks, but now Maryann's going to do something horrible, I just know it.'

David was next to arrive. Petra thought he was far from his usual joking self, so while Rick went off to set the dining room table for lunch, Petra took him aside and said, 'Something the matter?'

'Not really. It's just my parents' divorce. Not that they're fighting or anything like that, but everything's changing. Nothing's ever going to be the same again.'

She gave him a quick hug. 'I'm sorry.'

'So, what's up with you?'

'Nothing much, unless you count my mother playing cyber detective. It's Dodder, of course, and there's no chance Mum will ever be able to prove it, but just try and stop her. *And* she's talking of going to the school next week to confront Mr Constanza about cyber bullying.'

The doorbell sounded. 'Someone get that,' Thelma called out.

'I'll do it,' said David. In a few moments he was back with Jennie, Tal and Allyx. Jennie was serious; Tal was morose. Only Allyx was upbeat.

'Jeez, guys,' said Petra, 'what's wrong with you? We're supposed to be a cheer squad for Rick, but you look like you've just come from a funeral.'

'Rob Anderson's talking of moving in with Tal's mother,' said Allyx cheerfully, putting an arm around his waist and giving him a squeeze. 'Tal isn't all that keen on the idea.'

'But I'm guessing his mum is *really* keen,' said Petra.

That got smiles from Jennie, Allyx and David, but an irritated frown from Tal. 'It's okay for you lot to be

105

so happy about the situation,' he said. 'You don't have to live in the same house as the guy.'

Allyx grinned. 'Hey, I wouldn't mind. Rob is pretty hot.' Tal gave her such a disgusted look that she laughed aloud.

'So when's he moving in?' Jennie asked.

'He's not, until I agree.'

'Well, problem solved,' said David. 'You never agree and Anderson never moves in.'

'Oh, *sure*. Like no one's leaning on me to change my mind.'

'Lighten up, guys,' said Jennie. 'We're supposed to be cheering Rick up.' She looked around. 'Where is he?'

'Setting the table for lunch,' said Petra.

'Okay, remember not to talk about texting or games or videos in front of him. It'll just make him feel even more out of it.'

'Hey, speaking of videos,' said Petra, 'did any of you catch Kimba Nash's stab at acting on EgoWild? She sniffed, like, a hundred times. Nearly wet myself laughing. It was so bad it was awesome!'

Having set the table, Rick headed for the kitchen. He could hear his friends laughing as they discussed someone's attempt at acting. Then Allyx mentioned George's mini-blog plus video segments, which he'd started sending to everyone, twice a day, whether they wanted them or not.

'Even teachers, would you believe! I heard Babbage went totally ballistic when he saw the video George made of him at the local gym. It was gross!'

'Is everyone on for *Mutant Bloom* tonight?' David asked. 'Should be a blast.'

Mutant Bloom was the very latest interactive game, and it was already a bestseller. Rick had been looking forward to playing on the Five team, but now they were going ahead without a thought that he was missing out.

He paused outside the kitchen door, bleak resentment flooding through him. It wasn't fair. His friends were living in another world, one he'd belonged to only a few days ago. Hearing them talking about it made him feel even more isolated and alone.

Rick took a deep breath and straightened his shoulders. 'Hey,' he said, coming into the room.

'Hey, yourself,' said Jennie. 'How's it going, Rick?'

'Okay. Did Petra tell you about Maryann?'

'She's bad news,' said Tal. 'What did she want?'

'Rick,' said Petra with a hoot of laughter. 'She wanted Rick, but she didn't get him. In fact, he told her to get lost.' She gave Rick a big, cheesy grin. 'My hero.'

'I'm proud of you, dude,' said David. 'But watch out when you play *Worldstrider*. Don't turn your back on Princess Avenger. She won't have love on her mind this time. More likely she'll be aiming to sink her pink dagger right between your shoulder blades.'

Rick's stomach felt hollow. 'I can't play *Worldstrider*, remember? I'm a disconnect.'

'Sorry, I forgot.'

Unexpected rage suddenly filled Rick. His voice shook as he said, 'Easy for you to forget, David. Easy for all of you. You're still connected. If it happens to you, see how you like it!'

Petra sat beside Rick at lunch. 'About Manda,' she began.

'Don't want to talk about her.'

'Well, excuse me! I was going to offer to contact her for you. She must be wondering what the hell's happened to you.'

'I'm on it. You don't need to worry.'

Frowning, Petra said, 'What do you mean, you're on it? Come on, spill the beans. I won't give up until you do.'

Clearly reluctant, Rick said, 'If you must know, George says he can get hold of a phantom comm that acts as if it's a properly connected iZod. There's no Biobond recognition system on the phantom, but it still sends the correct signal to Farront to indicate a valid user.'

Petra stared at him accusingly. 'Hello? Correct me if I'm wrong, but I seem to remember you saying there was no way you'd do anything illegal.'

'I've changed my mind.'

'How much is George asking for the phantom? A lot, I bet.'

Rick glared at her mutinously. 'It's none of your

business. I don't want to talk about it anymore. And don't you mention it to anyone else.'

Petra put up her hands. 'Okay, have it your own way, but you're asking for *big* trouble.'

'I can handle it.'

'Sure you can,' said Petra, not sure at all.

Audrey Farront had made her own control video early that morning, and it was appearing everywhere – television channels, social networking sites on the web, the whole range of news services and entertainment podcasts, and even on closed-circuit advertising screens in supermarkets and stores.

Rick's grandmother had recorded the program, and announced as she was serving dessert that everyone could view it after lunch.

'But why?' said Rick, looking at the blank expressions around the table. 'What's the point?'

'These are your friends, dear. They're interested in anything that might affect you, and Audrey Farront will be talking about what her company's doing to help disconnects.'

When Rick protested that no one would want to watch anything so boring, Thelma said severely, 'None of us have seen it, so we have no idea whether it's boring or not.'

'It *is* boring,' announced David. 'I only watched a few moments on my iZod, but I felt my eyes glaze over.'

'A few minutes is hardly long enough to make a fair judgement,' Thelma pointed out.

Looking at the determined set of his grandmother's mouth, Rick groaned. 'Give in, guys. Resistance is futile.'

After the table had been cleared, everyone obediently trooped into the living room.

'This is embarrassing,' Rick whispered to Thelma as he sat down beside her. 'You're making out there's something wrong with me, just because I'm a disconnect.'

'Every day you're getting more depressed. Don't say you're not. I can see it with my own eyes.'

He felt his face grow hot as he realised she'd spoken loudly enough for his friends to hear. He looked around, catching Jennie's eye. She gave him a sympathetic smile. 'Hang in there, Rick.'

The program began with an image of the Farront logo, an eagle in flight clutching lightning bolts in its talons, and the words: AN IMPORTANT PUBLIC ANNOUNCEMENT FROM FARRONT INTERNATIONAL.

Then Audrey Farront appeared, calm and assured, in close-up. She wore a severely tailored navy blue dress. Her snow-white hair and caring expression made her seem reassuringly grandmotherly. Her voice was pleasantly modulated, her manner serious.

After introducing herself, she continued. 'I know I speak for every person at Farront International when I say how dedicated we are to providing the highest standard of communication services to the millions of people of all ages and walks of life who have chosen our company for their communication needs. We are constantly working to enhance our clients' communication experiences and to bring new and innovative products to the marketplace.'

'Yeah, yeah, yeah,' jeered David. 'Same old story. I told you it was boring.'

On the screen Audrey had become more animated. 'Now, exciting news. I'm proud to announce that Farront International will soon be releasing a radical new communicator, the iZod Excelsior, with matchless clarity, an expandable screen and three-dimensional projection. The iZod Excelsior also has an astonishing capability not offered by any other company. I refer to artificial intelligence, or AI, which can be customised to become your perfect companion. Your Excelsior will not only speak to you as one person to another, it will be your close personal friend, someone who is always there, who always cares about you as an individual.'

As Audrey went on to say that specifications and pre-ordering details were posted on the Farront website, Petra exclaimed, 'Cool! Can't wait to get one.'

'Tal, did you know about this new iZod?' David asked.

'I knew Farront was coming up with something big, but Mum wouldn't give me any details.'

Up on the screen, Audrey had become very serious. 'Sadly,' she said, 'I now must turn to a darker issue. All of us at Farront International were profoundly shocked, as you were, to learn of Barry Lyons and Ruth Byrne's impulsive attempt to take their own lives. Our hearts go out to family members and friends.' She cheered up slightly to add, 'We are immensely heartened by the most recent medical updates reporting that Ruth is out of danger and Barry is steadily improving.'

Two photographs appeared on the screen, one of Barry Lyons in tennis gear, proudly holding a trophy, the other showing Ruth Byrne with a tongue-lolling black Labrador.

'Did I tell you?' said Allyx. 'I've only just realised that I know Ruth. I met her a couple of times when our band played with the Hawthorne school band.'

'Omigod! What was she like?' Petra asked.

'Quiet. I don't remember anything particularly interesting about her.'

'Well, Ruth's interesting now,' said Tal, 'but what a way to do it.'

On the screen, Audrey had moved on to their disconnect status. '. . . this caused the two young people considerable distress. Farront International did provide iZod communication services to both Barry and Ruth, however our technical staff now believe the sudden disconnection was nothing to do with Farront, but entirely due to problems with the Commdat database, possibly in conjunction with malfunctions in the Biobond company's biometric recognition system.'

David had his comm out. 'The latest newsflash says Commdat is blaming Farront for the disconnections.'

'No one wants to accept responsibility for anything

anymore,' tut-tutted Thelma. 'It was a different and, frankly, a better world when I was growing up.'

There were suppressed grins all around, as they'd heard Thelma say this many times before.

David started to respond, but Thelma shushed him. 'This is the bit I want to hear.'

'. . . the exciting initiative mentioned yesterday by Dr Carter Renfrew – the Farront Clinics. The first of this chain of prestigious clinics, entirely funded by Farront International, will be under the supervision of noted psychiatrist, Dr Howard Unwin, and eminent psychologist Dr Carter Renfrew.'

Two images filled the screen. One was of Renfrew wearing a crisp white coat and solemn expression, the other a man with a shock of dark hair, fans of laughter lines at the corners of his eyes, and a deep cleft in his chin.

Audrey reappeared to say, 'The Farront Clinics will provide services specifically tailored to meet the needs of those suffering from communication withdrawal stress syndrome, also known as CWSS, as well as more serious emotional disturbances that may lead to suicidal thoughts. As part of our ongoing service to the community, these clinics will provide treatment free of charge to individuals assessed as being in genuine need of urgent intervention.'

She paused, then said, 'One final thought: Farront International is the world leader in the development and application of communication technology, such as the extraordinary iZod Excelsior. With such a position comes great responsibilities – responsibilities Farront has never, and will never shirk. In a society where it seems increasingly clear that profit alone is the driving force behind most companies, Farront International is proud, indeed honoured, to be widely acknowledged as a global corporate good citizen.

'A sincere thank you for your time and attention. Please do not hesitate to contact Farront International if you require further information.'

As the screen scrolled contact details, Rick whispered to his grandmother, 'I'm not going to that clinic, if that's what you're thinking.'

To his embarrassment, she didn't lower her voice. 'Rick, dear, the clinic is obviously of the highest standard. And *free*.'

Rick was relieved to see his friends were getting up and chatting to each other, but he still kept his voice at a near whisper. 'It's only free for serious cases, and that's not me.'

'Don't mumble, dear. Now, I know Dr Stein was helpful to you in the past, but he hasn't specialised in this new syndrome, whatever it's called.'

'CWSS. And I haven't got it.'

She patted his hand. 'Whatever you say, but I find it a comfort to know there's somewhere to go if you ever do happen to develop it.'

THIRTEEN

Early on Monday, Tal was on the sports field checking the final stats of his morning run – his shoes beamed information to a monitor on his wrist about distance, time, pace, heartbeat, blood pressure and respiration – when Jennie came jogging up to him.

'Tal, hi. Have you heard about Rick? Allyx messaged me after she couldn't get you.'

'Is something wrong?' he asked, immediately concerned. 'I haven't checked my iZod for a while.'

'It's an anonymous cyber attack like Petra's, only this time it's all about Rick's mental state. Someone's dug up how his family died and that he had to have psychiatric treatment.'

'Maryann Dodd,' Tal said with disgust.

'I guess. It's pretty vicious and it's everywhere on the web. Makes out Rick's crazy and likely to do something violent.'

Tal swore. 'Rick won't know a thing about it. We've got to get to him before he leaves for school.'

'Allyx is calling Rick on his grandparents' landline. She's going to tell him to stay at home, and then get her dad to drop her off at Rick's.'

As they headed for the changing rooms, Tal said, 'I'll go to Rick's too. You coming?'

'Try and keep me away.'

Ten minutes later Tal met Jennie outside the girls' changing room. 'I've just spoken to Allyx,' he said. 'She's at Rick's place with Thelma, but he isn't there.'

'He's not? Where is he?'

'Allyx said that when she called, Thelma answered the phone sounding really distressed. She told Allyx one of her friends had already emailed about the cyber attack. Thelma showed the email to Rick and he totally lost it. He went to his room and she heard him throwing things around, and then he stormed out of the house. Thelma has no idea where he's gone.'

'Oh, Tal,' said Jennie, 'Rick wouldn't do anything stupid, would he?'

'Of course not.' He made a face. 'But then, he is depressed . . .'

'And this could be the final straw.' She whipped out her iZod. 'I'll tell Petra and David. We've got to find him.'

They all met up at Rick's place. Thelma's face was drawn, but she had calmed down. 'I'm terribly worried about

Rick. He was in such a state when he left. I've talked to my next-door neighbour, Ron, who's a retired cop. He told me there's no point in reporting Rick missing to the police because they won't do anything until he's been gone for days. Ron says this happens all the time – kids getting upset and running away from home. Ninety per cent of them are back in a matter of hours.'

From their faces Tal could see his friends were thinking the same thing: what if Rick belonged to the ten per cent that didn't return within hours?

'We'll find him,' he said reassuringly to Thelma.

Had Rick been carrying his comm, it would have been simple to pinpoint his location using global positioning, but because he was a disconnect he'd left his iZod behind.

Keeping in touch with text messages, they split up and checked out anywhere Rick might go. Tal even went to Maryann Dodd's house in case he'd decided to have it out with her, but no one was home. After a fruitless search, Tal suggested they meet at Braidworth High, on the off-chance that Rick had cooled down and gone to school.

The five of them arrived within a few minutes of each other to discover the main topic at lunchtime was Rick. Because of the cyber attack, the fact that he had been under psychiatric care had spread like wildfire, along with the idea that he was likely to be dangerously unbalanced.

There had been a school shooting in Germany earlier in the year, when a mentally disturbed boy had killed or wounded several teachers and classmates. That the same thing might happen at Braidworth High no longer seemed impossibly far-fetched.

Tal was infuriated by the snatches of conversation he heard, but it was pointless to argue with those people who seemed perversely thrilled with the thought that a fellow student could be deranged.

'Certifiably crazy, that's what Rick Lawrence is.'

'Get out of here! He's not, is he?'

'They're saying he hears voices telling him what to do.'

'That happens to me all the time. Turns out it's my parents.'

'Oh, ha ha!'

'Hey, how about Rick Lawrence? Mental as. And he's got a gun.'

'Who's saying that?'

'Like, everyone.'

Tal went from fury to resignation. 'Guys, there's no way we can do anything about this ourselves,' he said to the others. 'I think we should go to the principal and ask him to do something.'

'Like what?' said Allyx. 'You can't stop people gossiping.'

'Red alert!' said David. 'Here comes Maryann with Kimba and Tiffany. She's got to be behind it, and the other two always back her up. I vote we start by ripping into them.'

'Excellent,' said Petra, her expression militant. 'Let's do it!'

Jennie shook her head. 'No, let's not. We'd be doing exactly what she wants us to do.'

Tal agreed. 'Maryann will play the innocent victim. We'll be the ones in trouble.'

Maryann, Kimba and Tiffany sauntered up to them. 'Look, Tiff,' said Maryann with a smirk, 'it's the psycho's little gang.'

'You're so unbelievably mean,' Jennie said. 'Rick's never done anything to you.'

Maryann smiled mockingly. 'Well, boo hoo.'

'Is the poor thing locked up yet?' asked Kimba, her voice full of exaggerated concern.

'I hope so,' said Tiffany. 'He's off his head.'

Maryann was obviously enjoying herself. 'And who knows what the nutso's capable of?'

'You'll soon find out,' said Petra with a grim smile. 'Here he comes.'

Rick, pale and with fists clenched, came striding towards them, his burning gaze fastened on Maryann. Sensing a dramatic confrontation, students rushed over to see the show.

For a moment, Maryann looked disconcerted, then her sneering smile reappeared.

Tal said urgently to David, 'Get ready to grab Rick if he tries to do something stupid.'

David started shoving his way through the growing crowd. 'If we can get to him.'

Jennie was close enough to put a hand on Rick's arm. 'Rick, don't.'

He brushed her aside. 'What have I ever done to

you?' he demanded of Maryann.

'Calm down,' she said, adding with a snigger, 'Anyone would think that you were off your rocker.'

Kimba clapped her hands. 'Good one, Maryann!'

Rick growled deep in his throat and took a threatening step towards Maryann. Alarmed, she shuffled backwards, lost her balance and sat down hard, her legs splayed inelegantly.

There was a ripple of laughter. Her face brick red, Maryann struggled to her feet. 'He pushed me! Everyone, you saw Rick Lawrence push me!'

'I didn't touch you.'

'Loser!' shrieked Maryann, flailing at Rick's face. He grabbed her wrists to stop her raking her fingernails across his eyes. She gave a piercing scream. 'Help! Help! somebody help!'

Alerted by the commotion, several teachers hurried towards the conflict.

Rick shoved Maryann away, then staggered as Tal and David seized him.

'It's over, Rick,' said Tal. 'Okay?'

'Dude,' said David, 'don't make it any worse.'

All the fight went out of Rick. He stood, head hanging, as Babbage, panting, pushed his way through the fascinated spectators.

'Jesus, son,' he said to Rick, almost in admiration. 'You've really done it now.'

FOURTEEN

First thing Tuesday morning, Principal Constanza called a whole-school assembly in the main quad.

Nobody seemed to be listening to the teacher on the dais, who was reading out notices and room changes in a bored monotone.

'Did you see that Ruth Byrne has got some big-deal agent to represent her?' Allyx said to David. 'There's talk of a movie of her life.'

'Yeah, and she's being paid a fortune for the live interview she's giving tonight. That's one messed up way to make money.'

Allyx shot David a disbelieving look.

'Stop talking down there,' called Ms Ingram from the sidelines.

The teacher reading the notices was still droning on, not seeming to care if anyone was paying attention.

'I've been asking around,' Mike whispered to Petra,

'but no luck finding anyone who knows for sure who started the cyber attack on Rick.'

'Why don't you believe me? It's the same person who cyber bullied me. Dodder. And I bet Kimba and all the rest of that crowd helped out.'

'What if it isn't Maryann?'

Petra glared at him suspiciously. 'Have you got something going with Maryann Dodd? You're always rushing to defend her.'

Mike smothered a laugh. 'Hell, no!'

'Admit it, Mike, it has to be Dodder. She's getting even with Rick for telling her to get lost.'

'When was that? Sunday? She wouldn't have had time to dig up all the stuff about his family dying and him seeing a head doctor.'

'But what if all the web searches about the plane crash and Rick's breakdown were done ages ago? She's been keen on him forever, so it'd be natural for her to want to find out everything she could about him.'

'Watch out,' hissed Jennie. 'Cabbage on the warpath.'

'Silence!' bellowed Mr Babbage. He glared at Mike and Petra. 'Another word and I'll have you both on detention.'

The teacher had finally finished reading the notices and stepped down. Principal Constanza, plump, round-faced and wearing a grey suit a little too small for him, shared a few words with an olive-skinned man, before climbing self-importantly onto the dais in front of the assembly.

The principal cleared his throat – an irritating nervous habit he had – and called for order, his amplified voice booming off the surrounding buildings.

'See the guy with the moustache,' said Tal to Jennie. 'He works for Mum's boss. His name's Joe Villabona.'

'What's he doing here?'

'No idea.'

'Quiet!' commanded a teacher.

The principal rocked forward on his toes and launched into his prepared speech, reading the words projected onto a transparent screen in front of him.

'As you must all be aware, yesterday a disturbing incident occurred. One of Braidworth's students, Richard Lawrence, precipitated a violent altercation with another student. He was removed from the grounds by the police and taken to a secure medical facility where his physical and mental health will be assessed. In the meantime, Richard Lawrence has been suspended from school until such time as he is judged no longer a threat to others.'

He paused, and David took the opportunity to say to Allyx, 'It's not fair to blame Rick.' He glowered at the back of Maryann Dodd's head, two rows in front of them. 'Maryann's the one who should be suspended. She set him up.'

'She did more than that,' said Allyx. 'Did you hear her tell the cops that Rick had psychiatric problems? And Constanza confirmed that Rick's had treatment in the past. That's what landed him in the mental ward.'

'Shhhh!' hissed Ms Ingram, glaring at them.

The principal coughed, then noisily cleared his throat. 'Events such as the violence yesterday make it imperative that we, both students and staff, are prepared well in advance to cope with potentially serious situations. Of course, Braidworth High has always had detailed disaster plans in place, but these need to be periodically updated to reflect changes in our society and in the nature of the emergencies we may face in the future. I am arranging for every parent and student to receive copies of the new contingency plans. Comments and suggestions will be welcomed.'

He stopped to look gravely around the quadrangle, as if expecting comments or suggestions to instantly materialise.

'Any idea how long before Rick gets out?' David asked Allyx.

'My dad says it'll take two or three days. They'll keep Rick under close observation and the doctors will do a psychiatric evaluation. When Rick checks out okay, he'll be allowed to go home.'

'David Segal! Quiet, please!' came Ms Ingram's sharp voice.

'Bloody Ingram,' he muttered to himself.

'Ms Ingram's nice,' said Allyx.

'And you, too, Allyx. Stop talking!'

'Bloody Ingram,' said Allyx with a grin.

Principal Constanza cleared his throat for the third time. 'And now I'm pleased to announce an enhancement to Braidworth High's already excellent student counselling services, which are always fully available to you all.'

'What a great way to get out of class,' scoffed David. 'I should have tried it ages ago.'

The principal continued. 'As you and your parents have been advised, tomorrow the eminent psychologist Dr Carter Renfrew is scheduled to speak to the school about the pressures and demands of today's world. Dr Renfrew will also be describing his exciting new research project, funded by Farront International. In addition, Dr Renfrew and his equally distinguished colleague, Dr Howard Unwin, will be running small group discussions for selected students, where there will be opportunities to learn more about Dr Renfrew's current project. As parental permission is required for those ultimately chosen as research subjects, comprehensive details are going out to parents this morning. Please also refer to the Braidworth website for further information on recruitment and payment scales.'

He paused to indicate Joe Villabona, then went on. 'Mr Villabona of Farront International has kindly agreed to speak with students interested in joining Dr Renfrew's research project. Please go to the hall at the beginning of lunch. Mr Villabona will also be at the school tomorrow to answer any further questions you may have and to walk you through the application process.'

David noticed Ms Ingram whispering furiously to Mr Babbage, who nodded as she spoke, his face set in a scowl. David nudged Allyx. 'Take a look at Babbage and Ingram. What do you think's going on?'

'Probably something to do with Dr Renfrew. You know Babbage can't stand him.'

'Babbage dislikes everyone,' said David. 'He probably even dislikes Babbage.'

Petra was called out of maths class later that morning to go to the principal's office. She was mortified to find her mother and father there, both impeccably dressed and wearing identical expressions of pained patience.

'Ah, Petra,' said Mr Constanza, ushering her to a chair. 'Your parents have been telling me about the cyber bullying you've had to endure. It's unconscionable, of course, that any Braidworth student should be attacked in this manner.'

'What's unconscionable is that nothing's been done about it,' said Petra's father. He was a slightly built man with a soft voice, but he projected a don't-mess-with-me aura that commanded respect.

Mr Constanza spread his hands. 'Mr Koslowsky, there's very little I can do. Cyber bullying has become a regrettable fact of life. Even teachers, myself included, have been targeted. Fortunately, although these attacks are distressing at the time, they soon die a natural death.'

'Not good enough,' snapped Petra's father, leaning forward in his chair. 'My time is valuable, Principal

Constanza. I expect at least one concrete suggestion from you before I leave for my next appointment.'

'I've already mentioned my suspicions about Lois Dodd's daughter, Maryann,' said Petra's mother.

Petra's heart sank. 'Mum,' she hissed, '*please*!'

Mr Constanza's soft face grew anguished. 'Lois Dodd is one of the most valued benefactors to the school. Her fundraising activities are invaluable. I can't accuse her daughter with no hard evidence.'

Petra's father stood. 'Then I suggest you find the evidence.' He put out his hand and gave the principal's pudgy fingers a hard shake. 'I'm afraid I must leave. Please inform my wife of the further steps you intend to take.'

When Mr Constanza had seen him out the door, Petra's mother said, 'We received notification that Dr Renfrew will be speaking at the school tomorrow.'

'Indeed, yes,' said the principal, rubbing his hands together and beaming. 'We are privileged to have a man of his stature visit Braidworth. He'll be accompanied by the renowned Dr Howard Unwin.'

'Your high opinion of Dr Renfrew is not shared by everyone, Mr Constanza. Perhaps you've seen critical items on the web about Renfrew and his theories. A group calling itself BrainSave is particularly persuasive. Its site posts original documents from researchers and health professionals who hold very unfavourable views of Renfrew's work. They see him as a pseudo-scientist, a threat to young minds.'

The principal's smile disappeared.

'I don't want my daughter involved in any way with Renfrew's visit to the school.'

'Mum, I'm not a little kid.'

Her mother silenced her with a look, then switched her attention back to the principal. 'Well?'

He ducked his head up and down, saying 'of course, of course' in a placatory tone. He cleared his throat, then added lamely, 'There is often controversy in the scientific field.'

Her voice frosty, Petra's mother said, 'My husband and I would normally support innovative research, but Renfrew's spurious experiments treat young people like lab rats. I'm surprised and concerned that you are permitting Renfrew to recruit subjects at Braidworth High.'

'Not exactly recruit,' he spluttered. 'I'd categorise it as alerting students to a valuable opportunity. They will be well paid for their time and trouble.'

'With money from Farront International – a company, incidentally, that you mention in laudatory terms on the school website. This is tantamount to stealth advertising.'

Meeting her formidable glare, Constanza said hastily, 'These are hard times for education. Braidworth needs considerable funds to allow us to continue with our special enhancement programs. Dr Renfrew has arranged for Farront to make a very generous donation to the school.'

'I see,' she said dismissively. 'I have another matter that concerns me, Mr Constanza. I wish to speak with

Ms Ingram, Petra's English teacher. I'm not at all happy with the grade Petra received for her last assignment.'

Petra shot her an agonised look. 'Mum, don't.'

Obviously relieved at the change of subject, the principal examined the interactive timetable displayed on a screen set into his desk top. 'Ms Ingram has a free period. If you give me a moment, I'll check if she's available.' He gave a nervous little cough. 'I must add that Barbara Ingram is one of our most respected teachers.'

'I'm not questioning Ms Ingram's ability, but her judgement in this one case. Petra has consistently received excellent grades in the subject. I can see no reason why she received a poor mark this time.'

'Mum –'

'Don't interrupt, Petra.'

While Mr Constanza made arrangements for Ms Ingram to come to his office, Petra tried again. 'About that assignment . . .'

'Wait until your teacher gets here. Then you can state your case for a higher grade.'

'But you need to know something.'

Ignoring her, Petra's mother checked her iZod. 'Will Ms Ingram be long, Mr Constanza? I have a business meeting it's imperative I attend.'

'Any moment –' He broke off at a knock on the door. 'I believe this is Barbara now.'

He murmured a few words to the teacher – no doubt, thought Petra, a warning that the parent she was about to encounter could be big-time trouble –

then waved her into the room. The principal retreated behind his desk, wearing a worried expression.

The English teacher was slender, with short, curly, copper-coloured hair and an engaging smile. 'Ms Koslowsky,' she said, putting out her hand, 'I've not had the opportunity to meet you before.'

Sensing an implied criticism, Petra's mother raised her elegant eyebrows. 'As my daughter has to this point received excellent grades in English, I saw no need for us to meet.'

'I gather your concern is the grade Petra received for her last assignment.'

'I'm aware it was a philosophical subject. I appreciate that evaluating essays on such topics might present difficulties, but as the standard of my daughter's work has always been high, I'm at a loss to understand how you could award her such a low grade.'

Quite unfazed, Ms Ingram said, 'You've discussed this with Petra?'

'Naturally. She had no idea why her essay had been marked down.'

'Mum, I tried to tell you earlier.'

Petra's mother glanced at her impatiently. 'Tell me what?'

'It wasn't all my own work.'

Clearly stunned, her mother repeated, 'Not your own work?'

'I didn't have time to finish the assignment.'

'Why not? We set your homework schedule every week. You had adequate time allotted.'

Knowing her mother would badger her until she came up with the truth, Petra said, 'I got caught up playing *Worldstrider* with Tal and the others. We were a team, I couldn't let them down.'

There was silence while everyone looked at her. Petra went on with a rush, 'When I realised there was no way I could finish the assignment before it was due, I went to this website where you can buy essays on practically any subject. You pay more than on other essay sites, because this one guarantees plagiarism checking programs won't work.'

'Obviously a false guarantee,' snapped her mother. 'Who told you about this website?'

'I don't remember . . . I think I found it myself.'

'How convenient.' She turned to Ms Ingram. 'No doubt you've had other cases of plagiarism?'

'Unfortunately, yes, as most teachers have.' Ms Ingram looked over at Petra. 'I imagine George Everett steered you to the website, Petra. Other students caught cheating recently have implicated him.'

Petra felt her face burning. It would be hell if George thought she'd dobbed him in. 'I don't remember who told me about the site, but it definitely wasn't George,' she said as convincingly as she could.

Not convincingly enough. 'I'll be speaking to Bruce Everett about his son's activities,' said her mother. 'Ms Ingram, please forgive me for needlessly taking up your valuable time. My daughter's written apology for her deplorable behaviour will be forth-coming.'

Mr Constanza cleared his throat. Frowning at Ms Ingram, he said, 'This is the first I've heard of Petra's plagiarism. Such matters should always be brought to my attention. Cheating's a very serious issue in education today.'

'It is, Mr Constanza,' she said, 'but a fair portion of Petra's essay was her own work. I felt confident that this was an isolated instance of poor judgement on her part and was unlikely to happen again, so I hesitated to brand her a plagiarist. I extracted a promise from Petra that she wouldn't do it again, and then I let the matter rest.'

The principal looked stern. 'We'll discuss this later, Ms Ingram.' He switched his attention to Petra. 'I'm sure, young lady, that your mother is as disappointed in you as I am. This is not the behaviour expected from a student of Braidworth High.'

'Sorry,' mumbled Petra, not meeting anyone's eyes.

'Rest assured my daughter will be delivering a much more adequate apology to you both.' Her voice icy, she said to Petra, 'I'll see you later at home. Your father and I will discuss a suitable punishment. In the meantime you can tell Mike he'll have to find another partner for the school dance on Friday.'

'But, Mum . . .'

'And I'm confiscating your communicator.'

This was worse than Petra had anticipated. Without her iZod she'd be just like Rick, cut off from everyone. 'Can't you just ground me?'

'I'm waiting, Petra.'

Unwillingly, Petra passed over her iZod. 'But if I don't have it I won't be able to do any homework,' she said hopefully.

'The completion of homework assignments is vitally important,' the principal put in.

'Don't worry, Mr Constanza, I plan to closely supervise my daughter's use of her communicator for school purposes, and for school purposes only.'

A few uncomfortable moments later, Petra and her furious mother left the principal's office.

'Petra, have you any idea how embarrassing this is for me?' she said tightly as they walked down the hall towards the front of the administration building. 'Your father and I didn't raise you to be a cheat.'

'What about smarts?' Petra retorted. 'They're not legal, but Dad got them for me. Isn't that cheating? And what about the music video? You know I wouldn't sound nearly as good without a technician to improve my voice. Isn't that cheating too?'

Her mother clicked her tongue in irritation. 'The situation's quite different. In those instances you are merely enhancing your natural abilities. However, in the case of the English assignment, you were passing off someone else's work as your own.'

'I can't see that they're different.'

'We'll discuss it at home – I can't waste the time now.'

Watching her mother stalk off to the visitors' parking area, Petra reached for her iZod to text the others. Wait until they heard what had happened!

She looked at her empty hand. This totally sucked. She might as well be a disconnect.

On her way back to class Petra rehearsed what she would say when her mother had cooled down. Somehow she'd have to persuade her to return the iZod. She heaved a deep sigh. Her dad she might talk around, but changing her mother's mind was next to impossible.

This was *so* not good . . .

FIFTEEN

Tal had hardly seen his mother since Saturday night, as she'd been working overtime on the PR crisis at Farront. But on Wednesday morning he took a break from training and found her in the kitchen drinking black coffee and staring moodily into the screen of her iZod.

'Hi Mum. What's up?'

'The usual – too much to do and not enough time to do it.'

'Did you know Joe Villabona was at school yesterday morning, and he's going to be there again today?'

She looked up, surprised. 'Really?'

'He's giving advice about how to volunteer for Dr Renfrew's research project.'

'That makes sense. Audrey's determined to use Carter Renfrew's high profile to portray Farront as a caring company.'

Tal grinned. 'Ruth Byrne's interview last night can't be much help.'

'Too true,' she said with a rueful shake of her head. 'The kids' suicide pact was bad enough, but having Ruth in cyberspace, sobbing over Farront's treatment of her and Barry as disconnects, plus the news that he's still in a serious condition in hospital, effectively paints the company as just another example of heartless big business. And in the last few days there's been an inexplicable spike in the number of teenage disconnects, almost all iZod users. You can see why countering negative publicity is an uphill battle.'

'It isn't working that Farront is publicly blaming Commdat for the disconnections?'

An odd expression of chagrin crossed her face. 'That's a sore point with me.'

'Why? Tell me.'

'I can't. It's confidential company business.'

'Oh, come on, Mum! You know I won't repeat it.'

'It's vital that you don't. It's only here at home that we're fully shielded from electronic snoops. Outside, anybody could be listening.'

'I get it, Mum. So what's the big secret?'

'If I have your word . . .'

She half-smiled as he mimed zipping his lips. 'I argued against it, but on Joe Villabona's advice, Audrey's established a secret task force to organise protests against Commdat. What will look like a spontaneous uprising of public indignation will actually be engineered by Farront.'

'Is that legal?'

'Probably, but it's unethical.'

'I don't get it,' said Tal. 'How come Villabona has so much influence? He hasn't even been with your company that long.'

'Joe's done a great job of selling himself to Audrey as an expert on the youth market – and to be fair, he does know what he's talking about. More importantly, he negotiated Carter Renfrew's association with Farront, including the unconditional guarantee of exclusive access to all of the research findings before publication. This could be a huge advantage if Renfrew comes up with valid data that can be used to refine the Excelsior artificial intelligence and develop future products and services.'

'I get the feeling you don't like Villabona much.'

She shrugged. 'It's irrelevant whether I like Joe or not. I have to work with him, however stressful I find it. On the surface we get on well, but that's to keep up appearances. In person Joe's charming, cooperative, and always says the right thing, but I get the strong feeling he's following some hidden agenda. I wouldn't trust him as far as I could throw him. For one thing, I'm positive I don't have his support as far as my promotion's concerned. In fact, I think he's subtly undermining me, and given Joe's influence on Audrey, it could be a serious problem.'

'What can you do about it?'

'Not much. Rob may come up with something I can use to put a dent in Joe Villabona's golden-boy image.'

His mother's ring tone sounded. Checking her iZod, she said, 'It's Victor calling.'

While she spoke with Victor O'Dell, Tal filled a bowl with cereal and poured himself a mug of coffee.

She finished the call and sighed. 'It sounds like Victor has beaten Joe to the punch. Audrey will be in a foul temper this morning. She was so sure that Victor would endorse Renfrew's research on his website and in his science blog. She couldn't have been more wrong. He called her at home last night to say that not only is he refusing to give his endorsement, he believes Renfrew's methods are so potentially dangerous that he intends to actively campaign against the program, starting today. When he spoke to me, Victor was on his way to a demonstration.'

Tal tried to imagine the ancient Mr O'Dell in the middle of a noisy mob, surrounded by riot police. 'Isn't he a bit old to be at a demo?'

'Victor certainly doesn't think so, that's why he's headed to Braidworth High.'

'You're kidding! The demo's at school?'

'It should be on the news.'

At her spoken command, the kitchen's paper-thin flat screen was filled with vivid extreme-definition images. A crowd of people milled around in front of Braidworth's entrance gates, many holding up flashing electronic protest signs. One of the swooping air cams focused in on a demonstrator's T-shirt bearing the words: 'Carter Renfrew = Voodoo Science'.

'There's Mr Babbage,' said Tal through a mouthful of cereal, 'and beside him is Ms Ingram. And that guy with the droopy moustache is Mr Marsfield, the laziest teacher in the school, maybe in the entire world.'

The crawl along the bottom of the picture advised: TEACHERS JOIN PROTEST AGAINST TODAY'S APPEARANCE OF FAMED PSYCHOLOGIST DR CARTER RENFREW AT BRAIDWORTH HIGH. AT ISSUE IS THE USE OF TEENAGE SUBJECTS IN RENFREW'S RESEARCH PROGRAM TITLED 'GOT TO BE CONNECTED'. 'DANGEROUS CHARLATAN,' DECLARES SPOKESPERSON FOR ACTIVIST ORGANISATION BRAINSAVE. DR RENFREW THREATENS LEGAL ACTION.

'Volume,' said Tal. The volume came up, filling the room with a buzz of voices and shouted slogans in hyper-realistic Encirclesound. Over cries of 'Protect our children!' and 'Renfrew scrambles brains!' someone yelled, 'Boycott Farront! Boycott Farront!'

'Oh God,' said Tal's mother, 'that's all we need. If a campaign to boycott Farront takes off, the company's in real trouble.'

Tal finished his cereal and gulped down the last of his coffee. 'I'm outta here. This is too good to miss.'

'Try not to get arrested,' she called as he left the kitchen.

He put his head back inside to say with a grin, 'I'll try.'

Rick's white-hot rage at Maryann Dodd's success in having him blamed for something he hadn't done had dwindled to simmering resentment. What he mostly felt now was boredom. Of course he didn't have his useless comm, but he had hoped the psychiatric wing of the hospital would provide a TV screen, even a radio, to pass the time. No such luck.

The two cops who had brought him here yesterday had been quite nice. The grey-haired one had clapped him on the shoulder and said, 'Women! You know the old saying, son: Can't live with 'em. Can't live without 'em.'

When Rick had pointed out that he could live without Maryann Dodd very well, the younger cop had said very seriously, 'Don't say anything like that to the doctors or anyone else. You might be joking, but they'll take you at your word.'

When Rick was admitted, he'd been given cotton pants with a drawstring at the waist and a shapeless T-shirt several sizes too large. Then he'd had a preliminary interview with a doctor who'd given him a quick physical examination and asked him a lot of questions about what he thought and felt. She'd listened to his answers with close attention, then handed him over to an orderly, who locked him in a small white-walled room with nothing in it but a bed jutting out from the wall, a metal wash basin and a metal toilet bowl with no seat.

Later he'd been taken out for more questions, given stew for dinner – an orderly watched Rick eat it with a plastic spoon – and then a nurse had asked him if he wanted a pill to help him sleep. Later he was sorry he'd said no, as the light remained on all night. He occupied himself looking for the lens of the camera he was sure was watching him, and at last located it. The metal door had an observation window, and he was aware from noises outside in the hall that he was being checked regularly.

Things were looking up this morning, as Rick was having a late breakfast with Dr Stein. The psychiatric facility at the hospital was decorated in soothing colours. Rick sat with Dr Stein in an interview room that had walls of the palest of pale pinks. The table and chairs were ivory white; the floor tiles a dusky rose colour.

Looking at the toast and honey and the glass of milk in front of him, Rick said, 'Can I have coffee? Milk's for little kids.'

Dr Stein shook his head. 'Coffee's far too stimulating,' he said lightly. 'At least, that's the theory.'

'Don't I need stimulating? I reckon they're saying I'm depressed.' He added bitterly, 'And who wouldn't be? Maryann flat-out lied when she said I hit her. She put on an act, screaming and carrying on, and everyone believed her.' His anger flaring up, he almost shouted, 'She's a bitch!'

'Now you've brought up the subject, let's explore exactly how you feel this morning.'

Embarrassed by his show of temper, Rick made an attempt at humour. 'Jeez, even I could be a psychiatrist. Nothing to it. All you have to do is keep asking people how they feel and look interested, whatever they say.'

'You've summed up my profession,' said Dr Stein, grinning, 'but let's keep it our secret.'

He flipped open a tiny camcorder, recited Rick's full name, the date, time and location, then said to him, 'To begin with, how did you sleep?'

'Not well.' He sent Dr Stein a beseeching look. 'Can you get me out of here? There's nothing to do, and I don't belong with mad people, anyway.'

'The admitting doctor's report makes it clear she found nothing to indicate you should be held for long-term treatment. If my assessment confirms, as I expect it will, that you're not a threat to yourself or others, there should be no problem having you released into your grandmother's care. Naturally there'll be a condition you are not to contact Maryann Dodd or any of her friends involved in the altercation.'

'I can't contact anybody. I'm a disconnect, remember?'

Dr Stein nodded. 'Okay, let's talk about that, and then we'll go through exactly what happened yesterday.'

'Aren't you going to ask me how I feel about it all?'

'Funny,' said Dr Stein with a laugh, 'I *was* about to ask you that.'

SIXTEEN

When Tal arrived at school, the demonstration outside the front gates was well underway. Looking around, he could see that the demonstrators now had a considerable audience made up of local residents, teachers, parents and students, all keen to see the show.

He could hear the whoop-whoop of media helicopters high overhead getting long shots and district views. Medium shots and close-ups were handled by the ten or so air cams, which hovered then dived to capture images at the radio command of their operators. Media vehicles were parked haphazardly along the edge of the road, their satellite dishes beaming pictures to anyone in the world interested in what was currently happening at Braidworth High.

Several air cams circled Victor O'Dell and his companion, a plump young woman with an explosion of frizzy brown hair, who was assisting him onto a makeshift platform to join Babbage and Ms Ingram at the front of the crowd.

Tal was impressed by Victor O'Dell's celebrity status. He was obviously highly regarded. People whistled, clapped and stamped their feet, and someone yelled, 'O'Dell rules!'

Once O'Dell was securely seated on the only chair on the platform, Babbage stated the obvious, saying, 'Victor O'Dell needs no introduction.' Applause from the crowd. 'His presence here today is testament to the concern he feels about unregulated research.'

'Let's hear it from Victor!' a demonstrator shouted. O'Dell shook his head and indicated that Babbage should continue.

Babbage, his amplified voice spreading out across the surrounding streets, said, 'Barbara Ingram and I don't often agree, but in this instance we're in perfect accord. A school is a place of learning, not a source of psychological cannon fodder.'

He paused, and obediently the crowd roared agreement, with only a few dissenting interjections. One was from a well-dressed woman near the front, who called out, 'Carter Renfrew is a respected doctor. And you? A couple of second-rate teachers.'

Another came from Tal's least favourite teacher on the staff, Mr Marsfield, who shouted, 'Science rules! Kids don't!'

On the platform, Ms Ingram took over. 'Renfrew's research for his project, Got to be Connected, employs untried testing methods,' she declared, speaking so loudly that her radio microphone blurred the sound. 'Our students are not guinea pigs to be used in hazardous experiments by Carter Renfrew for his personal glory!'

The crowd again roared approval and those with electronic placards scrolling brilliantly coloured slogans on both sides raised them high and shook them for emphasis. Tal noticed that 'Got to be Connected = Gotta B Disconnected' and 'BrainSave Saves Brains' were favoured messages.

Allyx, who with David had come up behind Tal, put her arms around his waist, gave him a squeeze and said, 'I gotta be connected to you.'

David groaned. 'Oh, *please*, none of this mushy love talk. Let's get serious here. If this demo goes for long enough, I'll miss Ingram's class.'

'Don't tell me you haven't done your English homework *again*,' said Allyx.

'Okay, I won't tell you.'

'You're out of luck, David,' said Tal. 'Here comes the principal and the cops. I'd say English is definitely on.'

Mr Constanza bustled out of the school gates, chanting, 'Excuse me! Excuse me!' He pushed his way through to the rickety platform. He was followed by four uniformed police officers with officially impassive faces.

The principal had trouble activating his radio microphone, but eventually got it working. 'This demonstration is over,' he bellowed. 'I'm ordering you to leave the area around the school property, or be arrested –' he paused to indicate the police officers – 'and charged with trespass or loitering.'

'You can't do that,' someone yelled back. 'We know our rights.' The crowd rumbled agreement.

'Down with Renfrew,' someone else shouted above the racket.

Cheers and claps were followed by a distinctly young voice calling, 'Down with Principal Constanza!'

Laughter rose from all sections of the crowd. As if this were a signal to leave, people began to disperse.

'Teachers will supervise an orderly return to scheduled classes,' boomed the principal. 'All students must go to their appropriate rooms without delay.' When this command had no appreciable effect, he said emphatically, 'At once. Immediately.'

'Good luck with that,' said David. 'I can't see anyone rushing to go anywhere.'

Realising that it would take some time to shepherd students through the gates and to their various subjects, Tal went over to say hello to Victor O'Dell. He found him concluding an impromptu interview with a TV reporter, watched by several hovering air cams. Tal arrived as he was saying, '. . . and death threats sent to my website this morning won't shut me up.'

One camera swept in for an extreme close-up, while the reporter, a gangly man with a lumpy, earnest face, tried to hide his delight at this exclusive scoop. 'Death threats, Mr O'Dell? You've actually received *death threats*?' He added hopefully, 'Are you saying that Carter Renfrew is behind them?'

'I have no idea who's making them, but I have a forensic cyber master tracing the sources.' He flashed his chalk-white teeth in a grim smile. 'The moment I have hard evidence, I'll splash the name or names all over the internet. Now, young man, no more questions.'

The air cams swooped away to take shots of the slowly depleting crowd. Victor O'Dell took Tal's arm. 'Nice to see you, Talbot. I'd appreciate it if you'd help me to my vehicle.'

'You drove here?' said Tal, thinking O'Dell was way too old to get behind a wheel.

'Marcia was my chauffeur,' he said, indicating the young woman who'd helped him onto the platform. 'She's my neighbour's daughter, in between jobs, so it suits us both. I still have a valid licence, but I have to admit my driving's not as sharp as it used to be, so I use Marcia when she's available.'

As they walked slowly towards the car where Marcia was waiting, Victor O'Dell said, 'What do you think of that fellow, Joe Villabona?'

'You're the second person to ask me that. Rob Anderson had the same question. I said he seemed okay.'

'Did Anderson tell you Villabona appears to have no past to speak of? Yes? Well, it might mean nothing more than he's worked in some secret capacity for the government, but I don't like mysteries. I've warned Grace to take care what she says and does.'

'Why? Because of the promotion Mum hopes to get?'

'There's a lot of official interest in the com-munications industry since the scandal broke about

Tacitcomm's deceptive marketing and outright fraud. Villabona could be a government plant, investigating Farront from the inside. Grace doesn't want to get caught up in anything like that.'

Marcia had a friendly, gap-toothed smile. 'Hey,' she said, 'good one, Mr O'Dell. I've been watching your interview live on my comm. How come you didn't tell me about the death threats? I'd have been super careful driving if I'd known.'

He shrugged. 'I often get threats, frequently with graphic details of what's going to be done to me. Talk is cheap. Mostly they're not worth worrying about.'

Marcia opened the passenger door so that Tal could help the old man into the seat. Before the door was closed, he leaned forward to say to Tal, 'Tell Grace that after I spoke with her this morning, Joe Villabona called on Audrey's behalf and asked my price. How much money would it take to shut me up?' He gave a cackle of laughter. 'I won't pollute your young ears by repeating my reply.'

Tal went thoughtfully back to Allyx and David, who were waiting for him by the front gate. Tal had been mildly interested when he and Rob had discussed the idea that Villabona might have protected status. But this new suggestion that he could be undercover for the government was alarming because of the implications it had for his mother.

As they joined the last of the students straggling onto the school grounds, David said, 'I'm thinking of volunteering for Dr Renfrew's program, mainly for the money. Things are a bit tight at home. How about you?'

'Wouldn't do it,' said Tal. 'It's messing with your mind.' Allyx nodded in agreement.

'Why do you think that? Just because the Cabbage and Ingram say so?'

'I know they're teachers, but they could be right,' said Allyx.

'Nah,' David replied derisively. 'That lot wouldn't know their arse from their elbow.'

Petra caught up with them. 'I missed all the fun,' she grumbled. 'My mother had me writing these stupid apology letters to Constanza and Ingram. Omigod, *hand write* them, then deliver them myself, would you believe! What's wrong with an email? I asked her. She went ballistic. You'd have thought I'd suggested texting the apologies.'

'Texting sounds fine to me,' said David.

'Not to my mum, it doesn't. So here I am, putting down that I'm really, really sorry. I mean, what more can I say? But surprise! That wasn't enough for Mum. She wants me to totally *grovel*.'

'I know a website where you can buy apology letters,' said David with an evil grin.

'Oh, shut up!'

'How are you going getting your iZod back?' Allyx enquired.

'I'm waiting until tomorrow, hoping Mum's softened up a bit by then.'

Tal snorted and said, 'How likely is that?'

'It's not,' Petra admitted, 'but I can't stand missing out on everything. I'm getting to know how Rick feels, and I hate it.'

David rolled his eyes. 'Poor Petra, must be agony.'

She sent him a scathing look. 'What's the latest with Rick?' she asked. 'Does anybody know?'

'My dad asked Rick's grandmother if there's any way he can help out,' Allyx said. 'Rick's seeing Dr Stein today. She's hoping that he'll be released tomorrow or the next day. But he's still suspended from school.'

Babbage, meaty fists on hips, confronted them. 'Are any of you intending to grace a classroom with your presence? You've got one minute before I start handing out detentions.'

'Great demo, sir,' said David, giving him an approving thumbs-up.

'This is your weak attempt to butter me up, is it, Segal?'

'No, sir,' said David, trying to look hurt at the accusation, but unable to hide a smile.

Babbage, all sarcasm gone from his voice, went on, 'It's a pity you don't take the issue seriously. I believe Renfrew's research poses a grave threat to susceptible minds. The only way to call a halt to his experiments is to rally public opinion against him.'

Struck by the science teacher's obvious sincerity, Tal said, 'What do you mean, susceptible minds?'

'Kids with mental or emotional problems, often undiagnosed, such as feelings of hopelessness, disguised depression, misdirected aggression, violent mood swings, and so on.'

Babbage's attention was suddenly caught by another group of students who were casually heading through the school gates in the wrong direction. He set off after them, bellowing, 'You kids there. I've got my eye on you!'

Petra shook her head in wonderment. 'You know, I think the Cabbage really, truly believes Dr Renfrew's a menace.'

'Okay, maybe he believes it,' said David, 'but that doesn't make him right.'

'Wait for me,' called Jennie. They all stopped walking to let her catch up.

'Where were you?' said Allyx. 'You missed all the drama.'

'Yes, I know,' said Jennie, making a face. 'The moment my parents saw the newsflash about the protest, they said I had to stay at home until it was over. Then Mum would drive me and Annie to school. I tried to tell them it was no big deal, but Dad said he didn't want to see me arrested. As if!'

'My mother made sure *I* missed it too.'

'Don't ask Petra why,' David warned. 'You'll be sorry if you do.'

'Red alert,' said Allyx. 'Mr Babbage is heading our way again.'

'Speed up, dudes,' said David, 'or the Cabbage will be telling us more about how Renfrew is a big, bad doctor.'

'You know,' said Tal, 'I've changed my mind. I'm going to volunteer for Dr Renfrew's research.'

D r Carter Renfrew, Dr Howard Unwin and Joe Villabona appeared on the school hall's stage to address an assembly of senior years. Tal, who was seated near the front with Allyx, noted that Renfrew's appearance had been spruced up with a well-tailored navy blue suit, crisp white shirt and red tie. Tal thought the doctor was probably wearing media make-up too, because at the barbecue his fair skin had been sunburnt and his nose peeling, but now his face appeared smooth and lightly tanned.

Principal Constanza cleared his throat before introducing the two doctors in glowing terms, and then extravagantly praising Farront International for its contributions to teenage mental and physical health.

Carter Renfrew was the first speaker. Tal was surprised to find his address to the students informative and entertaining. The doctor mentioned the demonstration that morning with self-deprecating humour, then spoke with disarming enthusiasm about his research and the positive results he expected to flow from it. In conclusion he mentioned that the medical building formerly known as The Carter Renfrew Centre would now be renamed The Farront-Renfrew-Unwin Youth Health and Counselling Centre, having as its patron Audrey Farront. 'For convenience, the facility will generally be referred to as The Farront Centre.'

Renfrew was followed by Dr Howard Unwin, smiling and affable, who explained how he had discovered and named communication withdrawal stress syndrome or CWSS.

'For those unfortunate enough to suffer from it, CWSS is a very real and highly upsetting experience. Dr Renfrew and I will be working together to continue my detailed analysis of the impact CWSS has on the nervous system. This research will facilitate our development of effective treatments and, I firmly believe, ultimately a cure.'

Following him, Joe Villabona spoke briefly. He noted Farront's support for the doctors' important work. For any student thinking of applying to be a test subject, he recommended attendance at one of the small discussion groups scheduled that afternoon. Villabona himself would also be available to answer any questions.

While the principal bustled forward officiously to thank the speakers and wrap up the assembly, Allyx said to Tal, 'You're not really serious, are you?'

'About being a test subject? Maybe. I'll tell you for sure after the group meeting this arvo.'

'But Tal, you were totally down on the idea. What changed your mind?'

'Not sure,' he said vaguely.

He couldn't explain it to Allyx without sounding like an idiot, but it all came down to Joe Villabona. The guy had manipulated Audrey into backing Renfrew's research, and now he remained closely involved in establishing the program. Why? What was the advantage to him? And were Victor O'Dell and Babbage and the others right to accuse Renfrew of dangerous experiments on kids' minds?

Underneath it all, the real reason had to do with Villabona being a threat to his mother's career. She used to love her work – now she was stressed and unhappy. Tal felt he had to try and do something, even if it were only turning up some extra bit of evidence to help discredit Renfrew. Damage to the doctor's reputation would reflect badly on Joe Villabona, and almost certainly undermine Audrey's confidence in Villabona's professional judgement.

Tal had to smile at the idea of being a knight in shining armour galloping to the rescue, but that was close to what he hoped to be.

Tal was last into the room where his discussion group was to be held. It was made up of eleven others, including David and George Everett – the latter completely absorbed with some weird-looking gadget. Yvette Sarno was cheerfully informing anyone who'd listen that she now had well over four thousand friends on MySpace, and was closing in on five thousand.

'They're not *friends*,' said David, 'they're just names. And half of them probably don't exist, anyway.'

'Like *you'd* know,' said Yvette. Seeing Tal, she smiled invitingly and patted the seat beside her. As it was the only spare in the semicircle of chairs, Tal was forced to take it. Yvette gave his arm a squeeze and told him he was looking extra cute today. 'Like, *seriously*.'

'Extra cute?' David sniggered. He was about to go on, when Dr Renfrew strode through the door.

'Sorry, I'm a little late. Now, who do we have? Let me check . . .' He consulted his iZod, then glanced up with a look of pleasure on his face. 'Talbot Blair. I'm delighted to find you here.'

'True, he is extra cute,' said David.

Renfrew frowned at the ripple of laughter. 'And your name is . . .?' he asked David.

'David Segal.'

Renfrew tapped away at his iZod for a moment, studied the screen for a few moments more, then said to David, 'You're excused.'

'What?'

'Please don't take this personally, but I'm afraid you don't meet the criteria for a test subject. Please leave.'

Stunned, David got to his feet. 'You backgrounded me?'

George, whose attention had been dragged away from his electronic device by the mini-drama, said, 'More likely an analysis of personality parameters, I'd say.'

'David doesn't actually *have* a personality,' said Yvette.

Fingers poised over his iZod, Dr Renfrew said to her, 'And your name is . . .?'

SEVENTEEN

Rick wasn't released until Thursday afternoon. Thelma came to pick him up in the lovingly maintained brown sedan that had been his grandparents' vehicle for as long as he could remember.

When they got into the car, Thelma gave him the welcome news that his grandfather was showing some improvement and had opened his eyes and tried to speak.

'What do the doctors say?'

'You know what they're like – they hate to commit themselves. "Cautiously optimistic" is the most Dr Morris would admit to, but I had a chat with one of the nurses – Eric, who's there most times we visit – and he said the swelling in Les's brain is going down and that's a very good sign.'

She squeezed Rick's hand. 'Things are looking up, dear. Soon we'll all be back to normal.'

'It won't be normal until I'm not a disconnect.'

Discomfited by the whiny note he could hear in his voice, he said more positively, 'Of course it's sure to happen soon.' He looked at her hopefully. 'It's been a week. You haven't heard anything, have you? The Facilitation and Support provider promised to notify you and the school the moment I was reconnected.'

'They haven't been in touch yet.' She squeezed his hand again. 'Until all this happened, I hadn't realised how important it was for you to be connected.'

'I'm nobody if I'm not.'

'Of course you're somebody,' she said stoutly. She released his hand to pat his cheek. 'You're Rick Lawrence and Les and I love you very much.'

Wriggling with embarrassment, Rick said, 'Thanks, but can we get going?'

Thelma double-checked everything around the vehicle before she pulled out of the parking lot. As usual, she drove very slowly and with great caution. Also as usual, this made Rick burn with frustration. When he had a car, he'd be a fast and decisive driver.

'A nice man from Farront International, Mr Villabona, came to see me this morning, just when I was leaving to visit Les. He said that because you were using an iZod from his company when you were disconnected – although Farront denies liability – he'd been authorised to offer you treatment absolutely free at The Farront Centre.'

Rick folded his arms and slid down lower in the seat. 'I don't need treatment.'

'Sweetie, I think you do. You weren't yourself when you got involved in that fight at school.'

'It wasn't a fight. I admit I lost my temper, but I didn't push Maryann. She made it look that way.'

'It's not normal for you to completely lose control, whatever cruel things they'd said about you. Mr Villabona told me behaviour like yours can be related to depressive illness.'

'He isn't a doctor, is he? I'd listen to Dr Stein, but not this guy. Anyhow, I'm not sick.'

A blast of horns indicated the traffic light had turned green. Thelma puttered into a snail-slow start, causing more horn blowing.

'Can't you go faster?'

'I'm not going to dash madly about like people do these days. It's just not safe.'

Rick groaned to himself as his grandmother went on to repeat a saying he'd heard her use at least a million times: 'Remember the tortoise and the hare. Slow and steady wins the race.'

'Yeah, yeah, yeah,' he muttered.

'What, dear?'

'Nothing.'

As she turned into their street, she said, 'Mr Villabona said he'd call by this evening to answer any questions you might have about the counselling his company is offering. He emphasised it would be free.'

'If I needed counselling, I'd go to Dr Stein. And you don't have to worry about the money, because my trust fund will pay.'

Thelma frowned at him. 'You know how I feel about your inheritance, dear. Apart from your monthly allowance, every cent of your parents' estate should remain untouched until you're twenty-one.'

Knowing that the lawyers controlling the trust fund would listen to Thelma before him, Rick sank further into the seat. 'Doesn't matter anyway. I don't need any treatment. I keep telling you, there's nothing wrong with me.'

'Mr Villabona —'

'I don't even want to meet him!'

'Manners, Rick! He's a guest in our house.'

'He's your guest, not mine,' he said sulkily.

'Please, dear, for my sake?'

Rick groaned aloud. 'Oh, all right. I'll listen to what he has to say, but that's all I'll do.'

By Thursday afternoon Petra was completely fed up with being an artificial disconnect. She'd never realised how much her time had been taken up by her iZod. Everyone was moving on without her. She was shut out of interactive games and, infuriatingly, David had pointed out that the team was doing perfectly without her input. She was missing out on her favourite blogs and gossip posts — in-jokes and references were going straight over her head. She hated having to rely on snippets of overheard information.

The only time she held the familiar shape of her

comm in her hand was when her mother supervised her boring homework assignments. That sucked!

This morning she'd caught her parents early, before they left for Garden Stuff. She'd tried pleading, even turned on quite convincing tears, but her mother had remained totally unmoved. Petra had then tried to persuade her father of the unfairness of it all, but he'd been just as unsympathetic.

In a final effort, she pointed out that if this went on much longer, there was a good chance she'd begin to develop symptoms of CWSS. 'Actually, I think I'm showing some signs of communication withdrawal already.'

It didn't have the effect she intended – her parents had been amused.

Her mother chuckled. 'You're trying to convince us you're sliding into a clinical depression because you haven't had the use of your iZod since Tuesday? Three days? Poor baby.'

After all that effort, the result was still no iZod, and not even an indication of when she might get it back. Her parents were totally forcing her to do something drastic.

Petra went in search of George. If he could get a phantom communicator for Rick, he could get one for Petra too. She was confident she could scrape up enough money to pay whatever it cost.

George was hostile when she did locate him. 'Oh, right! Like I'd want to do a favour for someone who dobbed me in to my dad. Get real, Petra.'

'It wasn't me, George. It was Ms Ingram. She got your name from other people you'd told about the website. Honest, I never said a thing.'

George's specs were sliding down his long nose. He shoved them back into place and glared at Petra. 'Don't give me that. It was *your* mother who called my dad. Now I'm grounded and Constanza has me on after-school detention for weeks. Thanks heaps.'

'Why don't you believe me? I never mentioned your name. I wouldn't do that to you.'

'Then why did your mum call Dad?'

'When Ingram said you'd helped other students cheat, Mum said she knew your father, and she'd call him.' Seeing George was wavering, she added, 'I'm really sorry, George, but I couldn't stop her.' Petra raised her shoulders in an elaborate shrug. 'Parents . . .'

'Yeah, they can be the pits.'

'So you believe me?'

'I guess.'

She looked at him with a hopeful little smile. 'You got a phantom comm for Rick . . .'

'Didn't have a chance to give it to him before the cops took him away.'

'So Rick can't use the phantom now, but *I* can.'

'Too late. Frank Arran has just been made a disconnect.'

Frank, who spent hours tinkering with electronic devices was, in Petra's opinion, George's equal in geekiness. 'Frank could build a phantom for himself, couldn't he?'

'Maybe he could, but Frank needed to be back online as soon as possible, so I sold it to him.'

Petra's heart sank. 'How long before you can get one for me?'

'Next week, maybe.'

'Next week? I'm going mad without my iZod.'

'Best I can do, and it'll cost you.'

He named a figure that raised her eyebrows. 'Omigod! That much? How could Rick afford it?'

'No idea. I don't ask questions like that.'

'For a friend, you could drop the price a bit . . .?'

'Petra, this is business. That's the going rate. Take it or leave it.'

She sighed. 'So much for Plan B. It's back to working on my mother again.'

When he got home from school, Tal was very surprised to see both his mother's car and Rob's little electric vehicle in the driveway. Tal had checked his iZod regularly during the day, and there'd been no urgent message from his mum, but even so a chill touched him. Something must be wrong.

He found them in the kitchen, huddled together at the bench, mugs of coffee in front of them and serious expressions on their faces. Tal's mother hadn't changed from her workday tailored suit, and Rob wore his usual garb of jeans and T-shirt.

They both looked up as Tal came in. 'Is something wrong, Mum?'

'My job may be on the line. Victor is scheduled to be on FinagleAlert's live chat this evening. Audrey's ordered me to persuade him not to appear.'

'But why?'

'Joe Villabona pointed out to Audrey that Finagle-Alert has a huge, well-informed audience. And more importantly, a politically active one. He's convinced Audrey that not only will Victor do irreparable harm to Farront's reputation, he will also encourage social activists to demand an investigation similar to Tacitcomm's audit. I argued that this was highly unlikely, but Joe won Audrey over by saying that further government scrutiny of the industry would mean we'd be looking at more government regulation down the line, something she's fought against for years.'

Tal's slow-burning anger over how his mother was being treated went up a notch. 'We've got to get rid of this Villabona guy.'

She gave him a tired smile. 'Amen.'

'Villabona may have a valid reason for warning Audrey,' said Rob. 'Victor's scheduled for a question-and-answer session about controversial issues in the communication industry. He intends to use Farront's financial backing of Renfrew's research, plus the free youth counselling services at The Farront Centre, as examples of cynical manipulation of public opinion, while the company actually cares little for the welfare of the individual young consumer.'

'I still don't see why it's up to Mum to do anything about Mr O'Dell.'

'Hah!' said his mother. 'That's exactly what I said to Audrey. Big mistake. She was livid because she'd already made a personal appeal to Victor to cancel the appearance, but he'd turned her down. Now she's made it my responsibility to stop him. Audrey didn't say it in so many words, but I get the picture – my hopes for promotion depend on getting Victor to shut up.'

'What did Mr O'Dell say when you spoke to him?'

She gusted a sigh. 'Both Rob and I have left messages asking for an immediate response, but Victor hasn't got back to us yet.'

'Hang on,' said Rob, as his comm's artificial voice announced an urgent item waiting for him on the FinagleAlert secure communications channel.

While Rob was tapping in a coded sequence to gain access to the channel, Tal said to his mother, 'Even if you do get Mr O'Dell to cancel tonight, what's to prevent him from attacking Farront tomorrow, or the day after?'

'Audrey's playing for time. The legal department is working full-time to find grounds for a court injunction to keep him quiet.'

Rob interrupted them. 'It seems Audrey's had her wish. Tonight's off. Victor's been in a car crash.'

Tal's mother leapt to her feet. 'A crash! Is he okay?'

'Cuts and bruises and a couple of cracked ribs. Because of his age, he's been admitted to hospital.'

'Poor Victor, he must be in pain. Which hospital? I'll visit him this evening.'

'Who was driving?' said Tal, visualising Marcia's cheerful smile obliterated by blood.

'A young woman – I don't know her name. She's all right except for a broken nose. She told the cops a ute sideswiped the car and ran them off the road.'

Tal's mother paced around the kitchen. 'Have they arrested anyone?'

Rob shook his head. 'Not yet. The ute was stolen some time last night. It was found abandoned less than a kilometre from the site of the accident.'

'Accident?' said Tal. 'Are you sure?'

'You mean the death threats?' said his mother. 'Victor's been getting them for years. He makes enemies because he's so outspoken, but no one has ever actually tried to physically hurt him.'

'Not until now. Rob said it – Audrey's had her wish. Victor O'Dell's off the air.'

'Tal, you can't be serious! Audrey may be ruthless in business, but she'd never condone anything like this. It's unthinkable.'

'It's been my experience,' said Rob, 'that if the stakes are high enough, many people find the unthinkable becomes the improbable, which rapidly changes to the possible.'

Finding himself with nothing else to do after dinner, Rick joined Thelma in front of the TV. If he hadn't been a disconnect, there were hundreds of things he could be doing right now. He particularly missed *Red*

Killer Guitar, where he'd been steadily improving as he played lead guitar with the avatars of the real Red Killer band. What a waste – the one advantage of being suspended from school was all the free time, and he had no way of enjoying it.

Slumped in his chair, he was half-watching Thelma's favourite live show, *Take the Carrot and Run*. Rick could not imagine why she found it entertaining. Both the studio audience and contestants shrieked and clapped hysterically when anybody won a prize, regardless of whether it was a gold-plated carrot or a million dollars.

The show was suddenly interrupted by a newsflash. 'Another near-riot at Commdat central offices,' said the voice-over announcer enthusiastically.

The screen showed an angry crowd milling about while police in riot gear tried to control them. Many of the demonstrators were young, and most of them held flashing signs demanding justice for disconnects.

'With the number of disconnects rising, and no action from Commdat or the government authorities,' declared the announcer, 'public frustration is at boiling point, and for good reason. Lives have been turned upside down, small business owners are facing ruin, students' education has been disrupted . . .'

The doorbell chimed. 'That'll be Mr Villabona,' she said, heaving herself out of her chair.

'Great,' muttered Rick.

'Now, dear, you promised.'

'Okay, okay.'

Rick turned off the TV, replacing it with electronic wallpaper – in this case an image of surf breaking on a beach. He folded his arms. He'd promised Thelma he'd be polite, but that didn't mean he had to be cooperative.

He slowly got out of his chair when Thelma, looking a little flustered, led two men into the room. Indicating the one with olive skin and dark moustache, she said, 'Rick, this is Mr Villabona from Farront International, and with him is Dr Unwin.'

'Please call me Joe,' Villabona said, flashing a smile as he shook hands. He wasn't much taller than Rick, but considerably more powerfully built, as shown by the way his bulging muscles strained the jacket of his suit.

'And allow me to introduce Dr Howard Unwin, co-director of The Farront Centre.'

Rick recognised him from Audrey Farront's PR video. His photo hadn't been retouched – he had the same thick black hair, regular features and luminous smile. But in person there was something about him that prickled Rick's skin. Perhaps it was his dry, limp handshake, or the way his smile never reached his eyes.

Seeing that Thelma was looking impressed, Rick decided he would make his lack of interest in Dr Unwin as obvious as possible. He seriously considered smothering a yawn, but decided it would be overkill. Instead he put on what he hoped was a totally blank expression.

'Well, Rick,' said Dr Unwin in a warm, sympathetic voice, 'you've been in the wars lately, I hear.'

When Rick didn't react in any way, Dr Unwin continued, 'Things aren't fair, are they? You did nothing wrong, and yet you were disconnected. And that's upset you. Yes?'

Rick became aware that Joe Villabona had stepped back from the one-way conversation, and was watching them with unnerving concentration.

Not at all put out by Rick's vacant stare, the doctor went on, 'And then you were unjustifiably attacked, and lashed out at those you thought responsible. I'm sure you never intended to hurt Maryann Dodd, but I'm guessing you couldn't help yourself. Am I right?'

'Rick, manners, please! Answer Dr Unwin.'

'Don't want to talk about it.'

Using a warm, understanding tone, Dr Unwin infuriated Rick by saying to Thelma, 'I know what Rick's inner self is experiencing. Bad feelings – depression, hopelessness.' He sent her a quick, electric smile. 'Fortunately, I can help.'

Villabona broke in to say to Thelma, 'I must remind you that there will be absolutely no charge for Rick's treatment. He can be admitted to the security-protected residential unit of The Farront Centre tomorrow, if it suits you both.'

His words jolted Rick. They were going to lock him up again?

To his relief, Thelma wasn't keen on the idea. 'A residential unit? Is that really necessary? Can't Rick stay here? I'm available to drive him for his appointment every day, if that's required.'

Unwin employed a lower-voltage smile as he said soothingly, 'I have found it preferable to have a patient like Rick under twenty-four-hour care.'

Patient? thought Rick. *I'm not your patient!*

'Dr Stein has been Rick's psychiatrist for many years,' said Thelma, 'and he's never suggested Rick join a residential program.'

Unwin nodded agreeably. 'Bernard Stein is a fine man, and a fine doctor. However, he has not specialised in the treatment of communication withdrawal stress syndrome, as I have. CWSS requires a unique approach available only to patients under my direct care.'

'No way am I going to be your patient,' Rick said. 'It's not going to happen.'

Thelma was obviously torn. 'Dr Unwin, if Rick feels that way . . .'

'I fully understand, but Rick's welfare is of paramount importance, and unfortunately at the moment he's not the best judge of what will help him. If I could speak to you alone for a moment, I can explain why it's far more advantageous for his mental health to have Rick stay at the clinic as our guest.'

Red rage bubbled up in Rick until he thought his head would burst. 'I'm going bloody nowhere!' he shouted. 'You can't make me!'

Storming out of the room, he yelled back over his shoulder, 'You can all get stuffed – the whole lot of you!'

EIGHTEEN

Tal's first period on Friday was an elective subject, History of Civilisation. He was sorry he'd ever taken the course. It should have been interesting, but it was taught by Mr Marsfield, the new teacher who had a sarcastic, jeering attitude and an almost total lack of interest in the topic.

Tal was seated at the very back of the room between Allyx and Jennie. In the row in front of them, George Everett was hunched over a razor-thin mini-notebook, no doubt working on something nerdy. Jennie, usually the most conscientious student of the Five, was playing with her iZod.

A documentary on early Rome was running on the students' desk screens – and being largely ignored – while down the front Mr Marsfield busied himself with his communicator, seemingly unaware of the racket his students were making.

Tal got up and went to George Everett's desk. 'Hey, I've got a favour to ask.'

George looked up from his mini-note. 'If it's about a phantom for Petra, forget it.'

'Nothing to do with Petra. I want anything you can dig up on this guy who's got no record of his past available – nothing personal, no work history.'

'The target's got protected status?' said George, obviously interested.

'I don't know. Some real experts have tried to find out more about him, but basically got nowhere.'

George grinned. 'You think I'll have better luck than the real experts?'

'I'm counting on it.'

Obviously pleased, George said, 'You've come to the right place.' When Tal mentioned money, George flapped his hand. 'Nah. It's a freebie. Sounds like fun.'

Tal gave him more information about 'the target', as George insisted they call Villabona – 'Never use names'. They arranged to meet the next day at George's place.

When he went back to his seat Allyx was pouting a little. 'I really missed talking with you last night.'

'Sorry, but I told you, I went with Mum when she visited Victor O'Dell in hospital.'

'He's going to be okay?'

'He's already bossing the nurses around.'

After a moment, Allyx said, 'And *Mutant Bloom* wasn't nearly as much fun without you.'

'Wasn't it?' he said, mildly irritated.

'This can't be true!' Jennie sat bolt upright in her seat, her gaze fixed on her iZod. 'Not Rick!'

'What about Rick?' Tal and Allyx whipped out their own comms.

'They're saying he's armed and dangerous.' Eyes wide, Jennie looked up from her iZod. 'It can't be Rick.'

On the screen of Tal's communicator, SECURITY ALERT INSTANT NEWSFLASH appeared blinking in red above a photo of Rick that had been taken at the school dance last year. Underneath Rick's smiling face scrolled: ARMED AND DANGEROUS. DO NOT APPROACH. SPECIFIC THREATS MADE. TWO WITNESSES REPORT SUSPENDED BRAIDWORTH HIGH STUDENT RICHARD LAWRENCE IN VICINITY OF SCHOOL ARMED WITH SHOTGUN –

The screen of Tal's iZod went blank. Simultaneously, four long blasts sounded from the electronic horn that usually announced the end of each period. All the desk screens displayed the words: CODE RED SECURITY ALERT. THIS IS NOT A DRILL. REMAIN WHERE YOU ARE AND AWAIT INSTRUCTIONS.

Tal's iZod came alive again, displaying the same message. Added below was: ALL TRANSMISSIONS CLOAKED FOR YOUR PROTECTION.

Mr Marsfield exclaimed, 'What the hell?' and got to his feet. He shook his communicator, then peered at the screen. 'Christ! They've cut us off.'

In the distance, multiple sirens wailed.

'Code red,' someone called out. 'That isn't good.'

'Run for the hills!' somebody else shouted, to chortles from the class.

'Rick Lawrence is out there with a gun!' yelled a student who had obviously seen the security newsflash.

The public address system crackled into life. An authoritative automated voice declared, 'Security alert, code red. The entire school is in lockdown. Students and teachers are not to vacate classrooms until instructed to do so. This is not a drill. Repeat, this is not a drill. The school is in code red security lockdown. Remain where you are and await instructions.'

There was silence for a moment, then a babble of noise exploded around Tal. Many were complaining about having their comms electronically cloaked, others were sharing misinformation about Rick, or discussing the best escape strategies to employ should an armed maniac enter the building.

'They've cloaked our comms so we can't tell anyone what's really happening.'

'That's not the reason. It's so *we* can't find out what's really happening.'

'How can I let my mum know I'm okay if my iZod isn't working?'

'Lawrence is going to kill Constanza because he suspended him then had the cops take him to the nut house.'

'No, it's Maryann Dodd he's after.'

'They say pretending to be dead is the best way to save your life.'

'Run zigzag. It makes you a harder target.'

'Quiet!' roared Marsfield. When he had most

people's attention, he went on, 'Don't leave your seats. I'm off to see what the hell's happening.'

'Teachers are supposed to stay in the room, too,' George pointed out.

Marsfield shot him a look of intense dislike. 'Mind your own business, Everett.'

The teacher stalked out, slamming the door behind him. Immediately most of the class rushed to the windows. The sirens were louder and a swarm of helicopters was fast approaching.

The sound of throat-clearing came over the public address system.

'Constanza!' chorused several students in unison.

'This is Principal Constanza speaking. Students, faculty, we have an emergency. Please remain calm. I repeat, please remain calm.'

'We're calm,' a student assured the public address system. '*So* calm.'

There were sniggers when someone added, 'Calm? We're practically unconscious.'

The principal said in grave tones, 'Braidworth High's website has received a series of credible threatening messages. Witnesses have reported seeing an armed individual in the vicinity of our school. The authorities are at this moment securing the area. Students and faculty are to stay in classrooms until advised otherwise.'

'I'm outta here!' someone yelled. 'We'll be sitting ducks if we stay.'

There was a murmur of agreement, and a number of students began to head for the front of the room.

Before they reached the door, it was flung open by Mr Marsfield. 'Get back to your desks immediately.'

Behind him in the hall, one of the long-time school security guards, known to teachers and students alike as Russell, stood holding his revolver. He was jumpy, swivelling his head around as though expecting an attack at any moment.

Russell moved to stand in the doorway, positioning himself so he could check the hall. 'Like I said, Mr Marsfield, the police have activated all the specialist squads. No one should be out there, especially students. You don't want to be shot by mistake.'

'The kid they're looking for should be easy enough to locate with GPS.'

'It seems he's not carrying a communicator,' said Russell, 'so the Global Positioning System is of no use.'

Marsfield wriggled his shoulders impatiently. 'How long are we going to be struck here? I've got appointments, things to do.'

'I'm sure we all have,' said the guard, unimpressed, 'but it's impossible to say how much time a sweep like this will take. Best lock the door and don't open it unless you're sure it's safe to do so. If something happens, use the call-back on the public address system.'

The guard stepped cautiously out into the hall and Marsfield shut and locked the door. Turning to the class, he said, 'Any of you know the damage a shotgun can do?'

'Lots,' said someone.

'Blow your head off, that's what. Cut you in half.' Marsfield broke the silence that followed by adding, 'Rick Lawrence is out there somewhere with a loaded shotgun. And he's gone apeshit. Totally apeshit.'

Time passed agonisingly slowly. Tension filled the air while everyone waited for something to happen. Outside, apart from the constant noise of hovering helicopters, there were distant shouts and an occasional siren.

Complaints about the comm shut-down grew louder and more resentful. One angry student pointed out that the total cloaking was unfair. They should at least be allowed to pass the time playing games.

With no communicator access to the outside world, the class split into groups, some talking quietly, others, including Mr Marsfield, crowding the windows and exclaiming whenever they saw anything.

'Look at those guys! I bet that's the anti-terrorism squad – see the body armour they're wearing.'

'Look, there's an air cam coming this way.'

Tal, Allyx and Jennie sat silently together. They couldn't believe Rick was being portrayed as a would-be killer on the loose, to be hunted down like a dangerous animal. There was little any of them could find to say, other than to repeat that it had to be a terrible mistake.

Tal noticed that George Everett was also silent, frowning over his illegally enhanced iZod, inputting sequences then pausing to review the result. At last he thrust his arm up in victory, exclaiming, 'Yes! I've broken through the cloak!'

'George, you're a genius,' said Allyx.

'True,' he said modestly.

George pumped up the audio on his iZod so everyone in the room could hear the news report. 'A police perimeter has been set up around Braidworth High School,' the announcer's fruity baritone declared, 'keeping out desperately worried parents and eager onlookers alike, while the police search for a deranged student who has vowed to kill.'

'Now they're showing a photo of Rick,' said George, looking at his iZod's screen.

The announcer continued, 'This is a recent photograph of Richard Lawrence – also known as Rick Lawrence – a suspended student of Braidworth High, who is described as mentally disturbed. In a series of postings to the school website, he has threatened to – and I quote – "blow away" teachers and students. Law enforcement authorities have issued a warning to the public not to approach Richard Lawrence under any circumstances. He is reportedly in possession of a double-barrelled shotgun and a supply of shells.'

There was a murmur of alarm in the room. Marsfield raised his voice. 'Settle down. The door's locked. No one can get in.'

'But with a shotgun, Lawrence could blow the lock away,' George pointed out.

This sobering thought started an avalanche of suggestions of what to do.

'We could get out the windows. It's not that much of a drop.'

'I say stay put. Russell said the cops could shoot us by mistake.'

'How about barricading the door with desks?'

'All the furniture's screwed to the floor. We haven't got any tools.'

'Get the principal on the call-back and tell him we've got to be rescued right now.'

'Why would he rescue us when the whole school's in lockdown?'

On George's iZod, the announcer was saying dramatically, 'As helicopters hover overhead, frantic parents wring their hands and terrified students crouch in classrooms, a systematic search is being made of every building, every room, any area where a crazed student might hide.'

'I wonder if our parents are out there, waiting,' Jennie said. 'I wish there was a way we could tell them we're okay.'

'There is,' said Tal. 'George's iZod is working. He could IM them for us.'

'No way,' said George, who'd overheard the conversation. 'If I do it for you, I have to do it for everyone. Besides, something's happening.'

'Dramatic developments!' boomed the announcer. Tal detected a trace of disappointment in his voice as he went on. 'The lockdown at Braidworth High is ending.

A thorough search of the grounds has failed to find any trace of armed and mentally disturbed student, Richard Lawrence.'

Almost immediately, the public address system broadcast the same message from Principal Constanza, with the welcome addition that the cloaking of comms was being removed. 'Under the circumstances, I am suspending lessons for the rest of the day and cancelling the school dance tonight. It will be rescheduled later.'

After a few cheers of relief that the ordeal was over, everybody grabbed their comms and began feverishly texting as they made for the door.

Outside there was confusion as students streamed out of the buildings, concerned parents flooded onto the grounds, and reporters interviewed anyone who looked the slightest traumatised – Tal was amused to see Yvette Sarno putting on a fairly convincing display of hysterics.

Tal, Allyx and Jennie met up with Petra and David in the crowd heading for the gates. 'I've got an IM from my dad,' said Allyx with a groan. 'He's waiting for me outside. He'll want to take me home, and I'd rather stay with you guys.'

Steven Grant wasn't alone. Standing with him was Jennie's anxious father and Rob Anderson, who Grace had asked to go to the school because she was stuck in a work meeting. Once Tal assured Rob that he was fine, Rob left for an important meeting of his own.

'Obviously my parents were too busy to bother coming,' Petra said bleakly.

Steven Grant shook his head. 'That isn't true, Petra. I'm here on their behalf. Your mother called me as soon as they heard the news. I've just been texting a message to say you're safe and well.'

'My mum won't even know there's been a drama,' said David.

'Why not?' asked Jennie's father, mildly scandalised by the failure of a parent to keep in touch.

'Mum works in a totally shielded zone, making drone reconnaissance flyers for the military. She doesn't get to use her comm until she leaves the plant.'

Petra had Tal make a call to her mother to repeat that she was okay. 'And tell Mum I could have called her direct if only I'd had my iZod.'

The call accomplished, Petra said, 'How about everyone comes to my place? We need a council of war. *We* know Rick wouldn't hurt a fly, but people are going to believe he's a stone-cold killer.'

'Allyx won't be joining you,' said Steven Grant firmly. 'No, Allyx, it's no use arguing. You've had an upsetting experience and I want you home with me.'

'Dad?' said Jennie with a sweet smile. 'I promise not to be home late.'

'Okay.' He kissed her cheek. 'You're sure about Rick? He isn't dangerous?'

'It's all a huge mistake.'

David said, 'Sure, we know they're wrong about Rick, but the cops don't. They'll shoot first and ask questions later.'

NINETEEN

An hour later the Five, minus Rick, sat munching toasted cheese sandwiches courtesy of Rosa.

Tal glanced around the little group, wondering if they felt like he did – strangely dislocated, as though the familiar world was not so familiar after all. The events of the morning seemed to have happened in some parallel universe, where Braidworth High could be locked down for the bizarre reason that Rick – *Rick*, who'd been their friend since kindergarten – had supposedly gone over the edge and was roaming the grounds with a shotgun, looking for people to kill.

Petra said indistinctly through a mouthful of sandwich, 'We've got to find Rick before the cops do.'

'Because he's a disconnect, he's got no idea what's going on,' said Jennie. 'My guess is he's just wandering around.'

'Then he won't be doing that much longer,' said David, who'd been monitoring the news on his iZod.

'There are pictures of Rick everywhere on the web, plus there's a reward for his capture being offered.'

'If he isn't wandering around, where would he go?'

'The games shop?' said Tal, remembering that, of all of them, Rick was the one who was the most into video games.

'Nah,' said David. 'Rick spends so much time there, the guy who owns it knows him. He would have turned him in by now.'

'This is so wrong,' said Jennie. 'I can't believe Rick had anything to do with those threats on the school website. He's disconnected, so he's got no way of posting them.'

'Maybe he got a friend to do it for him,' Petra suggested.

'Like who?' said David. '*We're* his friends.'

'And where's the shotgun supposed to have come from?' Tal asked. 'There's no way his grandparents would have a gun in the house.'

Petra agreed. 'It's all too dumb. Why would Rick tell everyone he was going to shoot up Braidworth High? It's like saying to the cops, "Please kill me".'

'Suicide by cop,' said David. 'Happens all the time.'

'Not Rick,' declared Petra. 'He isn't *that* depressed.'

'You can't say that, Petra,' Jennie pointed out. 'Even when Rick seems to be okay, he could be hiding how bad he feels.'

'That's true. You get isolated from everyone when you're a disconnect,' said Petra moodily. 'People find it hard to get in touch with you. I know all about it.'

David rolled his eyes.

Tal grinned at Petra. 'How about you give us all a big break, and get your iZod back? Tell your mum it's a safety issue, that you've got to have it to call for help if there's an emergency like today.'

Petra sighed. 'She'd never fall for it.'

Jennie stood up. 'Guys, while we're feeding our faces, Rick is out there somewhere. And he's in danger –'

David broke in. 'Thelma's being interviewed on TV. Maybe she'll say something that'll give a clue to where Rick might be.'

Seeing Tal and Jennie take out their iZods, Petra sighed despondently. 'I'll have to watch it on the big screen. I don't need to tell you why.'

'Please don't,' said David. 'I'm sick to death of the subject.'

They followed Petra to the entertainment centre. She keyed 'interview Richard Lawrence's grandmother' into the console and in a moment a list of possible TV sites appeared.

'Second from the bottom – the one with Bamber,' said David.

On the huge screen every line and wrinkle on Thelma's face appeared with less than flattering clarity. Although obviously stressed, her manner was direct and her voice crisp.

'I don't see the point in going over all this again. I've been asked too many questions today by too many people, Mr Bamber.'

Sleekly groomed Bamber, a celebrity interviewer so famous he only used a single name, said, 'No formality needed, Thelma. Just Bamber will be fine.'

He paused for her to respond. When she didn't, he said soothingly, 'I do understand how very hard this must be for you, Thelma – may I call you Thelma?'

This was clearly a rhetorical question, because he continued immediately, 'But I'm sure you want to help your grandson any way you can.'

'Naturally I want to help Rick. He's been wrongly accused of something he would never do –'

'Of course you believe that, Thelma,' he interrupted in a warmly sympathetic tone, 'and I'm sure you're right, but the huge audience watching this interview has yet to decide the truth of the matter. It would be of great help to know your grandson's state of mind.'

'Rick was a bit depressed because he'd been disconnected, that's all.'

'Let's talk about last night. Dr Howard Unwin's visit to your home upset Rick. Is that right?'

Thelma opened her mouth to answer, but Bamber was already saying, 'A short explanation for those who have just joined us. Dr Howard Unwin is a noted psychiatrist, and a co-director, together with Dr Carter Renfrew, of The Farront Centre, established by communications giant Farront International to research and treat youth health issues.'

His attention back on Thelma, he murmured, 'Please continue . . .'

'Mr Villabona brought Dr Unwin with him and –'

'Mr Villabona is a top executive with Farront International?'

Her lips tightened at this further interruption. 'Yes, Mr Bamber, that's correct.'

'And when Mr Villabona and Dr Unwin offered your grandson free treatment for communication withdrawal stress syndrome, also known as CWSS, Rick became angry?'

'He didn't believe he needed treatment. And anyway, Rick didn't like the idea of being a residential patient at the centre. I'm afraid he lost his temper and stormed off. Mr Villabona and Dr Unwin were very nice about it.'

'And this morning?' prompted Bamber.

'This morning Rick didn't want to go with me to the hospital – my husband's recovering from a bad fall – so I left him alone at home. When I got back, Rick was missing and the police were everywhere.'

'I believe you made a formal complaint about the way you were treated.' He gave a rueful shake of his head. 'Yet another case of police brutality.'

'Hardly brutality,' Thelma said tartly. 'Lack of consideration, more like it. And I didn't file a formal complaint. I did mention to the officer in charge that I'd been treated rudely. Perfect strangers, armed to the teeth, poured into my house demanding to know where Rick was. They called him a terrorist and shouted at me to show them where his weapons were stored.'

'You were understandably frightened.'

'I was understandably annoyed, Mr Bamber, to be treated this way in my own home. I told them Rick would never hurt anyone, that we didn't have a firearm of any description, and that I didn't know where Rick was at the moment, but I was sure he'd be back soon. I might as well have been speaking to a brick wall. No one listened to me. They just started with the same questions all over again.'

Bamber swung around to the camera. 'Richard Lawrence. Troubled young man, or dangerous terrorist? That is the question. We'll have answers for you right after our valued sponsors' important messages.'

A commercial for a home security firm filled the screen with graphic images of the dreadful things practically guaranteed to occur if people were too foolish to install the company's deluxe security system.

As the commercial showed a figure lurking in the shadows at the back of a mansion, Jennie said, 'I think I know where Rick could be. The treehouse. He's always loved it there.'

The elaborate treehouse in David's backyard had been a favourite rendezvous for the Five when they were growing up. Built by David's father with loving care, it perched in the embrace of an enormous old tree, and was still in good condition. Occasionally on summer evenings they would still climb up to sit in the warm darkness and talk things over.

It was an easy walk to David's place from Petra's home. On the way, Jennie said, 'Did you see the terrorist special teams this morning? If they find Rick . . .'

'If they find Rick they're liable to shoot him,' said David. 'Those guys are trained to take down a target fast.'

Tal quickened his pace. 'We're Rick's closest friends, so it's only a matter of time until they use our comms' GPS beacons to pinpoint where we are. We have to get to Rick fast and talk him into giving himself up.'

He didn't know why it hadn't really hit him before, but Tal was suddenly filled with an overwhelming sense of urgency. This was a life-and-death situation, not a game. It wasn't Rick's avatar that was being stalked, it was the real Rick, who would bleed real blood if he were shot.

'Hurry up,' he called over his shoulder as he broke into a run.

When the four of them arrived at David's place, Tal was amazed to see how neglected it was. Tal and the others hadn't been here since David's parents had split up. Now the house looked as though it were abandoned. The garden had been unattended for months. Weeds grew in profusion and unpruned bushes ran wild.

Clearly embarrassed, David gestured towards the garden. 'The divorce . . . Mum isn't coping all that well.'

'Shit happens,' said Petra. 'Don't worry about it.'

'Your mum's at work?' Jennie said.

'She won't be home until this evening.'

David led the way around the side of the house. The backyard was particularly overgrown, so they had to wade through tall grass to get to the treehouse.

The four of them stood by the thick trunk and looked up.

'Rick?' Jennie called. 'Are you there?'

Silence.

Crushed, she said, 'I was so sure this is where he'd be.'

Hands on hips, head thrown back, Petra bellowed, 'Move it, Lawrence!'

There was a rustle of leaves, then Rick's face looked down at them. 'How did you know I was here?'

'Jennie's psychic,' said Tal. 'Stay there. We'll come up.'

Soon they were all seated on the treehouse floor. The space had been roomy when they were kids, but now it was cramped. Taking up some of the area was a large backpack. 'I brought provisions,' said Rick, noticing Petra eyeing it.

'Why did you take off?' Jennie asked.

Rick drooped his head in misery. 'Thelma's going to put me in that clinic. I'm sure they'll persuade her. See, last night –'

'We know all about it,' Petra said impatiently.

Knowing the answer already, Tal asked, 'Did you know the cops are looking for you?'

Rick stared at him in astonishment. 'You're joking! Thelma called the cops just because I took off for a day?'

'I told you he wouldn't have a clue,' said Petra.

'Dude, you're a wanted terrorist,' said David.

'What? Is this a joke?'

'No joke,' said Tal. 'Someone claiming to be you posted terrorist threats on the school website. Whoever it was pretending to be you said he had a shotgun and he was heading to Braidworth High to blow away teachers and kids who'd laughed at him. The school was in lockdown this morning while cops and special teams searched the grounds.'

'Looking for you waving a shotgun,' Petra added, in case Rick didn't get the picture.

Rick was flabbergasted. 'It wasn't me! I never made any threats.' His face reddened with anger. 'It's bloody Maryann! Why won't she leave me alone?'

'Forget Dodder,' said Petra, 'we can deal with her later. Right now the big problem is what to do about you.'

He struggled to his feet. 'I'll tell them it's all a big mistake.'

'Sit down,' said Tal. 'It's not as easy as that. We can't just call and say to come and pick you up.'

Rick looked sick. 'Pick me up? I'm going to be arrested again? No way.' He grabbed his backpack. 'I'm outta here.'

'Where the hell will you go?' David asked.

'I don't know!' Rick sat down abruptly and buried his face in his hands.

Jennie put an arm around his shoulders. 'You have to give yourself up. The police are coming after you. They think you're armed and dangerous. You've got to show them you're not. Once they understand they've got the wrong person, they'll release you.'

Rick muttered something.

'What?' said Petra.

He lifted his head. 'I said I'd rather die than be locked up.'

Tal felt a surge of sympathy. Rick had done absolutely nothing to deserve what was happening to him. 'Hey,' he said, clapping him on the shoulder, 'it won't be for long. Like Jennie said, they'll let you go when they realise you were set up.'

Petra, apparently oblivious to Rick's distress, said, 'So what's the safest way to turn Rick in? We don't want to get shot doing it.'

'Involve our parents?' said David. 'Well, certainly not mine, but how about your mum, Tal? With Farront behind her, she's got influence.'

'Yes, but Farront is funding the youth clinic, and people seem awfully keen to lock Rick away in there.' He considered for a moment, then said, 'Rob Anderson. He'd be perfect.'

'Your mother's boyfriend?' said Petra. 'I thought you couldn't stand him.'

'He's okay . . . sort of. Besides, Rob works for FinagleAlert.'

'Great idea,' Jennie enthused. 'The police won't dare do anything stupid if FinagleAlert is involved.'

'Uh-oh.' David looked up from his iZod. 'Tal, you'd better get to Rob Anderson in a hurry. The police are blocking off streets in this part of Braidworth to conduct a house-to-house search.'

As if on cue, they heard the beat of helicopter blades and the yowl of sirens.

'Since I don't have my iZod,' Petra declared, 'they don't have any idea *I'm* here.' She added with satisfaction, 'And neither do my parents. It'll drive them mad not to know where I am.'

'Jeez!' David exclaimed. 'It's not all about you, Petra. Get used to it. Besides, Rosa would have told the cops you left with us.'

Tal made an urgent gesture for them to shut up. 'Rob?' he said into his iZod. 'It's Tal. Thank God I got you. We need your help. Desperately.'

Rick muttered, 'This is a nightmare. A total nightmare. I can't believe it's really happening.'

'Oh, it's happening,' said Petra, excited and apprehensive all at once. 'The trick is to survive it.'

TWENTY

They decided that the best thing was for Rick to surrender from the house, rather than have him clamber down from the treehouse when the police arrived in force. At the end of the call, Rob had told Tal that a news blackout was about to be imposed, along with electronic cloaking of all communication devices in the area. As he was saying this, they were cut off, and SERVICES SUSPENDED FOR YOUR PROTECTION appeared on the iZod's screen.

They waded through the high grass to the back of the house, while helicopters hovered overhead like malevolent dragonflies.

'It's a bit of a mess inside,' said David, unlocking the door with a handprint reader.

Rob Anderson had told Tal he'd make direct contact with the authorities at the highest level and explain that Rick was surrendering unarmed. At the same time Rob would use FinagleAlert's secure communication channel to send an urgent-item signal to all news outlets on TV and the web, giving the exact location of David's house. The media blackout would mean there'd be no real-time reporting of Rick's surrender, but images shot at the time could be used once the blackout had been lifted, which would probably be after Rick was in custody.

'I'm heading for the FinagleAlert chopper,' Rob had said to Tal. 'The pilot won't get permission to touch down near you, but we'll do it anyway and worry about the consequences later. So hang on – the cavalry's on the way.'

Tal devoutly hoped the cavalry would arrive in time, as the scream of sirens was now so loud they had to be just outside.

They crowded around the window in the front room, which was once used as an office by David's father and had been untouched since he'd left. A thick layer of dust covered everything and Rick immediately had a sneezing fit. 'Allergies,' he said thickly as he searched his pockets for a tissue.

Jennie handed him a small packet of tissues. 'This will cost you, kiddo.' Her tone was light, but Tal could hear the tremor in her voice.

'It could be a movie set,' said Petra, peering through the dusty slats of the plantation shutters. 'A whole bunch of squad cars have arrived and people are running around, and . . .' She squinted through the dirty glass. 'What's that? The thing like a little tank.'

'It's a robot ram,' said David, looking over Petra's shoulder. 'They'll use it to break down the door if we don't come out.'

'Then I'd better go,' said Rick without conviction. He smiled weakly. 'At least I'll get away from the dust.'

'Hold on.' Tal put a restraining hand on Rick's shoulder. 'Rob said to wait, if we can. He needs time to get here himself, but he also wants the media in position. If the cops know that they're being closely watched, they won't be tempted to start blazing away.'

Tal said this quite calmly, but his skin prickled as he imagined a volley of shots penetrating the wall and mowing them down.

'Occupants of the house,' boomed a loud, authoritarian voice, 'exit now, in single file with your hands clasped behind your necks.'

'Omigod! What do we do now?'

'Nothing, Petra,' said Tal. 'We stall for time.'

The amplified voice commanded, 'Refer immediately to your personal communicators.'

On Tal's iZod appeared: YOU WILL NOT BE HARMED. IF YOU ARE ABLE, IMMEDIATELY EXIT THE BUILDING SINGLE FILE WITH YOUR HANDS CLASPED BEHIND YOUR NECKS.

'*If we're able?*' said David. 'What's that supposed to mean?'

Jennie grimaced. 'I'd say they think it's possible that Rick is holding a shotgun on us.'

Rick, his face white, said, 'They're going to kill me, aren't they?'

Tal peered through the half-open slats of the grimy shutters. He let out his breath in a relieved sigh. 'Rob Anderson has just arrived.'

Rob walked unhurriedly down the overgrown front path, arms held out from his sides to indicate he was unarmed. A little pack of air cams hovered behind him, proof that at least some representatives of the media were in place. The cameras stopped five metres from the front door, obviously a perimeter set by the police, then they fanned out to shoot different angles of the house.

Once Rob was inside, Tal found himself shaking his hand. 'Thank God you're here.'

'Like the cop with the big voice told you, I'm all set to negotiate.'

'How come you've suddenly become a negotiator? Don't the police know you're with FinagleAlert?'

Rob grinned. 'Sure do, but now they believe I'm an expert siege negotiator too. It only took a word from the commissioner – I know him well – to convince them I was the man who'd persuade you all to surrender.'

'We're ready,' said Tal, leading him into the dusty front room.

Rob looked around. 'No shotgun?'

'Never was one,' said David.

'Where's our junior terrorist?' Rob asked. 'Hello, Rick, I guess you know you're famous. Your face is all over the web.'

Rick nodded miserably. 'No one is going to believe it, but I didn't make those threats.' He swallowed. 'What are they going to do to me?'

'You'll be taken into custody, at least temporarily, but first we have to get you safely out of the house.'

'How?' demanded Petra. 'What's to stop them shooting Rick as soon as he comes out the front door?'

'It's not going to happen. Follow directions and you'll be fine.'

Rick took a deep breath. 'Okay. What do I do?'

'You'll walk out of the house, your fingers laced behind your head. I'll be right behind you with a hand on your shoulder. Once outside, we stop until ordered to advance. When you reach the cops, they'll handcuff you.'

He bent his lanky frame so he could look directly into Rick's face. 'Now this is important. Don't make any statements, don't explain anything, don't answer any questions at all. Simply say you're waiting for your lawyer to arrive.'

'I don't have a lawyer.'

'You do now. FinagleAlert is arranging legal representation. We believe your case is an excellent example of police harassment. You were accused of terrorism on the flimsiest of unsubstantiated evidence and pursued as if you were a dangerous criminal.'

'You could sue for damages,' said Petra cheerfully. 'Like, zillions.'

'That's a long way in the future,' said Rob. 'First we get Rick safely surrendered.'

Rick straightened his shoulders. 'I'm ready.'

'What about us?' asked Jennie. 'What do we do?'

'As soon as Rick is handcuffed, you'll be given instructions. You'll be told to exit the house one at a time, hands behind your heads. Be prepared to be searched and maybe even handcuffed, until they're sure you present no danger. Then they'll search the house.'

'Search the house?' said David, bristling. 'Why?'

'To make sure no co-conspirator is hiding and to locate any weapons.'

'Oh, great,' David muttered. It was bad enough that the neglected outside would be featured on newscasts everywhere – now the cluttered, untidy interior would be too. 'Mum's going to love this.'

'Okay,' Rob said to Rick. 'Let's go.'

TWENTY-ONE

Rob had explained how they would safely exit the house, Tal thought wryly, but he hadn't mentioned that they'd be taken to the nearest police station to be interrogated, or that Rob himself would be arrested for an unauthorised helicopter landing in the nearby park.

Tal's iZod had been taken from him, so he had to make the one call he was allowed on a monitored police phone. His mother had said she was on her way, her voice half concerned and half aggravated.

Then he was left alone in a windowless interview room. It was an unpleasant place – the air stale, the walls a grimy grey. The only furniture was a battered metal table, which still had traces of its original green paint, and four metal chairs. High up in one corner of the dingy room the lens of a camera stared down. Set into one wall was a long, rectangular mirror. From watching countless crime dramas, Tal assumed it was a two-way mirror. He had the uncomfortable feeling that someone on the other side was watching him.

He waited with growing impatience. The sooner he set the cops straight about Rick, the sooner Rick could go home and Tal could too. It had been late afternoon when they'd all been brought to the police station. Without his iZod he didn't know what time it was now. For something to do, he got up and walked slowly around the table. That used up, at the most, ten seconds. Tal walked around the table the opposite way, then tried the door. It was locked. He sat on one of the uncomfortable metal chairs and rested his elbows on the table. If he had his iZod, he could occupy himself, but left alone in this dreary place without it, the minutes dragged by with agonising slowness.

His thoughts turned to the accusations Rick was facing. It was terrifying how easily people had been convinced that Rick was dangerous. What if he had been gunned down by a trigger-happy cop? It would have been too late then to discover that someone had deliberately set him up.

Rick was probably being interrogated right now. Of course he'd be denying everything, but it didn't matter how many times he declared his innocence, it meant nothing without proof that someone else had posted the threats to Braidworth High's website using Rick's name.

George had said Maryann Dodd's computer skills were excellent, but Tal wondered if she were good enough to break through the sophisticated firewalls the school's site used to block student hackers. And if not Maryann, then who? And why? That was the big question. Why was Rick the victim?

Tal was brooding over possible motives when the door was unlocked and two detectives entered the interview room. They introduced themselves as Detective Mentone and Detective Jetter. Mentone smiled cheerfully as he pointed out that Tal was not under arrest, but was merely there to help them understand what had happened. All through this Detective Jetter glowered at Tal. It was so obvious they were playing the good cop/bad cop script that he almost smiled.

Jetter looked perfect for the bad-cop role, with his heavy build, mean eyes and shaved head. As soon as they were all seated at the grubby table, he began. 'Where has Richard Lawrence hidden the shotgun and the ammunition?'

'There isn't a shotgun. There never was a shotgun. Look, you're wrong about Rick. He —'

'Just answer the questions, son, and you'll get out of here a lot quicker.'

'Don't be too hard on him, Fred,' said good-cop Mentone. When Jetter grunted disagreeably, Mentone went on. 'You can best help your friend by telling us everything you know.'

'Okay,' said Tal. 'This is what I know for sure: Rick's not a terrorist; he had nothing to do with the threats on the school website; he's never had anything to do with a shotgun, or any —'

'You forgot to mention Lawrence beats up girls,' Jetter sneered.

'Rick didn't beat up Maryann. Rick was angry because she –'

'He has a violent streak,' said Jetter, interrupting again. 'And to make things worse, the kid's got mental problems. It's obvious Lawrence is a time bomb, ready to explode.'

'No way! Rick isn't like that.'

Mentone smiled pleasantly. 'I get the feeling you've been friends for a long time.'

'Rick's been one of the Five from the beginning.'

Jetter leaned forward, obviously intending to intimidate. 'The Five? What's that? A secret society?'

'It's not a secret society. We're five friends. We have been since kindergarten. We've always been called the Five. It's a bit of a joke, actually.'

Mentone's friendly attitude abruptly changed. 'A joke? I'm not laughing.'

He pushed back his chair with a screech and stalked around the table to stand behind Tal. Placing his hands on the back of the chair, he bent over Tal to say, 'This group of yours – you have a cache of weapons? A secret meeting place?'

It was so ridiculous Tal laughed. 'Get real! We're friends, that's all.'

Jetter folded his thick arms over his chest. 'What if I were to tell you that when he was officially charged, your co-conspirator Richard Lawrence confessed to belonging to a terrorist cell.'

'That's impossible. I don't believe it.'

'You calling me a liar?' Tal jumped as Jetter slammed his hand down on the metal table. 'Level with us, son, or you'll be charged as an accomplice.'

There was a sharp knock at the door. A middle-aged, grey-haired woman with a commanding manner put her head into the room to say, 'Detectives? Out here, please.'

Tal decided he wouldn't say another word. He hadn't been arrested, so when his mother arrived, he'd leave with her. If that was a problem, she'd get him a lawyer.

The door opened again and the middle-aged woman came into the room. 'Thank you for your assistance.' She handed Tal his iZod.

He stood up. 'I can go?'

'Of course. Your mother's waiting for you.'

'What's happened to Rick and the others?'

'I'm afraid I can't discuss that.'

'Rick had nothing to do with those threats. He's been set up.'

She didn't reply, but held the door open for Tal. With a gesture, she indicated the way he should go.

Walking down the grimy corridor, he checked his iZod was working then sent a quick text to Allyx to say he was okay and would see her tomorrow.

His mother, grim-faced, was standing in the waiting area. Tal couldn't remember a time when he'd felt quite so pleased and relieved to see her.

'Mum, get me outta here!' Tal glanced past her, and

was astonished to find the other occupants of the waiting area were Joe Villabona and Carter Renfrew. 'What are –'

'Not now, Tal.' She grabbed his arm and propelled him in the direction of the door.

'Grace, we need to talk,' said Villabona, stepping in front of them.

'Later, Joe. I'll call you.'

He moved aside. 'Make sure you do. It's important – we both know that.'

When Tal and his mother got to the sliding entrance doors, she said, 'The media are here. Keep walking. Don't say anything.'

Outside it was rapidly becoming dark. They were met by a crush of media and curious bystanders. Glaring lights dazzled, air cams swooped, and reporters rushed to pepper them with questions.

'No comment,' Tal's mother kept saying in a monotone.

'Talbot! Talbot Blair! Look this way. What can you tell us about your friend Rick Lawrence? When did you suspect he was losing control?'

'Vultures,' Grace murmured.

Tal kept walking and eventually the members of the media returned to their stakeout of the station.

'What's the story with Villabona?' Tal asked.

'Just something to do with work. I don't want to talk about it now.'

Tal looked back over his shoulder at the brightly illuminated cop shop. 'I was told Rick had been arrested, but what about the others?'

'Petra, Jennie and David have already been picked up by their parents.'

'And Rob?'

'FinagleAlert's legal eagle is working to get him out on bail.'

Sitting in a no-parking zone was a black limousine with heavily tinted windows. In gold lettering along the side were the words: FARRONT-RENFREW-UNWIN YOUTH HEALTH & COUNSELLING CENTRE.

Tal halted and turned to his mother. 'Are Villabona and Renfrew here because of Rick?'

She nodded. 'His grandmother's in the station now, signing the papers to have him committed to psychiatric care at The Farront Centre. Dr Renfrew is here to formally take custody of Rick.'

'But how can he have custody, when Rick's been arrested for terrorism?'

She gave a short, unamused laugh. 'Oh, the police have cut a deal at the highest level. FinagleAlert's lawyer pointed out that there was embarrassingly little evidence to justify the full-scale manhunt and that Rick had an excellent case for harassment and wrongful arrest. Under those circumstances, the authorities are delighted to have him handed over to Renfrew and bundled away out of sight with the convenient label "mentally ill".'

'That sucks! Rick's going to totally hate it there.'

'I imagine he'd hate being locked up in a juvenile facility more,' she said dryly.

Once Tal was relaxed in the soft leather seat of his mother's Mercedes, he felt terribly weary, as if all the events of the day had suddenly hit him. Marshalling the last of his energy, he said, 'The first thing is to find out who set Rick up.'

She gave an irritated sigh. 'Don't get involved. Leave it to the police to investigate.'

'But you said yourself that the cops are happy to have Rick locked away as a mental patient. Why would they stir up trouble for themselves by keeping the case open?'

'God knows I've got enough problems at the moment without having you playing amateur detective,' she snapped.

'You don't understand, Mum,' said Tal. 'Rick would do anything for us. We have to do the same for him.'

When Petra's mother had picked her up from the police station, her expression had been so coldly furious that Petra had hardly said a word, not wanting to provoke a bitter argument.

Now that they were home, her mother took her into the study and handed Petra her iZod. 'Your father and I have agreed you can have your communicator back. This is not because you deserve a break. You don't. It's because in an emergency such as the lockdown at the school, we need to be able to speak with you in person, not rely on someone else to tell us where you are and that you're safe.'

Petra felt like kissing her iZod. Connected again! 'Oh, that's great, Mum. Thanks.'

'Nothing else has changed. You're still grounded. In fact, I'm extending the period by a month.'

'A month? But Mum –'

'Don't waste your breath arguing. It would have been a different story if you'd stayed here this afternoon, and not gone haring off with the others to find Rick. Your impetuosity got you arrested.'

'I wasn't arrested. I was "helping the police with their inquiries".'

'Whatever you care to call it, the embarrassing fact remains that you were detained by the police. I had to physically push my way through hordes of media outside the station in order to collect you. I'm sure you'll agree this is *not* good publicity for Garden Stuff. Your father's still at work, attempting to repair the PR damage.'

Hot tears burnt Petra's eyes. 'That's all you care about, isn't it? It's Stuff! Stuff! Stuff! What about how I feel? What about Rick, locked up as though he's raving mad, when he's not?'

'I can't do anything for Rick at the moment, but I've already spoken with Thelma Lawrence to offer my support. As for your feelings, Petra, your father and I never fail to listen to what you have to say, but you can't expect us always to agree with you.'

'All right, you listen, but you don't trust me. You and Dad monitor everything I do. It was okay when I was young, but I'm not a little kid anymore.'

'It's natural that we would want to protect you.'

'Protect? Fine. But you're *smothering* me.'

'Let's talk it over this Sunday in our family discussion time.'

'What a great idea,' said Petra sarcastically. 'Let's talk and talk until we're blue in the face. It won't make any difference. Nothing changes in this family.'

There was silence for a moment, then her mother said, 'When I was growing up, I remember feeling just the way you do. And my father said something I never forgot: "You don't have the family you want: you have the family you've got."'

Rick panicked as soon as he saw his grandmother with Dr Renfrew and two orderlies in crisp white uniforms. Tears ran down Thelma's face as she choked out, 'Rick, dear, this is for your own good.'

'Don't do this to me!'

Dr Renfrew nodded to the orderlies, who moved quickly to seize him. Rick struggled wildly. 'I'm not going with you! You can't make me!'

The doctor stepped forward, a pneumatic hypodermic in his hand. Rick pulled away, but it was no use. He felt a faint sting on his arm and then a rush of calmness.

'It's the newest thing,' he heard Renfrew say to Thelma. 'A short-acting drug that almost instantly calms the patient without causing any sleepiness, confusion or loss of motor skills, although the ability to speak is temporarily affected.'

A wedge of police officers cleared the way to the limousine. As questions were shouted and cameras darted, Rick walked tranquilly with an orderly on either side – Felix and Luis by their name tags. It wasn't really necessary to guard Rick, because his body was far too relaxed to respond to his brain's urgent commands to resist.

Followed by media vehicles, the limousine drove smoothly across town. 'There's the centre,' said Felix.

Situated at the edge of Braidworth's upscale industrial park, the subtly floodlit building was a graceful structure surrounded by beautifully landscaped grounds.

However attractive it was, Rick thought, it was still going to be his prison.

Already a knot of reporters was gathered at the front entrance. The limousine turned down a side road leading to the back of the building. The pursuing media vehicles were stopped by an electronic gate, which blinked off only long enough to let the limousine through.

Unhindered, the air cams soared above the gate and zipped after them, to witness Rick being efficiently whisked out of the limousine and in through the back entrance.

Inside, the soothing colours reminded Rick of the hospital's psychiatric unit, although this was far more luxurious. His feet sank into the soft, beige carpeting, the neutral walls held what looked like original paintings – some abstract designs, but mostly peaceful landscapes or seascapes – and there were vases of flowers in pastel shades everywhere.

They took a lift to the fourth floor. Rick walked compliantly between the two orderlies as they approached a sleek white desk with the sign Secure Wing Patient Admissions. Felix, who seemed to be the friendlier of his two escorts, said, 'You're going to like it here, Rick. Trust me.'

Dr Renfrew had been right when he'd told Thelma that it was a short-acting drug. Rick could feel the tension returning to his body and he found he could speak again. 'What's to like about being a prisoner?'

The other orderly, Luis, gave a sour laugh. 'Sure beats what the cops would offer you, kiddo. Here you get your own room with attached bathroom. In police detention you get to share a cell with who knows what? An axe murderer, a sexual deviant? You name it.'

Seated behind the desk was a stout woman with brassy blonde hair and an empty, professional smile. A name plate identified her as Gloria. She said to Felix, 'Dr Unwin has already completed this patient's admission details. I just need to check that he's been body searched.'

'The cops did that for us, Gloria.'

Rick felt his face grow hot as he remembered the indignity of the strip search he'd been subjected to at the police station.

'Very good,' she said. She handed over a paper-wrapped parcel. 'Tomorrow we'll arrange hot meals with the kitchen, but for tonight here's a packet meal for Rick. Please take him to room eight.'

'How did she know who I was?' Rick asked as they walked down a short hallway.

'You're famous, kiddo,' said Luis with a mocking smile. 'Pretty well the whole world knows you, at least for a few minutes more. Then someone else will do something outrageous and take your place.'

SECURE WING said the sign. In smaller letters it advised, NO UNAUTHORISED PERSONS PERMITTED.

As the drug wore off, panic flooded through Rick again. Once he was in the secure wing he'd be trapped. He looked around desperately. Could he get away from these two guys? Was it best to try to hide, or make a run for it? The media must still be waiting for something to happen. If he could get outside, he'd yell for help.

Luis took his arm in a very firm grip. 'Hang in there, Rick. You'll be okay.'

Felix stared into the lens of an iris reader and with a click the lock on the heavy white metal door opened. 'After you, Rick. Let's get you settled in.'

He tried to remember the route they'd taken since coming into the building, but everything was fuzzy. The dull thud of the heavy door closing behind him filled him with utter despair. He'd been abandoned by Thelma. The doctors would keep him here forever.

He had one hope, he told himself – his friends. And Tal's mother worked for Farront. Maybe Tal would persuade her to do something.

Room eight was pleasant enough, with cream walls and pale blue carpet. The bed had a darker blue quilt. The only other furniture was a small round table, a blue upholstered chair and a small chest of drawers. Inside the drawers were pale yellow cotton pants with a drawstring and matching top, identical to the clothes Rick had been told to change into when Felix and Luis had brought him into the room. They'd taken away his own clothes.

There was no window, but a screen set into the wall mimicked an outside view of rolling green hills dotted artistically with trees. The sky was slowly darkening as it would be in reality and the grass rippled as if touched by an evening breeze. Rick expected there'd shortly be a soothing sunset depicted in pretty colours. Apart from watching the artificial view, there was nothing to do except listen to faint, bland music piped into the room.

He'd eaten the almost tasteless cheese sandwiches in his meal pack and was sitting on the bed deciding whether to have a shower in the utilitarian little bathroom before going to sleep, when he heard a faint click as the electronic lock on the door disengaged.

'Ah, Rick. How are you settling in?'

Rick imagined the satisfaction of punching the smile off Dr Unwin's face, but that would probably earn him another injection, or worse. He said, 'I want to go home.'

Carter Renfrew shook his balding head as he closed the door behind him. 'Not possible, I'm afraid, until you've fully recovered.'

'There's nothing wrong with me.'

'I know you believe that,' said Dr Unwin sympathetically, 'but it's common for depressed patients to deny they're ill. After treatment you'll realise what it's like to be normal.'

He wanted to scream 'Let me go!' but forced himself to sound cool and reasonable. 'Look, I don't need any treatment from either of you. Dr Stein's my psychiatrist.'

'Dr Stein is no longer involved with your case,' said Renfrew. 'Your grandmother has signed the papers to make Dr Unwin and myself your sole medical caregivers.'

'Thelma can't do that. I must have some say in who my doctors are.'

Dr Unwin wore his understanding smile. 'I don't think you appreciate your situation, Rick. First, in the law's eyes you're too young to make medical decisions for yourself. Second, you're extremely fortunate not to face the courts as a terrorist. Being admitted to the centre as a patient is a far preferable fate, I assure you.'

'I'm not a terrorist. Someone else made those threats.'

Dr Renfrew put a fatherly hand on his shoulder. 'It's quite possible that you don't remember doing it, Rick, but the evidence is clear.'

'What evidence?' Rick demanded, shaking Renfrew's hand off.

'We'll approach the issue during your treatment,' said Dr Unwin.

'I refuse. I won't cooperate.'

Dr Unwin's smile evaporated. 'Get this straight, my boy. You don't leave the clinic until Dr Renfrew and I agree our treatment has been successful. If you aim to go home soon, you'll cooperate. If you'd prefer to stay here indefinitely . . .' He shrugged. 'Your choice.'

'I want to see Thelma.'

'No visitors until you're appreciably better.'

It was hopeless. No matter what he did, he couldn't escape. He took a deep breath. 'If I agree, what sort of treatment are you talking about?'

Dr Unwin gave him a small, satisfied smile. 'That's much better, Rick. Have a good night's sleep. We'll talk over the details tomorrow and begin your regimen as soon as possible. You'll be back home before you know it.'

As the doctors moved towards the door, Rick said, 'This regimen – what will you do to me?'

'Nothing to be worried about,' said Renfrew with a dismissive gesture. 'A few simple tests, a brain scan, perhaps mild medication.'

'That's all?'

Dr Unwin smiled. 'That's all.'

TWENTY-TWO

Tal had been so exhausted when they'd arrived home that he'd had a bowl of soup and gone up to bed. Before going to sleep he'd checked his text messages. Allyx sent her love and said how much she missed him, Petra exuberantly advised everyone her mother had caved and she had her iZod back, Jennie and David both said they were in big trouble with their parents, who didn't appreciate the notoriety that came with being featured in the national media and everywhere on the web.

Tal slept in and came down for a late breakfast the next morning. He poured himself a glass of orange juice and commanded the wall screen to display a digest of the local weekend news. The major item was the capture of Richard Lawrence, alleged teenage terrorist.

Yesterday Tal had watched from the house as Rick and Rob had walked slowly towards the waiting cops. Rick had been roughly seized and thrown to the ground before his hands were handcuffed behind his back. Seeing it from the camera's point of view gave Tal quite a different perspective. The edited close-ups made the whole scene even more dramatic than it had seemed to him at the time.

Tal found it unsettling to view himself exiting David's house, followed at intervals by the others. He hadn't seen this yesterday, but as Petra left the house she'd stuck her tongue out at the camera. Her parents were going to love that!

The screen switched to a sleek black limousine speeding past media trucks and reporters. The crawl at the bottom of the screen announced that Richard Lawrence, allegedly responsible for Friday's terrorism red alert at Braidworth High, was now a psychiatric patient at the new Farront Centre, under the joint care of the famous Dr Carter Renfrew and the eminent Dr Howard Unwin.

Tal put slices of bread in his mother's space-age toaster and attempted to hit the correct sequence of buttons to produce acceptable toast. He was puzzled: why, even before Rick's arrest, had Dr Unwin and Joe Villabona been so keen to admit Rick as a patient? Did it have something to do with Rick being a disconnect? Maybe it was because Rick was a disconnect who had a history of depressive episodes, so he might be more likely to suffer CWSS.

Perhaps it was a strategy to head off legal action by Rick's grandmother. A smart lawyer could probably persuade Thelma to sue Farront, claiming that the stress of being disconnected had driven Rick to lose his mind. Thelma's case would be weakened if a jury heard she'd accepted Farront's offer of free medical care for treatment that would otherwise be very expensive.

He rescued his toast, which was burnt in the corners and still white in the middle. He tossed the slices, deciding to have fruit salad instead.

Tal tried to visualise what being a patient in the psychiatric wing of The Farront Centre would be like. His image of mental hospitals came from graphic e-novels and horror movies, so in his mind's eye he saw Rick strapped to a table with dozens of wires attached to his head. Villabona, perfectly groomed, stood coldly watching while Rick struggled to free himself. Creepy music played in the background. Meanwhile, wild-eyed Dr Renfrew stooped over a control panel, finger poised to send electricity zapping through Rick's brain.

He chuckled aloud at his fantasy. Reality would be entirely different. Rick was likely relaxing in a comfortable room, glad to be away from the cops and their grotty station.

'Rob was in jail all night,' said Tal's mother, coming into the kitchen. 'He's just been released and is going straight home to get some sleep.'

'Rob was great with Rick yesterday,' said Tal sincerely. 'I really think he may have saved Rick from being target practice for the cops.'

His mother raised an eyebrow. 'So Rob's not so bad, after all?'

'Not so bad,' he conceded.

'You okay to get your own lunch? Victor is recovering well, so he's being released from hospital this morning. I'm going to pick him up, take him home and settle him in.'

'No problem. Have you heard how Marcia is?'

'Victor says she has a broken nose and two black eyes, but otherwise she's fine. Marcia's been badgering the police to find the hit-and-run driver who caused the accident, but they haven't even got a suspect yet.' She sniffed. 'I smell something burning.'

'Your toaster burnt my toast. It always does. I think it's possessed by an evil spirit.'

She laughed. 'You represent the next step in evolution, right? But you have trouble operating a toaster. It's a worry.'

His mother's smile disappeared when he said, 'Mum, about Villabona. At the cop shop yesterday – what was that all about?'

Her expression grew bleak. 'Basically, Joe's influence on Audrey is growing every day. Before he joined the company, Audrey had no problem with my relationship with Rob. She took it for granted I'd make sure my professional and personal worlds never overlapped. Even when FinagleAlert began to investigate Tacitcomm, Audrey still accepted that I kept my private life with Rob entirely separate from my work.'

'And Joe Villabona changed her mind?'

'He's done more than that. I didn't see it at first, but from the time Joe joined Farront, he's been working to drive a wedge between me and Audrey.'

'Why?' said Tal. 'How does it help him?'

'I don't know.' She rubbed her forehead fretfully.

'If Villabona has something to hide, he'd hardly like having a colleague with links to FinagleAlert around, would he? The last thing he'd want is someone snooping into his business.'

'You could be right. I'm positive Audrey's ultimatum about Victor's appearance on FinagleAlert came direct from Joe. And now he's well on the way to persuading her that Rob is using me to cause trouble for Farront. From things that Audrey's said, Joe's suggesting that Rob is seeking material for an exposé of Farront's business practices. Rob's also supposed to be on the lookout for trade secrets to sell to Audrey's competitors.'

'But why would Audrey believe that?'

'Joe can be very persuasive. It helps him that Audrey is paranoid about the company's continuing success. Her father built Farront from nothing into a communications giant. Audrey is constantly comparing her achievements to her dead father's, and striving to do better than he did.'

'And last night? What was so important?'

'Audrey's asked Joe to discuss with me in depth my so-called "conflict of interest" between Rob and my job.'

'Seems to me,' said Tal, 'that the guy's trying to force you to resign.'

'If so, he'll be waiting for a long time.' She gave a grim smile. 'Of course, Audrey could fire me.'

Tal went to George Everett's house that afternoon. He'd thought long and hard about his intentions for Joe Villabona. No way could he tell his mother or Rob Anderson – they wouldn't let him get involved in anything illegal, however excellent the reason. And his mother would be shocked if she learned Tal was willing to reveal confidential information about Farront.

Rob and FinagleAlert might discover some of Joe Villabona's secrets, but the vital facts about him would be buried so deep that it would take extraordinary skill to find them. George wasn't just brilliant, he wasn't at all constrained by laws protecting electronically stored information. And Tal knew that if George were caught, he himself would be at risk.

It was worth it. Like a spider sitting in the centre of a web, Villabona was linked to many of the bad things that had happened lately. Since he'd appeared on the scene, Audrey's attitude towards Grace had changed for the worse, to the point where her career was now in real jeopardy. Villabona had persuaded Audrey to establish The Farront Centre and install Dr Renfrew and Dr Unwin to carry out research that Victor O'Dell condemned as dangerous to young minds. And there was Victor's hit-and-run accident – if it were an accident.

Lastly, Rick. There was something odd about his disconnection and how keen Villabona and Unwin had been to talk Thelma into having Rick admitted for treatment. Tal was convinced that the fake terrorist threats were not the work of Maryann Dodd, spiteful though she could be. Tal thought Villabona would have the expertise to set Rick up, but what was in it for him?

George Everett's large family lived in a rambling house that was comfortably run-down. The peeling paint and sagging wooden steps up to the front verandah were part of the building's relaxed charm.

Tal made his way around a haphazard pile of kids' bicycles, climbed the sloping stairs, and was about to knock on the front door when it was flung open. A stream of kids came rocketing out and down the stairs. They grabbed the bicycles and disappeared noisily down the street.

'Thank God the noisy little creeps are outta here,' said George. 'Come in.' He led the way down the uncarpeted hall. 'Hope you don't mind, but I asked Frank Arran over. He's good, maybe better than me in some areas –' he winked – 'but don't let him know that.'

George opened a door that advised in roughly painted red letters that anyone who entered uninvited could expect to die horribly.

'How many kids in your family?' Tal enquired.

George made a face. 'Don't ask. Every time I look, there seems to be another one.'

The room was so packed with electronic equipment that there was very little space left over. Tal followed George as he squeezed his chubby body between two loaded benches, to discover Frank Arran sprawled in a chair, staring fixedly at a monitor.

'Yo,' he said absently, waving a hand at Tal.

Where George was plump, Frank was skinny, with long lank hair that fell over his face. Like George, he was wearing an ancient T-shirt bearing the faded words, JOIN THE NERD HERD, and even more disreputable shorts. Tal felt positively overdressed in jeans and plain white T-shirt.

Looking around, Tal wondered how George could afford all this expensive electronic equipment.

As if reading his mind, George said, 'Who paid for this stuff? Me. I've been creating applications for communicators, mainly iZods, but also apps for BeauBrutes and Cascaders.' With a satisfied smile, he went on, 'I made more than my dad last year.'

'Wow.'

Becoming business-like, George said, 'Now about your problem . . .'

'Before we start, I've got a question. Does Maryann Dodd have the skills to hack into the school website and post the terrorist threats Rick was supposed to have made?'

George shoved his sliding specs into place as he thought it over. 'It's unlikely. She hasn't got the patience. Dodder's best at cyber bullying. That's her strength.'

He pushed a moth-eaten office chair in Tal's direction, and plopped down in a similar seat. 'Frank's keen to help, if that's okay.'

'Sure.'

'So what do you want us to find out for you?'

Tal outlined the two areas of interest involving Villabona. The first concerned his mother's career at Farront. The second, Rick's welfare, which brought Renfrew and Unwin into the picture.

As he spoke, George tapped notes into his mininotebook. He broke off to say, 'Getting the info on your targets one, two and three involves doing things that aren't strictly legal, so it's good we have a MAD situation here.'

'A mad situation?' said Tal, puzzled.

'The nuclear stand-off between Russia and the States last century? They could wipe each other off the face of the earth. That's mutually assured destruction, also known as MAD.'

'Gee, thanks for the history lesson,' said Tal dryly.

'Anytime. Now, this is how MAD works for us: I can't tell anyone you've been giving me classified stuff on Farront, because if I do, you'll dob me in for major hacking; you can't tell anyone about my hacking, because if you do, I'll blow the whistle on you for disclosing confidential company information. MAD keeps us both honest.'

'Keeps me honest, too,' said Frank, tapping away at the keyboard while he glared at the computer screen.

'Remember,' said George, 'that unless you're in this room, which is fully shielded, or somewhere else you're absolutely sure has an impenetrable electronic curtain, you have to act as though every communication you send and receive is being actively monitored.'

'Big Brother is watching you,' said Frank. 'In fact, he's watching all of us.'

'Isn't that a bit paranoid?' said Tal.

George grinned. 'Maybe not paranoid enough. Big Brother *is* watching. Believe it.'

Rick felt as though his brain had been removed and replaced with tightly packed cotton wool. He dimly remembered having breakfast and then getting terribly sleepy. After that, nothing, until he woke to find himself lying on a metal tray that was slowly moving backwards. He squinted down his body and saw that the tray was withdrawing from a tunnel in the centre of a huge white machine. A cold breeze was blowing from the tunnel and chilling his bare feet.

It was an effort to keep his eyes open, so he allowed them to slide shut.

'Very satisfactory scan,' said a male voice behind him. 'Note the effect of the drug on the patient's frontal lobes.'

The voice was familiar. In his imagination Rick saw a handsome, smiling man. A smile he loathed. He concentrated on dredging up a name. Dr Unwin. Dr Howard Unwin.

Dr Unwin went on. 'He'll be an excellent subject for research once we induce severe depression.'

'I'll arrange to intensify sensory deprivation,' said a second voice. Who was this? Another face swam into Rick's mind. Someone famous. Rick had the name – Dr Renfrew.

Dr Unwin said, 'Then we'll administer a second severe emotional shock to precipitate the necessary clinical depression.'

'I'm not sure of the ethics –'

'Jesus, man! It's a bit late in the game to develop moral principles. You've bent the rules before, now all you have to do is bend them a bit more.'

After a pause, Renfrew said, 'Of course you're right,' although he didn't sound entirely convinced.

'Did Joe get into Stein's files?' said Unwin briskly, changing the subject.

The fuzziness was rapidly leaving Rick's mind. He immediately knew who Dr Stein was. He had very blue eyes and a soft, pleasant voice.

Renfrew, sounding more confident, said, 'Joe's nothing less than a computer genius, so he didn't have any trouble copying the entire case file. The boy's a classic case of survivor guilt.'

'Excellent! We can work on that aspect under drug-induced hypnosis.'

Although he knew he should be alarmed at what he was hearing, Rick felt strangely detached. Some sense of self-preservation kept him very still and breathing slowly and evenly. What would they do to him if they discovered he'd woken up and had been listening to their conversation?

'I still have some reservations,' said Renfrew. 'In my opinion, he'll be suicidal if we administer the entire program of treatment you're suggesting.'

Clearly impatient, Unwin said, 'The patient will be

on suicide watch twenty-four/seven. He won't have an opportunity to hurt himself.'

'But —'

'I haven't got time to discuss it now. We'll talk later. Buzz for Luis, will you?'

Rick heard Dr Renfrew ask for Luis to come to room three, and then the sound of receding footsteps as the two doctors left. Just in case someone else was watching, he kept his eyes shut.

'Okay, Rick. Rise and shine.'

Pretending to waken, Rick dragged open his eyes. 'What?' Bending over him was a medical orderly. 'Luis?'

'That's me, kid. Now let's get you up on your feet and walking.' He helped Rick stand. 'Here, put these slippers on.'

For a moment Rick considered telling Luis what he'd just heard. But what if Luis went to the doctors and told them he'd been awake when they had thought he was unconscious?

Instead he asked, 'What have they been doing to me?'

'You'll have to ask your doctors.' There was a note of suppressed anger in Luis's voice. Then, relenting, he said, 'You've had a brain scan using the very latest equipment. Now, no more questions. You're going back to your room.'

'But there's nothing to do there.'

'Not my problem, kid.'

As they were walking down the hallway towards the

clinic's secure wing, Luis said, 'I've got a message for you from your grandma.'

'Is Thelma here? Can I see her?'

'No visitors until Dr Renfrew and Dr Unwin say so.'

'Jeez . . .'

'Look, kid, I'm bending rules doing this, but your grandma begged me. Everything's supposed to go though official channels, so don't breathe a word to anyone, okay?'

'Okay.'

'It's your granddad. He's much, much better. This morning he was wide awake and able to sit up in bed. The doctor told your grandma the signs were excellent for a complete recovery.'

Rick found himself smiling for the first time in days. 'Really? That's great.'

'Play it cool. You're not supposed to have any messages from outside that haven't been cleared by Dr Renfrew or Dr Unwin, so don't let anyone know you've heard the good news.'

'I don't understand why I can't get messages from Thelma and my friends.'

Luis shrugged. 'Part of your treatment, kid.'

Back in his room, Rick found the artificial view had been switched off, leaving a blank cream wall to stare at. And the faint music had gone too. He told himself he didn't mind: he could sit and think how great it was that his grandfather was so much better.

Five minutes later he was up and examining the ceiling and walls again for the pinhole lens he knew was there. This was the psychiatric ward, so he had to be under constant surveillance. And he'd just heard Dr Unwin say he'd be watched twenty-four/seven. A horrible anxiety began to rise in him, but he pushed it away.

He couldn't find the lens, so with absolutely nothing to capture his attention, Rick flung himself down on the bed. Maybe they were trying to drive him mad with boredom.

Two words popped into his head: *sensory deprivation*. Rick had an idea what it meant. He'd ask Luis next time he saw him.

With a shudder, Rick faced what he had deliberately avoided thinking about. Unwin had said *suicide watch*. The doctors were going to play with his mind until he fell into such despair he'd want to die.

'No way,' he said, then louder, 'No way!'

TWENTY-THREE

At school on Monday everyone was still talking about Rick and the lockdown and how practically everybody had something on a social networking site, starring themselves. Yvette Sarno's hysterical turn for the media was a popular clip, with opinion evenly split between those who approved and those who shared David's derisive view of Yvette's acting abilities.

'She's a total ham,' he was saying to Tal and Jennie, when Petra came rushing up.

'Omigod, have I got news for you! You're not going to believe what my mother's done!'

'She's sold Garden Stuff and given the money to a charity for disadvantaged garden gnomes?' Tal suggested.

'Very funny,' said Petra, laughing in spite of herself, 'but no. Mum's setting up a committee of parents and teachers to fight cyber bullying. I thought she'd forgotten all about it, since the attacks on me have pretty well dried up, but I should have known better. My mother never forgets anything.'

'This is all very interesting,' said David, 'but get to the point, if there is one.'

'You'll never guess who volunteered to chair the committee. Lois Dodd!'

'You're kidding?' said David, a delighted smile spreading over his face. 'Your mother doesn't know Maryann is queen of the cyber bullies at our school?'

'*She* knows about Maryann, but Dodder's mother has no clue.'

'This could get nasty,' said Jennie.

'Yes, couldn't it?' said Petra cheerfully.

Laughing, David said, 'Dodder's mother will curl up and die when she discovers her darling daughter caused the lockdown.'

'We don't know for sure that she did,' said Tal. 'I asked George his opinion and he said it was unlikely.'

'Then who?' said Jennie. 'We know it wasn't Rick.'

'That's what I want to talk to you all about,' said Tal, 'but it has to be at my place after school.'

'Why your place?' Petra frowned. 'I'm grounded, remember? I'm supposed to go straight home.'

'Because our house is protected by an electronic curtain. I'm not going to say anything else now. I'll explain this afternoon.'

'I still think Maryann had something to do with it,' said David. 'At the very least she spread the stories about Rick seeing a psychiatrist. I vote we front up to her at lunchtime.'

Petra was all for it. 'Great idea! She deserves everything she gets.'

'I don't know,' said Tal doubtfully.

'I agree with Petra and David,' said Jennie. 'You're outvoted, Tal.'

When classes were released at lunchtime, the four of them waylaid Maryann Dodd in the hallway before she could meet up with her clique.

'We're here to congratulate you, Dodder,' said Petra. 'It's not everyone whose mother leads a cyber bullying committee.'

Maryann would normally pounce on anyone who called her by the nickname she loathed. Instead she looked a bit sick and said, 'Thanks. Now, if you don't mind . . .'

'We mind,' said David.

'Omigod,' said Petra. 'Imagine what your mother will say when she finds out it was *you* who pretended to be Rick and made those terrorist threats.'

Maryann's customary superior manner had deserted her. 'I didn't. Please believe me.'

'Then who?' said Tal.

'I only know it wasn't me.'

'It's a crime to make a terrorist threat,' Jennie pointed out.

Petra added, 'And Rick could take you to court and sue you for what you've put him through.'

'I haven't put him through anything.'

'Come on, Dodder,' said David. 'Admit you set Rick up. And you didn't give a thought to the fact the cops could kill him.'

Maryann appeared genuinely upset by the accusation. 'I tell you, it wasn't me! It had to be Rick himself, or somebody else. It isn't something I'd do. You've got to believe me.'

'It's exactly the sort of thing you'd do,' Petra said with scorn. 'Remember the great time you and your lame friends had last week attacking me online? And what about making everyone think that Rick was nuts?'

Maryann was fast regaining her usual arrogant attitude. 'Okay, I might have had something to do with posting messages about Petra.' She shot a vicious look in her direction. 'And I'm not sorry. You deserved it.'

'And what about Rick?'

'So what if I found out he'd been a bit of a mental case in the past? I thought people should know, that's all.'

'You're such a bitch,' said Petra in disgust.

'Say what you like about me, but I never posted those threats to the school's website.'

'Do you believe her?' David asked the others.

'You know,' said Jennie, 'I think I do.'

Petra called Rosa and said she'd been held up at school. 'I'll come up with a convincing story later,' she said to the others, who were sitting around in a comfortable little room Tal's mother called the lounging area.

After Tal had told them about his visit with George Everett, he said, 'You can't tell anyone about this. Play dumb if it ever comes up because –'

'What about Mike and Allyx?' interrupted Petra. 'Are we going to keep them in the dark?'

'I'm not sure,' said Tal.

'The fewer people who know, the better,' Jennie pointed out. 'None of us wants to end up in jail.'

'Yeah, yeah,' said David. 'We get the picture. And no talking about it on our comms, in case our messages are being scanned.'

'What do we do about Rick?' said Petra. 'We can't just leave him locked up.'

'Can't his grandmother get him out?' David asked.

'No way,' said Petra. 'Mum's spoken with Thelma. She believes having Rick committed was the best thing she could do for him under the circumstances. When she signed the papers she gave the doctors complete control. They're not allowing him any messages or visitors – he can't even see Thelma. And Renfrew and Unwin have the final say whether Rick stays or goes.'

'Then he'll stay,' said Tal. 'and it worries the hell out of me what they're doing to Rick while they've got him.'

Jennie looked appalled. 'You can't mean the doctors are experimenting on him.'

'We have to get Rick outta there,' said David decisively. 'Tal, you're starting Renfrew's research project at the centre sometime this week, aren't you?'

'Wednesday afternoon.'

'Okay, then you'll be our eyes inside. All you have to do is find out where Rick is and how to get through the security.' He added with a grin, 'Simple, really!'

Tal took out his iZod. 'I'll get a floor plan of the centre. With a bit of luck it'll indicate where the psychiatric ward's located.' After a moment, he swore.

'What's wrong?' Petra asked.

'It looks like I've just been made a disconnect.'

Rob came for dinner that evening. When he arrived, Tal said, 'The hot news is that I've suddenly become a disconnect. Even Mum can't find out why, or get me connected again.'

'It's so frustrating, Rob,' she said. 'I've just had a very interesting conversation with Ken Yeats, the head of Farront's connectivity services. He said he's sorry, but even for me his hands are tied and he can't do anything to help.'

'Wait until you hear why,' said Tal.

'Ken told me that for months Joe Villabona has been stacking connectivity services with his own people, to the point where Ken feels he's on the verge of being forced out. Now Joe's instructed Ken that from now on each case of teenage disconnection is to be referred to Farront's public relations department. Restoration of the customer's service is to be given a very low priority.'

Rob folded his lanky body into a lounge chair. 'I think I can throw some light on the situation.

FinagleAlert has been analysing the pattern of disconnects for the Big Three over the last year. In the last few months there's been an inexplicable surge in the number of young people using Farront's iZods who have become disconnects. No one was paying all that much attention to this, until those two kids made their dramatic suicide pact.'

'The ubiquitous Ruth and Barry,' said Tal's mother. 'Did you see the boy's now out of danger? And like his girlfriend, he's trying to sell his story.'

'He won't have any luck,' said Tal. 'It's all ancient history now.'

'It won't be ancient history if a scandal breaks over deliberate disconnections,' said Rob with a wry smile.

'It's something to do with Unwin and Renfrew, isn't it?'

'Yes, Tal, I believe you're right. As I see it, the majority of disconnections for young iZod users are deliberately engineered. And prior to becoming disconnects, a significant number had applied, or had already been accepted, for Dr Renfrew's research. Their psychological profiles could be used to select subjects for the stressful experience of disconnection.'

'Apart from those profiles, Renfrew and Unwin would also have access to the data Farront keeps on every client,' said Tal's mother.

'Including Rick?'

'Of course.'

Tal said to Rob, 'Dr Renfrew had background info on every person who'd applied to be in the small group discussions about his research. David and I were in the same group. I got accepted for the program, but David didn't. Renfrew checked out his background, then told him he could go. He did the same with half the group.'

'I'm not at all happy about you being in Renfrew's program.'

'Hey, Mum, you want me to dip out after he's gone to all the trouble of making me a disconnect?' Tal laughed as he added, 'Let's face it, people don't come much saner than me, so I'm going to be a big disappointment to the guy.'

Rob shook his head. 'Not at all. I think Renfrew's focus is on highly stressed disconnects, but for valid research results he needs the whole range of responses, including yours, plus a control group who haven't been disconnected. And Renfrew's program is a gift to Dr Unwin, who can use it for his research into CWSS without having to spend the time and money to assemble the full range of subjects himself.'

Tal's foreboding about what could be happening to Rick intensified. 'Rick's a special case, isn't he?'

'I'm afraid so,' said Rob. 'He has a history of depression and suicidal thoughts. He's likely to have extreme reactions to continued disconnection, and that makes him a perfect research subject, particularly now that he appears to have had a breakdown.'

'Rick was set up, you know he was!'

Rob spread his hands. 'Maybe, but why?'

'So they could experiment on him, and no one would know,' said Tal. 'They've got him locked away at The Farront Centre, and they're not allowing him any visitors, not even his grandmother.'

'I may be able to find out how he's doing,' said Rob. 'As of yesterday, FinagleAlert has an informant on the centre's staff. We didn't have to recruit the guy, he contacted us a few days ago, saying he had serious misgivings about the treatment of some patients.'

'Was Rick one of them?'

'No details as yet, but I know he has access to all areas of the centre, and that must include the psychiatric unit. I'm meeting him for the first time tomorrow to work out the logistics.'

'He's a paid informant?' said Tal's mother, dis-approving.

Amused, Rob said, 'This guy's not a whistleblower, putting his job on the line to go to the authorities. He's got a family dependent on him, so he needs the extra money. Besides, he'll be taking a big risk with his job. As long as the information he gives us is accurate, FinagleAlert is happy to pay him.'

'What's his name?' Tal asked.

'Sorry, can't tell you that.'

'But since I'm going to be at the centre for Dr Renfrew's research, he could pass any information he had through me.'

'Not an option,' said his mother.

Rob agreed. 'For security reasons, it's essential to restrict the number of people involved. Also, you've got a personal interest in your friend's welfare, which could cloud your judgement.'

'Well, could you ask him to give a message to Rick from me?'

'Sorry, no. It'd be asking him to take an unnecessary risk that could compromise the whole undertaking.'

'Okay,' said Tal, thinking that they'd freak if they had any idea of the risks he and the others were going to take. He got to his feet. 'I'm going for a run before dinner.'

'Don't be too long.' Half-serious, Grace added, 'I'm warning you, I won't be happy if you're late.'

'I'll go by Allyx's place and break the news I'm a disconnect.'

He didn't mention it would be a lightning visit, because his real destination was George's house.

Allyx was upset about Tal's disconnection. 'I hate this already! Can't your mother do something?'

'She's tried. No go.'

'But without your iZod, we can't call each other, or text, or send videos, or *anything*.'

'It'll only be temporary.'

'How temporary?'

Tal lifted his shoulders in a shrug. 'Don't know.'

'See you tomorrow night?'

Tal grimaced. 'Sorry, I'm going with Mum to visit Victor.'

Frowning, Allyx said, 'Do you have to? It's not as if you know him all that well.'

'I'm not making a social visit. Remember, he's seen a detailed outline of Dr Renfrew's research plans. I want to ask him what parts of the program are likely to be applied to Rick.'

With a sigh, Allyx said, 'All right, so tomorrow's off. What about Wednesday night?'

'Should be okay.'

'So pleased you can make it,' she said with deep sarcasm. 'Do you have a few minutes to spare for me right now, or do you have an urgent appointment?'

Tal didn't want to say that he was on his way to give George a hacking assignment. Although it hadn't been resolved whether Allyx and Mike should be told about using George's skills, Tal had decided not to mention anything to Allyx. Because her father worked for Brownbolt, she'd be put in a difficult position if she learned confidential information about Farront and had to decide whether to pass it on to her dad or not.

Trying to make a joke of it, Tal said, 'An urgent appointment? How did you guess? Mum said if I came home late for dinner tonight, I'd find myself homeless, and out on the street.'

'Funny,' said Allyx, not smiling.

He was almost out the front gate when Steven Grant called him back. 'Tell Grace I need to see her rather urgently about something confidential, so please don't mention this to anybody. I'll fit in with any time that suits her, and I think it's best if we meet at your place. I don't want to use a comm to set this up – it's not secure.

If you tell Allyx a time when your mother's available, she'll pass it on to me.'

Jogging to George Everett's house, Tal thought about Steven Grant's odd request. He'd seemed nervous, stroking his beard and then smoothing his thick greying hair. Tal had been tempted to ask if it had anything to do with the rash of teenage disconnections. But if Mr Grant was this secretive about seeing Tal's mother, there was no way he was going to reveal what it was about to Tal.

The front door of George's place was wide open. On the way out was Becca, one of George's sisters, who was in the year below Tal. In comparison to her brother, Becca was as up-to-date with the latest fashion styles as one could be.

'Go right in,' she said. 'You know where his room is.'

Tal went down the hallway to George's door and knocked.

'Get lost!'

'It's Tal.'

'Come in.'

Once he was seated on a ratty office chair, he said, 'I'm a disconnect.'

'Want me to get you a phantom? It's not cheap.'

Tal shook his head. 'Not yet. If I'm disconnected for too long, maybe.'

George's chair creaked as he leaned back. 'You've been disconnected *and* you're in Dr Renfrew's research group. Not a coincidence.'

Tal was impressed. 'You've seen the connection?'

'I've been very busy,' said George, rubbing his hands together. 'Frank, also. He has a special interest, since he's disconnected too.' With a chuckle, he added, 'It's a blast, as long as you don't get caught.'

'Rob Anderson was just telling Mum and me that FinagleAlert has been looking at how many young people have had their iZods disconnected.'

George nodded as Tal detailed the main points Rob had made. 'I haven't had time to go into it at that depth, but everything you're telling me fits in with what I've got.'

'And Joe Villabona? Anything on him?'

George puffed out his chest. 'You're looking at a guy who's been reading employees' files in Farront's human resources department.'

'Villabona's?'

'Target One's file.'

'Do we have to call Villabona, Renfrew and Unwin Targets One, Two and Three? Wouldn't it be simpler to use their names? You did say this room is fully shielded.'

Obviously annoyed, George snapped, 'It's part of my professional protocol.'

'Oh, in that case . . .' said Tal, hiding a smile.

His good humour restored, George went on, 'There was extra protection on Target One's file, but it didn't stop me.'

Missing his iZod already, Tal checked the time on an old wristwatch he'd dug out of a drawer full of bits and pieces. 'George, my mother will kill me if

'I'm late for dinner, so give it to me fast.'

'You got it. First, this target's qualifications – which could be fake, but I don't think they are: he's a near-genius in the computing field. Second, he's invented a brilliant cover story to explain the lack of detail in his work history.'

'Whatever this cover story is, Audrey Farront fell for it completely and gave him an executive job.'

'It is pretty good,' George conceded. 'The target claims to have spent years working for the government as an expert fighting cyber terrorism at the very top. And according to him, the department where he worked is so secret that very few people even know it exists.'

'Why did he leave?'

'The reason he gave is burnout. "The intolerable pressure" is how he put it in his job application, which he backed up with official-looking documents with areas blacked out because of national security concerns. Printed at the top of every page was a warning that revealing any information contained in the document was a federal crime.'

'Did anyone in human resources check if they were genuine?' Tal asked.

'Audrey Farront did it herself. Any contact had to be through a protected government email address. The reply, also by secure email, confirmed everything Target One had said. No surprise that I found the address no longer exists. The whole thing is a scam, but a very convincing one.'

'So he's definitely a phony?

'Yep, but he's good. Get this, Target One says this top-secret department still contacts him for help when a particularly bad cyber attack occurs.' George shook his head in grudging admiration. 'Nice touch!'

'Jeez,' said Tal, checking the time, 'I've really got to run. Before I go, have you got anything on Rick?'

'Working on it. Call around on Wednesday night. Frank'll be here. We should have something for you then.'

'FinagleAlert's negotiating with a potential informant on The Farront Centre staff who called in the last few days. I know whoever it is has direct contact with patients, but Rob wouldn't give his name.'

'Leave it with me,' said George.

TWENTY-FOUR

For Rick, everything had become a fuzzy, depressing blur. Batteries of tests and endless questions were interspersed with intervals of restless sleep in his room, where the ceiling light never went out. When he complained about the light, Dr Renfrew merely said, 'It stays on. Security reasons.'

Rick was aware his thoughts were becoming paranoid, but why not? He wouldn't put anything past Dr Renfrew and Dr Unwin. For one thing, he half believed the reason he felt so sleepy and confused all the time was because the doctors were putting drugs in his food. Hunger, plus the novelty of having something to do, made him eat the contents of each tray anyway.

With no way to tell the time, or even if it were day or night, Rick tried to rely on the pattern of his meals to mark the passing of the days. The trays were shoved through a narrow slot at the bottom of the door. Breakfast indicated it was morning, lunch was always some sort of salad, and a hot dinner showed it was the evening. Then a disturbing thought surfaced. What if they were serving breakfast at night, just to confuse him?

When he was taken out of his room for further tests and questions, Rick was always accompanied by Luis or Felix, the only people he ever saw other than the two doctors. Neither orderly would let him know what time it was. 'Can't tell you. Why? Just following instructions.'

When Rick had asked Luis about sensory deprivation, Luis had hesitated, then said he couldn't discuss anything about Rick's treatment.

'That's what they're doing to me, isn't it?'

'Like I said, I can't discuss your treatment.'

Looking back, Rick realised that Luis may have indirectly answered his question. By saying he couldn't talk about Rick's treatment, he'd implied that sensory deprivation was part of it.

It made sense: Rick's world had shrunk to two rooms, a bedroom and bathroom. There was nothing to listen to, nothing to watch, nothing to do, and no one to interact with, except the doctors and the two orderlies.

What made it worse was that knowing all this was no help. Rick knew the isolation was getting to him. Sometimes he felt like screaming and beating at the door, but mainly he found himself struggling against a pervasive hopelessness that made him hardly care what happened to him.

Rick had used the flimsy plastic cutlery to eat the contents of his dinner tray – an almost tasteless stew and a doughy bread roll, plus an insipid custard dessert in a plastic bowl – and was drinking the last of his fruit juice, when he heard the snick of the door's lock disengaging.

White-coated Dr Renfrew and Dr Unwin came in, both looking very grave.

'No, don't get up, Rick,' said Renfrew. 'I'm afraid we have some bad news for you.'

A horrible feeling of dread skewered Rick's heart. 'What is it?' he heard himself say, as though from a long distance away.

Dr Unwin came over and put a comforting hand on his shoulder. His customary smile absent, Unwin said solemnly, 'We're asking you to be brave, Rick.'

Rick shrank away from his touch. 'Brave about what?'

Dr Renfrew gave a heavy sigh. 'It pains me to have to tell you this, Rick, but it's your grandfather. I'm so sorry. He never regained consciousness. He died this afternoon. Your grandmother was by his side as he slipped gently away.'

Before he could think, Rick blurted out, 'I know that isn't true!'

Unwin gave Rick's shoulder a gentle squeeze. 'It's normal to be in denial, but I'm afraid you have to accept reality, however painful it is. The truth is, you will never see your grandfather again.'

Liar! thought Rick, anger burning away the grey lethargy that had come to fill him. If Luis hadn't passed on the message from Thelma that Les was awake and sitting up in bed, Rick might have believed them.

'I want to see Thelma.'

Renfrew shook his head regretfully. 'When I spoke to your grandmother she told me she was too upset even to think of visiting you at the moment. Later, perhaps.'

Another lie. Thelma would never pass up an opportunity to see him.

'We'll leave you alone, to grieve in private,' said Renfrew, turning towards the door.

Rick leapt to his feet. 'When's the funeral?' he demanded. 'I have to be there.'

Unwin, clearly surprised at Rick's vehemence, said with warm sympathy, 'I understand entirely. It's natural you would want to show respect to your grandfather, but I hope you appreciate why it's impossible for you to leave the centre. Your mental health is simply too fragile.'

'Stop feeding me all those drugs, and my mental health will be fine.'

Unwin chuckled. 'Oh, come now, Rick,' he said indulgently. 'The very idea is laughable. This is simply a delusion of yours that isn't –'

Rick's fist hit Unwin in the middle of his smarmy smile.

Dr Renfrew called out, the door was flung open and Felix and Luis rushed in to grab Rick and wrestle him to the floor. As he felt the sting of a sedative being injected into his arm, Rick had the satisfaction of seeing that his punch had badly split Unwin's lip.

That's going to put a crimp in the doctor's oily smile,
was Rick's last thought before he lost consciousness.

'**H**ow's Allyx handling your disconnection?' Tal's
mother asked on Tuesday evening, as they drove
to visit Victor O'Dell.

'Okay, I suppose, but she misses us being in contact
all the time.'

Tal winced to himself, recalling Allyx's hostile
reaction that morning at school when he'd told her he
wasn't available on Wednesday night. He hated to lie,
but he couldn't say he'd be seeing George, because of
course she'd ask why. The excuse Tal had come up with
was half true. He'd pointed out that on Wednesday
afternoon he was having his orientation meeting for
Dr Renfrew's research project at The Farront Centre.
He said he'd checked and found the session was open-
ended and likely to run well into the evening. He'd
suggested a date on Friday instead, since his mother
had nominated Thursday evening for Allyx's father to
call by. Allyx had said she'd get back to him. They'd left
it at that.

Turning into O'Dell's driveway, his mother
commented, 'I'd feel claustrophobic if I had that close,
moment-by-moment personal contact you kids take
for granted. To me it would be suffocating.'

'You're getting old, Mum.'

'That must be it,' she said, laughing.

Victor O'Dell was surprisingly spry for an old man who'd been in an accident bad enough to total his car. He greeted Tal and his mother enthusiastically when he answered the front door. 'Thank heavens! I'm dying of boredom here. Being without wheels is more than an inconvenience, it's an unwelcome change in lifestyle.'

'How are you feeling?'

'Fine, Grace, fine. My ribs are strapped and I'm a bit stiff, but the cuts and bruises are healing fast.'

Using a walking stick, he made surprising speed down the hallway to the kitchen. 'I've got the coffee on, and Marcia dropped in with a sponge cake she'd just made.'

'How is Marcia?' Tal asked once they were seated at the old wooden kitchen table.

'Her nose is taped and she's got two black eyes.' He gave a creaky laugh. 'You interested in her? You could do a lot worse, Talbot. Marcia's a fine young woman.'

It was ridiculous, but Tal's face felt hot. Amused at his discomfiture, Tal's mother said, 'Allyx is Tal's steady girlfriend, Victor. You met her at the barbecue.'

'Ah, yes, another fine young woman.' He winked at Tal. 'But you're much too young to even think of settling down. Take my advice and play the field.'

While O'Dell poured the coffee from an antique percolator, Tal's mother cut the sponge cake. Marcia had been generous with both the icing and the filling of whipped cream and raspberry. Tal took a bite and found it delicious.

'See, my boy? Marcia can cook too. *And* she has a sense of humour.'

He seemed ready to enlarge on Marcia's other excellent qualities, but Tal's mother said, 'I'm concerned for your safety, Victor. I don't see any extra security, even though Rob strongly advised you to get more protection. After that hit-and-run you can't afford to take any chances.'

'Don't worry, Grace, I'm not in the slightest danger now. Audrey Farront has effectively muzzled me with injunctions claiming I've set out with deliberate malice to ruin her company's reputation. My legal guy is working on it, but in the meantime I can't say a word about Farront without running the risk of landing in court.'

'My, my, Farront's lawyers *have* been busy,' she said with a cynical smile. 'This afternoon FinagleAlert was slapped with a slew of injunctions too.'

Tal hadn't heard anything about this. 'What about?'

'Pretty well anything a creative law firm can think up,' his mother said. 'Among other things, FinagleAlert's accused of copyright infringements, releasing stolen documents, industrial espionage, defamation and slander, invasion of privacy, and so on.'

'Legal games,' said Victor contemptuously.

'Rob says FinagleAlert's lawyers believe nothing will stand up to a challenge in court, but in the meantime the injunctions have the effect of smothering any criticism of the company, Audrey herself and, indirectly, Renfrew and Unwin.'

O'Dell said scathingly, 'Audrey's been taken in, hook, line and sinker. Until all this happened, I considered her a tough but ethical businesswoman. Now she's so desperate to get the results of Renfrew's research incorporated into the new iZod Excelsior that she'll turn a blind eye to that unholy trio, Renfrew, Unwin and Villabona.'

'Speaking of Dr Renfrew,' said Tal, 'my friend Rick Lawrence is locked away in The Farront Centre's psychiatric unit under Renfrew and Unwin's care.'

'Care?' snorted O'Dell. 'That's not how I'd describe it. Brainwashing is a more accurate word. Or in the case of your friend, who has, I believe, a history of depressive illness, I'd call it torture.'

'Torture!' Tal's mother exclaimed. 'Surely that's an exaggeration.'

'The pity is, I'm not overstating anything, Grace. Quite the contrary. Sensory deprivation, where the subject is isolated and cut off from the outside world, can be a devastating experience for someone with mental or emotional problems.

'When I reviewed Carter Renfrew's research plans, as Audrey had requested, I immediately had serious misgivings about several procedures. Most disturbing to me was Carter's willingness to utilise this SD technique. When I told him so in no uncertain terms, Carter babbled something about how sensory deprivation was a valuable tool to strip away the surface of the patient's personality and reveal the true self underneath. Naturally I told him this was dangerous nonsense, but he's too puffed up with pride at his fame and influence. Refused to listen to me.'

'I get what sensory deprivation is,' said Tal, 'but what's it for?'

'There are some positive applications. Certain meditation techniques use it to remove outside distractions and attain transcendence. Religious retreats and prayer circles may use modified SD to enhance the spiritual experience. However, it's far better known as a method of interrogation or as a form of torture.'

'So this could be happening to Rick right now, and there'd be no way to stop it?'

'I share your outrage, Talbot, but there's little to be done if his grandmother has officially given Renfrew and Unwin the power to make all medical decisions. Unless she takes legal action to remove Rick from their care, he stays where he is.'

'Thelma Lawrence was pressured to sign the papers,' said Tal's mother. 'She was given the impression that it was either commit Rick to the centre, or have him arrested for terrorism. The truth was that the authorities were looking for a way out, embarrassed that they'd overreacted and there was no hard evidence against Rick at all.'

'Problem solved, Grace. Explain the true situation to her, make sure she gets a good lawyer, and her grandson comes home.'

'Not going to happen,' said Tal. 'Thelma told Petra's mother that she believes Rick is better off at the centre.'

His mother nodded agreement. 'I've spoken to Thelma too. It seems to me that she feels guilty about committing Rick, and has persuaded herself that she did the right thing. Underneath I think she's beginning to have doubts. I'll talk to her again and see if I can change her mind.'

'So for the moment Rick is stuck there.' said Tal.

O'Dell grimaced. 'What makes it all the more unfortunate, Talbot, is that sensory deprivation works particularly well on your age group, because you're so accustomed to a continuous stream of communications all day, every day. When that stimulating torrent is cut off, your brain, to say the least, isn't happy. In fact, it may resort to hallucinations in an effort to replace the missing input.'

Picturing what Rick was suffering at the hands of doctors who were supposed to heal, not hurt, Tal felt a steely determination to do something practical to save him. No matter what it took, no matter what Tal and the others had to do, Rick was getting out of that place.

On Wednesday Tal was on the lookout for George, and caught him between classes. Checking that no one could overhear, he asked, 'Okay if Jennie and David come with me tonight?'

'No Petra?'

'She's grounded, but she's trying to work something out.'

George grunted. 'She would.'

He brightened noticeably when Tal said, 'Let's order in pizza. I'll pay.'

'You'll need heaps. Frank'll be there too.'

Tal visualised George's crammed room. 'Where are we all going to sit? With Frank, there'll be five of us.'

'Six,' said George morosely. 'Petra will make it, you can count on it.'

The sliding entrance doors of The Farront Centre were set into a wall of glass, so the foyer was full of light. Tal counted fifteen others in the orientation group. He recognised four students from Braidworth High. Three he didn't know personally, the fourth was Frank Arran, who for a change was dressed respectably in trousers and a plain blue shirt.

While the group was waiting to be escorted to the research facility, Tal said to Frank, 'I didn't know you'd applied for this.'

'The money's nice, but I was going to give it a miss until I was made a disconnect. Now I want to find out why.'

A three-person security team – two male guards and a woman – checked the list of names, then led them to the lifts. The research facility was on the third floor. Tal noticed that on the lift's control panel the fourth and fifth floors were marked as restricted entry, for authorised personnel only.

Individual identity cards were distributed from

the research facility's reception desk. Once the guards had made sure that each person had his or her correct ID, they were given a stern instruction that these had to be clearly displayed at all times when in the centre.

Each person was assigned a locker. Visitors to The Farront Centre were banned from using any electronic devices. Tal wondered how many others in the group were disconnects like him and Frank, so didn't have comms to lock away anyway.

The group was shown around the research facility by a young guy with a white lab coat and a haughty manner. His name tag held only one word: Graeme.

'Questions?' Graeme asked at the end of the brief tour, his tone indicating he was not expecting any.

When someone asked where Dr Renfrew was, Graeme said with a touch of impatience, 'You won't be seeing Dr Renfrew or Dr Unwin unless you earn a gold rating, which will indicate you are a superior subject for "Got to be Connected" research.'

'More money?' a skinny, sharp-featured girl asked.

Graeme agreed that gold-rated subjects were paid more generously.

'That's so not fair!'

Graeme frowned. 'It's a privilege to be part of Dr Renfrew's groundbreaking work at any level. Those of you who don't achieve a gold rating will nevertheless be included in the research, but to a lesser degree.'

'What happens if you don't even make that lower rating?' Frank asked.

'Then you'll be thanked for your time,' Graeme snapped, 'asked to surrender your ID and shown the door.'

The next step of the orientation session was run by a severe, efficient woman called Stella. With genuine enthusiasm, Stella pointed out how fortunate they were to be considered for Dr Carter Renfrew's cutting-edge research.

'You have the opportunity to be part of scientific history,' she assured them. 'Any questions? No? Let's get to work.'

In a short time she had the group silently sitting at desks filling out answers to page after page of personal questions. Many of them puzzled Tal. For instance, did it really matter what foods his most hated meal would contain, or if he believed in ghosts, UFOs and out-of-body experiences, or what his very earliest memory was?

Stella and two assistants then took the orientation group to a lab, where everyone was seated in a separate cubicle to perform various tasks. Tal found that his task – pressing a button each time a light of a certain intensity momentarily appeared on the monitor – soon became tedious. Identifying a sequence of words flashed for a fraction of a second was only slightly more interesting. These were followed by hearing trials, where Tal wore earphones and responded each time he heard a certain arrangement of tones.

He was rapidly coming to the conclusion that being a research subject was going to be very boring.

At the conclusion of the testing Graeme reappeared to announce that at the next session, on Friday afternoon, brain scans were scheduled for all new participants in the program. 'Metal objects interact with the scanner,' he said, 'so don't wear jewellery or carry anything metallic.'

After collecting their equipment from the lockers, the group was escorted out of the building by the same security team that had met them at the beginning of the session. Tal noticed the guards were much more casual this time, chatting among themselves as he and the others straggled to the front doors, where their identity cards were scanned.

The sleepy-looking guard supervising the scanning raised his voice to say, 'Remember, you need your IDs to get into the building and also to leave it. Don't forget to bring them with you. No card, no entry.'

Once they were outside, Frank said, 'See you tonight,' and loped off to collect his Solarscoot from the security rack near the entrance.

Tal caught a shuttle, and when he was seated, he shut his eyes to run through everything about the layout and the security procedures he'd observed at the centre. He'd compare notes with Frank this evening.

It was maddening not to have his iZod or a mini-note to record the information while it was fresh in his mind. He'd have to rely on something really primitive, like a pen and paper.

TWENTY-FIVE

The empty pizza boxes were haphazardly piled on top of an already overloaded bench. George had squeezed everyone in by clearing a larger space in the middle of the room. He'd also provided enough seating with an assortment of stools and a rickety kitchen chair he'd arranged in a rough circle.

George had been right: Petra had made it. 'I snuck out,' she said, when asked how she'd managed to get around being grounded. 'Mum and Dad are at a Garden Stuff meeting with suppliers that'll go on for ages, and Rosa's watching some mushy movie marathon and thinks I'm in my room.'

Frank Arran pointed out that all Petra's parents needed to do was check the global positioning on her comm and they'd know she wasn't in the house.

'Think I'm dumb? I left my iZod in my bedroom.' She looked over at Tal. 'Can we get going? Mum will check on me when she gets home, and I'd better be there when she does.'

'Okay,' said Tal, 'we've talked it over enough, so let's start planning exactly what we'll do. We have two related objectives: rescue Rick; and bring down Villabona, Renfrew and Unwin.'

'Targets One, Two and Three,' George corrected.

'Enough with the targets,' said Petra impatiently. 'We've already been through this, George, and everyone's agreed that we'll use names.'

He slumped in his chair, mumbling to himself.

'If we discredit the doctors and Villabona, the Farront company will suffer damage too,' David pointed out. 'What about your mum, Tal? If it gets out that you're involved, she could lose her job.'

'Her job's on the line, anyway. Joe Villabona's trying to get rid of her.'

'Let's concentrate on the most important thing – rescuing Rick,' said Jennie.

'We all agree that has top priority.' Because Tal couldn't use his comm, he'd had George print out information from government building records. He passed out the pages, which showed architectural floor plans for each storey of the then-named Carter Renfrew Centre.

'The lifts to floors four and five are restricted to authorised personnel,' Tal said. 'Floor five is Dr Renfrew's penthouse suite. That leaves floor four. Check the north-west corner, where there are no windows. It's marked Secure Wing. That's got to be the psychiatric ward. Behind the security door there's a series of small rooms, each with a separate bathroom. A couple have the bed, toilet and basin in the one room.'

'Like prison cells,' said Jennie.

'So how do we get in?' David asked.

Tal glanced at George, who'd stopped sulking and was wearing a smug expression. 'Okay, George, what've you got?'

'Oh, nothing much. Just the name of FinagleAlert's informant at the centre.' Gratified at the attention this got, he went on. 'Luis Cardova. His job description says he's an orderly, authorised to enter restricted areas.'

'Tell us how you know that,' demanded Petra.

'It took a while, I can tell you. I hacked into the centre's personnel files and got a list of employees, which included contact information. I figured, since Tal had said the guy had first called FinagleAlert in the last few days, that he would have used FinagleAlert's Totally Secure Tip-line, which is supposed to be hacker-proof, but I got in. Then all I had to do was compare comm numbers with FinagleAlert's tip-line records for the last couple of weeks. And there he was – Luis Cordova.'

'George is a top cyber master,' Frank said, quite sincerely. George smiled.

Tal recalled how confident Rob was about the effectiveness of FinagleAlert's security measures. 'When this is over, Rob Anderson's not going to be happy to learn FinagleAlert's records can be hacked.'

'The system will show that security has been breached, so Anderson will already know, but I've made sure there's no way to trace anything to me.'

'Let's get back to Rick,' said David. 'This Cordova guy is no use to us unless we have a clear idea of what we're going to do.'

'Tal and I need a bit of time to find out how things work at the centre,' said Frank, 'and if there's a realistic chance we can get Rick out.'

'Frank, are you sure you want to get that involved?' Petra asked. 'What I mean is, we're willing to run the risk of being caught because Rick's one of us and we can't leave him there. But it's a risk you don't have to take.'

'I'm in, if that's okay,' said Frank, looking around the circle.

'Just don't expect me to be a hero too,' George announced, patting his plump stomach. 'As you can see, I'm not much into action stuff. I'll be behind the scenes only.'

Rick could hear the beat of blood in his ears, the whisper of air as he breathed and the faint rustle of clothing when he moved. Otherwise there was absolute silence.

He was lying on his back on a hard, unyielding surface. He felt as though his arms and legs were made of lead and to even open his eyes would take a huge effort. It was tempting to drift back to sleep, but a faint stirring of curiosity made him struggle to a sitting position and look around.

Dizziness swamped him and he had to lie down again until it subsided. When he cautiously sat up he found he was on a slab of hard grey plastic jutting from the wall. At one end was a neatly folded grey blanket. There was no pillow.

It had been boring to be locked up in the other room, but at least it had been comfortable, with carpet on the floor, a proper bed and a separate bathroom. This was far more spartan – even worse than the room he'd been locked in at the hospital. The floor, walls and ceiling were all painted the same dreary grey. The only items that gleamed in the bright, flat light were a stainless steel toilet and a stainless steel hand basin. The room lacked a table, a chair, a chest of drawers. One thing Rick did find, however, was the lens of the surveillance camera, positioned out of reach in the ceiling.

Rick ran his hands over the featureless metal door – grey, of course. It had a slot at the bottom, which indicated that perhaps they intended to feed him. Not that he felt hungry. In fact the thought of food made him feel nauseated.

How had he got here? Memory came back in bits and pieces. With anger he recalled how they'd lied to him about his grandfather; how they'd said Thelma didn't want to see him. He felt a quick stab of delight when he remembered splitting Dr Unwin's lip.

He jumped, startled, when a voice boomed from the ceiling. 'Perhaps you wonder why you've been moved to this accommodation.' Squinting, Rick could make out the tiny speaker beside the surveillance cam.

The voice – Dr Unwin's – went on. 'Your behaviour is unacceptable. Violence will not be tolerated. Until you learn to control yourself, all privileges are withdrawn.'

'What privileges?' Rick shouted. 'Being kept a prisoner, is that a privilege?'

Silence.

Either Dr Unwin had gone, or he was quietly waiting, observing what Rick would do.

He told himself to stay calm, to sit down and relax, but impotent rage boiled up in him, and Rick found himself hammering at the door with his fists and yelling words that would have shocked Thelma deeply.

'**T**hrough Farront, Joe Villabona's tied to Renfrew and Unwin,' said Tal, 'and he's obviously got things to hide in his past.'

'Maybe he has,' said Petra, 'but we should concentrate on Dr Renfrew and his research. We know he's experimenting on Rick, for instance.'

'We don't actually know that for a fact,' said Jennie. 'Anyhow, Dr Unwin's the one who's a psychiatrist, and everyone knows they're all mad. I think we should go after him.'

'Hold it, dudes!' Everyone looked at David. 'How about George tells us what he can do for us, before we worry about who to target?'

George leapt into lecture mode with wholehearted enthusiasm. 'Cyber warfare covers lots of things,' he began. 'There's cyber espionage, where a company's classified information is stolen and distributed to competitors or sold to the highest bidder.'

'Nix that,' said Jennie.

'Then there's denial-of-service attacks, where large numbers of computers, usually without the owners' knowledge, have been programmed to overload the target company's website with so many incoming messages that the site crashes.'

'We know all about botnets,' said David. 'No use to us.'

'Then there are worms and viruses –'

'George, cut the lecture and get to the point. I've got to get home before my mother does.'

George grinned at Petra, who was perched uncomfortably on a too-small stool. 'Here's something Petra knows all about – a cyber attack. And I figure that's the way we want to go.'

'I know we want to get the doctors,' said Jennie, 'but what about the others who could get hurt?'

'Like who?' said David.

'Like people who work for them. They could lose their jobs.'

'Tough,' said David. 'My mum always says you can't make an omelette without breaking a few eggs.'

Petra broke in. 'I know from experience how foul a cyber attack can be. I found the best way to handle it was to pretend it wasn't happening. What's to stop these guys from doing the same and ignoring the attack?'

'It won't be something they *can* ignore,' said Frank. 'You all know how cyber bullying starts with a few people, then more and more join in? Well this will be a million times larger. If we do it right, once the cyber attack is underway it'll be totally unstoppable.'

Clearly miffed that Frank had taken over, George said, 'The idea is to swamp the web with sensational stuff about the targets, true where possible, but made up if necessary. I'll make sure to involve every part of the internet – all the social networking sites, the media sites, the blogosphere, online forums, et cetera, et cetera.'

Frank said, 'You know how we all pass on videos that send people up and make us laugh? Literally millions of people see the good ones, so videos that ridicule these guys can be really effective.'

'What about medical associations?' David asked. 'If they get enough complaints, they investigate.'

'Good idea.'

'And how about anti-psychiatry organisations?' said Jennie. 'We could send anonymous tip-offs to groups like Clear Minds Forever or Psycho-trist Anonymous.'

'Malpractice,' said Petra. 'I bet those two have patients who've sued them.' She got to her feet. 'I'm outta here.'

'Before Petra goes,' said Tal, 'do we all agree that George and Frank will get together a team to start and maintain the cyber attack?'

'The Geek Gang,' Petra named them as she went out the door.

TWENTY-SIX

The front door chime sounded. Tal's mother checked her iZod, which displayed images from the house security cams. 'It's Steven and Allyx.' A few minutes later, she was leading them into the living room. 'Sit anywhere. Make yourself at home.'

Even when Allyx's father was casually dressed, Tal thought, he never seemed to relax. His jeans had ironed creases and his dark maroon sports shirt looked brand new. He was sitting stiffly in the lounge chair, fretfully tugging at his neat beard, until Allyx murmured to him, '*Dad*, forget the beard.'

'Sorry.' He dropped his hand, embarrassed.

A prompting glance from his mother prodded Tal to say, 'Can I get you something to drink?'

'No thanks. Grace, I suppose you're wondering what this is all about.'

'I certainly am.'

'Two words: Joe Villabona.'

She was startled, then intrigued. 'I definitely want to hear this – but I have a request. Rob Anderson's working in another room. He has a keen interest in Joe Villabona. Would you mind if Rob sat in?'

'Not at all.'

Allyx followed Tal when he went to collect Rob. When she caught up with him, he swung around to face her. 'What's up?'

'Tal, you absolutely have to get a phantom from George Everett.'

'That'll cost a bundle. Besides, it's illegal to have one.'

Entreaty in her eyes, Allyx said, 'Please? I can't stand what you being a disconnect is doing to us. You don't seem to be the same person.'

Exasperation tinged Tal's voice. 'I'm the same person. I haven't changed in the few days since my iZod died. The only thing that's different is that I'm disconnected, and that won't be forever.'

'Listen to yourself. You're annoyed with me just for talking about it.'

He *was* annoyed, he realised. He'd noticed how short-tempered he'd become in the last couple of days. 'I've had a lot on my mind,' he said. It was a lame excuse, but better than nothing.

'And that's another thing,' Allyx said resentfully. 'You're keeping something from me, you and the others. I was talking to Mike, and he agrees with me. He says Petra's acting all mysterious, and when he asks what's going on, all she'll say is, "My lips are sealed." '

Tal's mother came out into the hall. 'Tal? Are you going to take all night?'

'We'll talk things over later,' he said, feeling a touch of guilt. Had he been right to exclude Allyx from their plans to rescue Rick?

'Fine!' Allyx turned and marched back to the sitting room.

Tal collected Rob, who was so fired up at the mention of Villabona's name that he hurried ahead and was already shaking hands when Tal came through the door.

'Steven, nice to see you again. Hi, Allyx.'

Tal tried to catch Allyx's attention, but she pointedly avoided eye contact. *Okay*, he thought, *be that way.*

'Good that you're here, Rob,' said Steven. 'I'm hoping FinagleAlert will ultimately be involved in exposing Villabona's criminal activities.'

Tal went on full alert. Perhaps whatever Allyx's father had on Villabona could be used in the cyber attack they were planning.

'Is it all right if I record our discussion?' Rob patted his pockets in an effort to locate his camcorder.

'No, I'm afraid it's not all right. I have my career to protect.'

Rob put up his hands. 'No recording.'

Steven glanced at Tal's mother. 'Grace, I shouldn't even bother asking, but this house is fully shielded, isn't it?'

'Farront's electronic curtain is the best in the business.'

'Fighting words, Grace.' He forced a smile, obviously trying to ease the tension in the room. 'Brownbolt's curtain is equal, if not better.' His smile faded. 'Since yours is a Farront system, there's a chance it may be compromised.'

'By Villabona?' said Rob. 'No worries. I've set up FinagleAlert's security system to run a check on the shield's integrity every ten seconds, twenty-four/seven.'

Steven ran a hand over his hair. 'What I have to say is strictly confidential. I've already sworn Allyx to secrecy. I must have the same undertaking from all of you.'

'You've got it,' said Tal's mother. Tal and Rob both nodded.

'I can't have anything traced back to me.'

'Nothing will be,' said Rob. 'You have my guarantee.'

Steven took a deep breath. 'Okay, here it is. Joe Villabona has approached Brownbolt's top executives, including me, with an offer he describes as priceless. He, of course, has a price – a hefty one. For a considerable sum, to be paid into an off-shore bank, Villabona will provide highly secret data from Carter Renfrew's mapping of the teenage brain and how it applies to the new iZod Excelsior. As a bonus he'll throw in Howard Unwin's CWSS work on the link between teen disconnection and clinical depression.'

'Why would your company risk buying stolen research findings? It could ruin Brownbolt if it got out,' said Rob.

Steven tugged at his beard. 'I hate to admit it, but my company is at a distinct disadvantage as far as teens are concerned. Once Farront's iZod Excelsior is released, it will give Farront a nearly unbeatable sales lead. We're developing a similar AI application for our BeauBrute communicator, but we're lagging behind Farront. With access to Renfrew's research on how kids' brains process information, Brownbolt would become competitive in this vital segment of the marketplace.'

'Are we *that* vital?' Tal asked.

'Yes. Because of your age group's dependence on all forms of electronic communication, you make intensely loyal and reliable consumers. At Brownbolt we've taken to calling teens "connection addicts".'

'Our product research shows the same thing,' said Tal's mother. 'Teenagers have a craving for connectedness that can become an obsession. That's why disconnection hits them so hard.' She glanced at Tad, adding with a smile, 'Perhaps not all of them.'

'And there's more,' Steven said. 'Using Renfrew's brain-mapping techniques, it will soon be possible to tailor specific advertising strategies to take full advantage of teens' dependence on connectedness. We'll be able to predict confidently which of our potential products and services will be successful and which are likely to fail. The saving to the company in development time and money would be enormous.'

'I still find it hard to believe that your top executives would willingly get involved in a criminal enterprise like this.'

'You're too innocent, Grace. It's not a moral question for my fellow executives. They're busy weighing up the risk factor – whether the huge advantages are worth possible exposure to ruinous legal proceedings. The fact it's industrial espionage on a grand scale isn't an issue.'

'And Dad can't do anything about it,' said Allyx. 'At least, not without losing his job.'

'Allyx is right. I'm telling you all this because there's nothing I can do personally without destroying my career, and I can't afford to do that. What I'm hoping is that you can stop Villabona at your end.'

'Isn't it possible Villabona will self-destruct?' Tal asked. 'For all he knows, someone at Brownbolt could be planning to go direct to Audrey with the news he's selling Farront's secrets.'

'Villabona's a highly skilled operator,' said Rob. 'He would have been carrying a nullifier to disrupt any attempts to record him on video or sound, and I'm betting the material he brought to the meeting as proof he had access to confidential data was in electronic form and programmed to self-destruct within a short time.'

'Exactly right,' said Steven. 'As a matter of course we made a recording of the meeting, but as you say, it was nullified. And attempts to read and copy the data he'd left with us initiated an instant destruct command. It was a smooth operation. My guess would be that Villabona's done something like this before.'

'Unless Rob and FinagleAlert can come up with convincing evidence against him, the only hope is for me to persuade Audrey that Joe is a con artist and a criminal,' said Tal's mother. 'Frankly, I don't like my chances.'

Steven shook his head. 'I'd have thought Audrey Farront, of all people, would be impossible to fool.'

'Don't be too hard on her, Steven. I can see why Audrey fell for Joe's story. He presented himself as a can-do guy, a specialist in electronic communications and cyber warfare, with impeccable references and contacts at the highest level of government.'

Rob nodded. 'As Grace says, Villabona looks great on paper, but more importantly, he also delivers the goods. His organisational skills and computing abilities are excellent. So, unfortunately, is his ability to manipulate people, particularly Audrey Farront.'

Steven Grant gave a dispirited sigh. 'So what do we do?'

'FinagleAlert will keep digging,' said Rob, 'until we turn something up.' He made a face. 'I wish I had something more concrete to offer.'

Tal wished with all his heart that he could say what he was thinking: *Just wait a while. A cyber war is coming that'll sweep Villabona away.*

I hope . . .

TWENTY-SEVEN

After first period at school on Friday, Tal, Petra and David stopped to talk on their way to maths.

Allyx passed them by. She didn't slow down, but waved acknowledgement that she'd seen them. She didn't smile.

'What's up with Allyx?' Petra asked Tal. 'She froze me out when I said hi before rollcall.'

'What's Allyx's secret?' David mocked. 'I'd freeze you out myself, if only I could find a way.'

'So not funny.' She turned to Tal. 'Well?'

Tal had tried to talk to Allyx last night, as she was leaving with her father, but she'd shrugged him off. Without a comm, he couldn't contact her, so he'd got his mother to text Allyx a message, sending his love and saying he'd see her the next morning. There'd been no reply.

'Allyx doesn't much like me being a disconnect,' he said. 'Plus she and Mike have been comparing notes, and he told her you were acting all mysterious.'

'I didn't tell Mike a thing!'

'Whatever, Allyx knows something's going on, and she hates being left out.'

'Why did you drop hints to Mike that you were hiding a big, fat secret?' David enquired.

'I didn't have to drop hints. Mike knows me well enough to know something was up. Anyway, it was left to me and Tal to decide whether to tell Mike and Allyx, so it's nothing to do with you.'

Jennie came hurrying up to them. 'George wants Maryann Dodd on the cyber team.'

'No way!'

'Hold on, David,' Jennie said. 'George says she's great at cyber bullying, and that's what this is going to be, but on a grand scale.'

David folded his arms. 'No Dodder. She can't be trusted.'

'We don't have to trust her,' said Petra. 'We just have to use her. And what about Kimba and Tiffany?'

'George mentioned them too.'

'No way!'

'Get a grip, David,' said Petra. 'You're starting to repeat yourself.'

At lunchtime Tal went in search of Allyx, finding her chatting with a group of other girls. 'Can I see you for a minute?'

'You can see me for a lot longer than that, if you

like,' said Becca Everett, with a flirtatious smile. The others laughed.

'Are we going to get together tonight?' Tal asked, when he and Allyx had moved away.

'I don't think so.'

'Oh, come on, Allyx!'

She flushed with anger. 'No, you come on! You've got some important secret you won't share with me.'

'I'll tell you when I can.'

'You don't trust me.'

'That's not the reason.'

Eyes flashing, Allyx said, 'You being disconnected sucks. Most of the time I don't know where you are or what you're thinking. We never talk.'

'We're talking now,' he pointed out.

'You know what I mean, Tal. We can't do anything online together. We can't share everything like we did before. I hate it!'

Surprised by her intensity, Tal said, 'Hey, it's *me* who's disconnected. I'm the one who can't do anything, not you.'

Allyx turned and began to walk away. Looking back, she said bitterly, 'I knew you wouldn't understand.'

Tal found the second session at the centre rather more interesting than the orientation. Frank and Tal had discussed striking up conversations with the security team, because, as Frank said, it was basic psychology to be more relaxed with people with whom you had some sort of relationship, particularly if he and Tal came over as pleasant and non-threatening.

The guards were the same three who'd escorted them to and from the research facility, their name tags identifying them as Cilla, Mitch and Brad. Tal guessed Cilla was about his mother's age. Mitch was middle-aged, overweight and had a mean face. Brad, the other guy, looked only a few years older than Tal.

While waiting in the foyer for everyone in the group to arrive, Tal struck up a conversation with Cilla, while Frank chatted with Brad. Later, standing in the line for their brain scans, Tal and Frank compared notes.

'Cilla is really nice,' said Tal, 'but she takes her job seriously. While we were talking she kept checking around to make sure everything was okay.'

'Brad's too lazy to be serious about his job,' said Frank. 'He makes it obvious he's bored out of his mind.'

'So what did you talk about?'

'Sport, mainly.' Frank grinned at Tal's expression. 'Surprise! It is possible for a geek to be into sport.'

Once the brain scans for the whole group were completed, Graeme appeared, just as officious as before, and haughtily read out the names of the eight members of the group who had made the gold-rating list. Tal and Frank were both on it.

'What about me?' yelled the skinny girl who'd complained about money in the first session. 'I should be gold too.'

'If I didn't read out your name, you're not gold material.' Graeme looked pleased to be saying this.

When she continued to protest loudly, Graeme spoke into his comm. The young guard, Brad, entered the room. 'Yeah? You called?'

Graeme's lips twitched irritably at Brad's casual attitude. 'Please escort this young woman off the premises.'

She was led away, still objecting.

At the end of the session Tal sidled up to Cilla. 'Guess what? I'm a gold-rated research subject.' He hoped it came over as naive enthusiasm.

She smiled. 'Really? I'm so impressed.'

With nothing to do that evening except school assignments – since his disconnection, homework for each subject was provided in printed form – Tal decided to go for a run. He headed in the direction of George's place, intending to call in for a progress report. When he jogged up to the sagging front fence, he saw Becca sitting on the stairs to the verandah.

'We meet again,' she said with a wide grin. 'Is it too much to hope that you're stalking me?'

'You wouldn't be that lucky,' said Tal, laughing.

'Have you and Allyx broken up?'

'No,' he said curtly, feeling irritated with both Becca for asking, and Allyx for making it possible for Becca to ask. 'Is George in?'

'My brother is always in,' said Becca, getting up to let Tal past. 'Honestly, it's a joke when Dad grounds him, because George spends most of his time in his room anyway.' Becca gave Tal a shrewd look. 'He's doing something for you, isn't he? Something big?'

'Maybe.'

Becca gave a gurgle of laughter. 'I don't know the target, but I do know it's a cyber attack. George asked me if I'd help out.'

Tal blinked at her, which amused Becca even more. 'I *do* know a lot about cyber attacks. George isn't the only nerd in the family.'

'You're calling yourself a nerd?' said Tal, eyebrows raised.

'A nerd in heavy disguise,' said Becca. 'And if anyone asks, I'll deny it.'

Rob had taken Tal's mother out to dinner, and they came in shortly after Tal arrived home from seeing George.

Over coffee, Rob said, 'I've been telling Grace about the latest stuff FinagleAlert's dug up on Villabona, Renfrew and Unwin.'

'Anything interesting?'

'Definitely. For starters, Renfrew's almost broke.'

'But he must have made heaps,' said Tal.

'I hope Renfrew's a better psychologist than he is businessman,' Rob said sardonically. 'He's made a lot of money, but has squandered most of it with unwise investments. A few months ago he was desperately trying to scrape up funds so he could continue his teenage brain research.'

'This is where Joe steps in,' said Tal's mother. 'It must have seemed too good to be true, but I guess Renfrew wasn't going to rock the boat by asking too many questions.'

Rob went on. 'Renfrew urgently needs the backing of a huge company like Farront and, right on cue, Villabona appears and says not to worry, he'll introduce him to Audrey and then help persuade her to pour money into the research. And what does Villabona ask in return? Full access to Renfrew's findings, which as we know from Steven, he intends to sell under the table to any company willing to pay his price.'

'Do you think Renfrew's getting a cut?'

'I doubt it, Grace. He's got what's most important to him – funding for his research. If Villabona goes down, Renfrew will want to be in a position to say, "I knew nothing about it".'

'I don't understand,' said Tal, 'how Villabona would know that Dr Renfrew badly needed money, and at the same time just happened to have something of great value to Audrey.'

'I suspect Villabona had other potential victims lined up, should the deal with Renfrew not work out. I believe he plans way ahead, moving into a city with a new identity and using his skills to find people like Renfrew and Audrey to manipulate.'

'Renfrew's a fool, and Joe's a crook, but the one that really chills me is Howard Unwin,' said Tal's mother.

'And he's supposed to be taking care of Rick,' said Tal, feeling a chill himself.

'As a renowned child psychiatrist, Unwin provides excellent window dressing for The Farront Centre,' said Rob, 'but he has some dark things in his past. Villabona would certainly know about the malpractice lawsuits brought by parents against the doctor. Unwin was accused of experimenting with psychiatric drugs unauthorised for use on children, and also of submitting young people to harsh regimens that not only failed to achieve what he promised, but in some cases made the patient much worse.'

'Why isn't he in jail?'

'Principally, Tal, because he's a very rich man. Most of these malpractice suits were settled before going to trial. Unwin paid the families enough money to keep them quiet. They signed non-disclosure documents that would mean forfeiting every cent of the settlement if anything about the legal action was revealed. Those few cases that did end up in court never resulted in a conviction. Witnesses didn't turn up, or had unexpected memory lapses. It's obvious they were paid off, but nothing was ever proved.'

'I don't get why Unwin's involved in the centre,' said Tal. 'From what you say, he doesn't need the money.'

'Can you be too rich? Unwin has an expensive lifestyle to maintain. Also, I'm sure Villabona is aware of Unwin's past problems, so perhaps he's blackmailing Unwin into cooperating.'

'Tell Tal what your informant said.'

'Grace, what's the point? No one can do anything.'

'It's about Rick? Is he okay?'

Rob grimaced. 'It seems the doctors told Rick they had bad news. His grandfather had died without regaining consciousness.'

'That's awful.' Tal frowned. 'I'm surprised I haven't heard about it.'

'You haven't heard because it isn't true. Les Lawrence is well on the way to complete recovery. And Rick knew it was a lie, because our informant had secretly passed on a message earlier from Thelma Lawrence saying his grandfather was awake and doing well. Understandably, Rick lost his temper. He punched Unwin in the mouth.'

'Good for Rick! I hope he did some damage.'

'Apparently he split Unwin's lip. He didn't have time to do anything else because he was immediately restrained and sedated. Our informant says he's been moved to a basic room with nothing in it but the bare necessities.'

'Before you ask,' said Tal's mother, 'I've spoken to Thelma Lawrence. It was a waste of time, because Dr Unwin has been dropping by with glowing reports on Rick's progress. Unwin told Thelma that Rick's responding well, but she can't visit yet because he has to be kept isolated for a little longer. Thelma sincerely believes Rick's getting the best possible treatment.'

Tal was thinking furiously. George had told him that the earliest the cyber attack could be launched was the middle of next week. It had to be sooner.

He made a snap decision. 'Rob,' he said, 'your informant's name is Luis Cordova.'

TWENTY-EIGHT

Tal had to be content that Tuesday would be day one. It would take until the end of the week to fully launch the cyber attack, despite Tal, David, Petra and Jennie fretting over Rick's captivity and trying to speed things up.

'Look,' said George. 'I understand about Rick, but from what you say, his grandmother won't budge unless there's a tidal wave of bad stuff about the doctors. And that takes time.'

Tal knew that getting Thelma to change her mind and demand Rick's release – and having Renfrew and Unwin agree to it – was a long shot. It was far more likely they'd have to attempt to rescue Rick themselves.

In the meantime, Frank and Tal continued to attend sessions at The Farront Centre. They were getting to know the staff members and become familiar with their routines, including Luis Cordova's.

Rob had been astonished, alarmed and furious all

at once when he'd realised that Tal knew the name of FinagleAlert's informant. 'Someone's broken through our supposedly hacker-proof security. I'm sure you know who it is. I want a name.'

'Tal, tell Rob who it is.'

'No, Mum, I won't. The hacker doesn't matter. Rick matters.' Switching his attention back to Rob, he said, 'Rick needs to hear from his friends that he isn't alone and some day soon he'll be back home. That's the reason I wanted to know who your informant was.'

'What do you intend to do, Tal? Walk up to Luis and announce you're a friend of Rick's? He's got no reason to trust you, so he'll tell you to get lost.'

'That's where you come in,' said Tal. 'When Frank and I meet with the guy, he needs to know we're above-board.'

'Tal, you can't ask Rob to do that.'

'Grace is right. I won't jeopardise Luis's position at the centre.'

Tal didn't bother to hide his anger. 'What about Rick's position? Don't either of you care?'

'Of course we care,' said his mother, 'but this isn't the way to go.'

'All I'm asking is for a simple message to be passed on to Rick. If you won't help, I'll approach Luis Cordova cold and try to talk him into doing it.'

He had seen that Rob was wavering, so he'd said persuasively, 'The guy's given him a message before without a problem.'

'Just a few words of support?'

'Yes.'

With obvious reluctance, Rob had said, 'Okay.'

Tal, Petra, David and Jennie had a final strategy session at Tal's before the cyber war was launched. There was a strange mood in the room. Everyone was tense, but not serious. There was lots of talk and brittle laughter.

Calling the meeting to order, Tal reported on his and Frank's meeting with Luis Cordova in a crowded coffee shop. 'Rob had shown him pics of us, and we knew what he looked like, so when he asked if he could share our table, we said sure.'

'What's this Luis like?' said Petra.

'Ordinary looking, but sort of intense and a bit sarcastic. One good thing – he's really angry about Rick. He said it's wicked, the way he's been treated.'

'So what's he doing about it?' David asked.

'For starters, he's going to tell Rick not to give up, because we're working on getting him out.'

'We know Luis is authorised to go anywhere in the centre,' said Jennie. 'Do you think he'd be willing to get you and Frank into the psychiatric ward?'

'It's not impossible. Frank and I hinted we might be planning to spring Rick ourselves, and he didn't fall about laughing. The trouble is, we couldn't say too much because we weren't sure Luis could be trusted not to tell Rob Anderson.'

'Speaking of trust,' said Petra. 'Now that Mike's absolutely sure something big is about to happen, he's started really bugging me about it.'

'This close to launch, no one can be let in on the secret,' said Tal. 'That includes Mike.'

'And Allyx?' Petra asked.

'Yes, Allyx too.'

'Dudes,' said David, shaking his head, 'you're worrying about the wrong people. I reckon parents are going to be the real problem.'

'Our parents just think of us as kids,' said Jennie. 'At least in my family. It'd never occur to them that we could run a full-scale cyber war.'

'Wrong, Jennie. Sooner or later they're going to guess it's us,' Petra declared. 'My mum is already asking why I joined the after-school debating club, which is my excuse for being home late. So far it's worked, but if Mum checks and discovers I'm never there, she'll go ballistic.'

'You'll come up with some convincing story,' said David. 'You always do.'

Petra looked complacent. 'True.'

Every person participating in the cyber attack had been sworn to absolute secrecy. George had been persuasive regarding Maryann, Tiffany and Kimba, so to David's chagrin they joined Becca and a team of self-styled geeks under the leadership of George and Frank.

Tal was amazed at how eager everyone was to take

up the challenge, risky though it might be, especially in the early stages. Once the attack had gained momentum, the huge volume of electronic messages generated would make the chances of detection more remote.

Led by Maryann and her clique, the attack commenced with a blizzard of venomous postings about Dr Renfrew and Dr Unwin on bulletin boards, blogs and social networking sites. They followed this up by using other people's names to send inflammatory responses to their own postings.

Meanwhile, Frank was distributing defamatory – but very funny – short videos mocking the two doctors and Farront International to sites like YouTube and ItsaZoo. Frank's work soon inspired imitators, and a whole series of video skits ridiculing the two doctors appeared. Renfrew was usually depicted as a wild-eyed mad scientist; Unwin as an ever-smiling quack. These skits gained a virulent life of their own as they were copied and recopied across the internet.

Some members of the team hacked into the doctors' own websites, making alterations and linking them to other websites, including dummy sites. George was particularly proud of the one he'd created, QuackRenfrewQuackUnwin, accusing the psychologist and psychiatrist of treating human subjects like lab rats. Disturbing photographs were included, some of dubious origin. There was a listing of legal actions taken against Howard Unwin but never completed because they'd been settled out of court to avoid damning publicity.

The radical anti-psychiatry protest group Clear Minds Forever jumped on the buzz and declared war on The Farront Centre, picketing the building every day while wearing death's head masks. Images of members being arrested appeared almost immediately across the web.

Similar groups opposed to psychiatry and clinical psychology, such as Psycho-trist Anonymous, provided even more ammunition to be used against the doctors, including details of Unwin's drink-driving arrests, complete with unflattering mug shots, and the claim that many of Renfrew's books and articles contained plagiarised material. Popular blogs repeated and embellished these allegations.

Within two days the weight of the negative publicity forced Renfrew and Unwin to respond with vehement denials of wrongdoing, which generated even more responses, both for and against.

The spotlight now fell on Audrey Farront. The whole topic of deliberate disconnections was opened up and anecdotal stories of the horrors of being a disconnect began to circulate.

Barry and Ruth, the most famous of the disconnects, signed contracts with an international pharmaceutical company to appear in advertisements launching a new anti-depressant drug for teenagers.

Tal was impatient to nail Joe Villabona, but Frank pointed out that to the general public he was a shadowy figure, not nearly as interesting as doctors abusing patients or huge companies manipulating their customers. Frank believed the best strategy was to play up Villabona's links to both Renfrew and Unwin – guilt by association. The next step was to emphasise his role as a man of mystery, who possibly was a master criminal.

The only clear head shots of Joe Villabona had been taken by Uncle Ian at the barbecue. When Tal begged him not to tell anyone that he'd provided the images of Villabona, Uncle Ian was puzzled but agreeable. 'Not even Wendy, eh?' he chuckled. 'Good to keep women a bit in the dark, you'll find.'

Uncle Ian's pictures of Joe Villabona were in extreme close-up and extraordinarily clear. With a pulsating red arrow stabbing at his image, and the words, MYSTERY MAN . . . MASTER CRIMINAL? above his head, Villabona's face began to pop up all over the internet.

During this hectic time, Tal hardly saw his mother, as Audrey had everyone at Farront working long hours to combat the barrage of attacks on the company. One morning she did waylay him and asked if he were involved in any way.

'Mum,' he said with a laugh, 'I wish. This is cyber master stuff. Way out of my league.'

Rob Anderson was harder to handle. 'All right, Tal, I'm sure you've got something to do with it. It's no co-incidence the targets are Renfrew, Unwin and Villabona. And you know at least one hacker skilled enough to break into FinagleAlert's system. What's the story?'

'There's nothing I can tell you.'

'A nice evasive answer.'

'It's the only one you'll get from me.'

Rob gave him a long, hard look. 'Remember the law of unintended consequences. Innocent people are going to suffer.'

Tal remembered Jennie's comment about people being hurt. He kept his face neutral. 'I guess you'd call it collateral damage,' he said lightly, but the thought continued to nag at him.

Tal and the others marvelled as the cyber storm George and his team had created became an overwhelming tsunami.

'This is way out of our control now,' George said with satisfaction. 'It's got a life of its own.'

On behalf of Audrey and the two doctors, Farront's law firm sent out thousands of 'cease and desist' letters promising catastrophic legal action. These attempts to intimidate or discredit their critics were largely unsuccessful, not only because of the virtual anonymity the internet provided and the sheer volume of attacks, but also because it was extremely difficult – often impossible – to establish in each case who was legally responsible. Was it an individual? The company hosting a site? The internet provider?

The storm did not abate. Social news aggregators featuring the most popular web stories had Farront and the doctors appearing on the most-viewed listing day after day. Tal noticed with grim pleasure that Joe Villabona had joined them under the designation, 'Farront's Mystery Man'. Speculation about his real identity was rife and several online gambling sites were taking wagers on who he'd turn out to be.

By the end of the second week, prodded by this intense public interest, professional medical associations and government bodies announced official inquiries into the allegations. An audit of Farront International was proposed. High profile politicians, sensing that these were potent issues in the electorate, climbed on the bandwagon too, promising all would be revealed, no matter what the cost.

'Who would have thought,' said Petra, 'we'd be quite *this* successful in such a short time?'

George wore a Cheshire cat grin. 'As a matter of fact, I did.'

TWENTY-NINE

The notoriety of The Farront Centre co-directors ensured a constant media presence outside the building, with banks of hovering air cams and bunches of reporters waiting for a glimpse of one of the major players in the drama. Clear Minds Forever's daily demonstrations and outrageous street theatre provided excellent back-up news images, guaranteeing a regular police presence that often led to arrests. And there was always footage to be gained from interviewing members of staff, or patients and their families as they came and went.

Because they'd been rated as gold subjects, Tal and Frank now attended sessions every weekday. At first they and the other research subjects were accosted by reporters and followed by air cams, but as the days went on and nobody in the group said or did anything newsworthy, the media lost interest.

On Thursday of the second week, only two security guards met the group in the foyer.

'Where's Mitch?' Tal asked Cilla. 'Is he sick?'

Cilla's mouth tightened. 'He was fired for selling his story to the jackals outside.'

When Cilla smothered a yawn, Tal said sympathetically, 'You look tired.'

'We're shorthanded, so I'm working double shifts.'

'Brad too?'

Cilla glanced over at Brad, who was leaning against the ID scanner and chatting with Frank and Scot, the guard operating the machine.

With uncharacteristic openness, Cilla said, 'Brad hasn't the energy for one shift, but he likes the overtime money. The roster has him down for two shifts, though he's a no-show half the time.'

Tal thought Brad's laziness could be useful. He was wondering whether to comment on it, or let the subject drop, when Cilla said contritely, 'Please forget I said that. We're all under a lot of pressure, but that's no excuse. It was quite unprofessional of me.'

The group was escorted to a lab and told to wait for Dr Renfrew. He was rarely involved in the day-to-day testing, but this afternoon he was overseeing an experiment to establish the pattern of brainwaves that would efficiently carry out computer commands by thought alone.

Renfrew was running late, so there was plenty of time to talk. Frank leaned over from an adjacent cubicle to ask Tal, 'Did you notice the staff seems to have shrunk? There's not as many people around.'

'Cilla told me security's shorthanded, so they're tired from working extra shifts.'

'Security's not the only one,' said Frank. 'The medical section's short-staffed too. Scot, the guy on the scanner, was saying reporters have started following staff members home and harassing their families with a tiny air cam that's so new even I haven't seen one. It's called the Snooper because it's small enough to sneak into houses and hide, so it can record private conversations.'

'Jeez,' said Tal, 'everyone will need a personal nullifier soon.'

'And Scot says it's not just the media. People are turning up and behaving like tourists visiting celebrities' homes. They climb over fences, knock on doors and peer through windows.'

'Totally weird.'

'Some of the staff are so fed up they've resigned,' said Frank. 'And others have been caught selling stuff to the media and been given the bullet.'

We started all this with our cyber war, thought Tal, *but we never meant things like this to happen to ordinary people.*

He shoved this uncomfortable idea out of his mind. 'Tomorrow's looking good,' he said, knowing Frank would realise Tal was referring to Rick's rescue.

'This might help. Brad says rumour's going around that Renfrew is heading for a nervous breakdown.'

As Frank was speaking, Dr Renfrew came into the lab. He did look like a man under tremendous pressure. His face was grey, his eyes heavy, his body language defeated. He'd obviously lost weight, as his clothes hung loosely on him. For a moment Tal felt a pang of sympathy, until he thought of Rick locked away in a cramped cell.

'We need a final meeting,' he said. 'Tonight at my place? Mum won't be there. She's working late, as usual.'

'Okay. I'll text everyone the code word.'

'Thanks. I'd do it if I could,' Tal said, angry that such a simple thing as texting was closed to him.

Being a disconnect was worse than he'd imagined. When it had first happened to Rick, Tal had privately thought his friend had overreacted, and that Petra had exaggerated her despair when her mother had confiscated her iZod. Now he'd experienced the isolation that came with being a disconnect himself, Tal wasn't so judgemental.

He realised he'd taken for granted the way his comm put him in touch with everybody he wished to contact, no matter what time it was or where they were. The device he'd held in his hand could bring the whole world to him, so he could share events as they were happening. He could surf the internet, research the most obscure subjects, laugh at the funniest videos . . .

Tal was disconcerted by the sense of loss. Giving himself a mental pep talk helped, but he still couldn't escape the feeling that everything important was passing him by. Allyx hadn't been wrong when she'd said he'd changed. Usually an optimist, now he had to fight off negative thoughts. Things he previously found mildly irritating now had the power to make him furious.

He said to Frank, 'It's driving me mad being a disconnect. How much does a phantom cost?'

'Phantoms? They're illegal,' snapped Stella from behind them. She usually had two assistants helping her set up experiments, but today she was the only person fitting subjects with wired caps designed to amplify brainwaves.

'Illegal,' she repeated. 'Do you know someone who has a phantom communicator? It should be reported to the authorities.'

Frank jerked his head to toss a strand of lank hair out of his eyes. With a friendly grin, he said, 'Hey, Stella, you're working way too hard. It isn't fair. Someone should be helping you.'

'Humph,' she grunted, but she was obviously pleased.

She began fitting Tal with a wired cap. As she tested the circuits, he said, 'Is there a problem with Dr Renfrew? He looks ill.'

Stella was indignant. 'Poor man, who wouldn't be, what with all the scurrilous attacks on his reputation? And if that isn't enough, Dr Unwin starts throwing his weight around.' With a snort, she added, 'Anyone would think Howard Unwin was the centre's senior director.'

'Stella?' Dr Renfrew called out, his tone fretful. 'I *was* hoping to start this experiment today.'

'Coming.' Stella dropped her voice to say, 'You boys are not to repeat what I said about Dr Unwin. He doesn't need any more trouble.'

'Oh, I think he does,' said Tal, once she was out of earshot.

Tal, Frank, Jennie and David were ready to start the meeting, but Petra was late. 'What excuse did you use to get here tonight?' David asked, when she finally arrived.

'I told Mum I'd be at a rehearsal to prepare for a debate we're having with another school.'

'Good luck with that!'

'It'll work. She and Dad are fully occupied at the moment. They've just heard a rival chain of garden suppliers plans to open a store in our area. Mum won't have time to –'

'Tomorrow's the day,' said Tal, interrupting, 'and it can't come too soon. I've got some news about Rick that isn't good. When I saw Luis earlier he said that because of the sensory deprivation and the drugs he's been given, Rick's starting to hallucinate. He told Luis he keeps seeing people out of the corner of his eye, but when he looks around his cell, there's no one there.'

There was silence for a moment, then David swore, and Jennie said, 'Can we really trust Luis to help us?'

'I'm sure we can,' said Tal. 'Luis is upset because Rick's getting worse each day. He says there could be permanent damage to Rick's mind if he's kept isolated in those conditions much longer.'

'Tomorrow's Friday,' said Frank. 'The media like to close the week with a big story. That's good for us.'

'I've made a checklist,' said Tal. 'I'll start with Frank and me. Luis will get us up to the fourth floor and through the security door into the psychiatric area. At the moment Rick's the only patient in the ward. He's watched by a surveillance system that's supposed to be checked regularly, but Luis says they're low on staff. As a back-up, the system's monitored twenty-four/seven by a computer programmed to detect unusual patterns of movement or sound.'

He glanced over at Frank, who raised a can of spray paint. 'Armed and ready to fire.'

'Will that work?' said Jennie doubtfully.

'The computer will record it as a malfunction,' said Frank. 'Trust me, I'm a geek.'

Tal went back to his handwritten list. 'Dr Stein?'

'He's cool,' said David. 'Just waiting for the word.'

'Jennie? Clear Minds?'

'I've met with them twice. Their leader, Hugo Z – the hairy guy with the big beard – says they're really keen to help. He joked that they'll use any excuse for a riot.'

'Clothes for Rick?'

'Jeans and a T-shirt,' said Petra. 'And thongs. He can slip them on quickly.'

'ID?'

'I used my ID as a template and made one for him,' said Frank. 'The Centre doesn't have the latest scanner system, so it should work without any trouble.'

'How about George?'

'He's all set to spread the story that something

sensational will be happening at the centre tomorrow afternoon,' said Frank.

Tal consulted his list. 'Last item – exit strategy.'

'Under control as long as David doesn't blow it,' said Petra.

'Oh, please! *Me* blow it?'

'Stop it, you two,' said Jennie. 'This is serious. Tomorrow all of us could be arrested, and end up in a cell like the one Rick's in now.'

THIRTY

Tal and Frank arrived a little early for their Friday session at The Farront Centre so they could chat with the media. Tal noticed that the number of spectators was larger than usual and that the ranks of the Clear Minds Forever protesters had swelled.

'The word is, a big story's breaking today,' said one reporter in the media crowd that had gathered around Tal and Frank. 'What do you kids know about it?'

Frank said, 'We've heard all these rumours inside the centre about the doctors blaming each other for what's happened.'

Tal added helpfully, 'People are saying Dr Renfrew and Dr Unwin are at each other's throats.'

A flurry of questions followed. Tal put up his hand. 'The only thing we know for sure is that one of the doctors will be coming out here to make an important announcement some time this afternoon.'

When Tal and Frank entered the building, Cilla, who'd had an excellent view of the media through the glass wall of the foyer, said to them, 'And what was that all about?'

Tal shrugged. 'The usual. They're after a sensational story.'

'Vultures,' said Cilla, glaring at them through the glass.

'You said they were jackals last time,' said Tal, grinning. Cilla didn't smile.

When everyone had arrived and Scot had scanned their IDs, Cilla and Brad escorted the group to the lifts.

'Aren't you hot in that?' Brad asked Frank, who was wearing a loose black woollen jumper and oversized black tracksuit pants.

'I'm feeling awfully cold. Think it's the flu.' He backed this up with a hacking cough.

Brad rapidly stepped away. 'Don't give it to me! I've got a big weekend coming up.'

Dr Renfrew was again administering the thought command experiment. Subjects who had scored particularly well in the previous day's tests were being asked one by one to control a cursor on a screen while being distracted by a random sequence of loud noises delivered through earphones, blasts of hot air to the face and eyes, and electric shocks to the fingers.

Tal had had so-so results the day before and was spared the ordeal. But Frank had scored high – 'My superior mind,' he'd chortled – so Renfrew called for him first.

While Stella was preparing Frank for the experiment, Dr Renfrew said, 'Before someone raises the issue, let me assure you that the electric shocks, delivered through the finger clips you see Stella attaching, may sting a little but are entirely harmless.'

When Frank's turn was over he came back to Tal shaking his fingers. 'Those electric shocks really hurt. The guy's a sadist.'

Tal had continued wearing the old watch he'd found in the bits-and-pieces drawer at home. He kept anxiously checking his wrist, until at last it was time. 'Now,' he said to Frank.

Tad excused himself to go to the restroom. While he waited for Frank to follow and Luis to turn up, Tal looked himself over in the mirror. His sandy hair was too long, but he'd had no opportunity to get it cut. Nor had he kept up his training regimen, so he wasn't as fit as usual.

'This cyber-warring takes up a lot of time,' he told his reflection.

'Talking to yourself is the first sign of madness,' said Frank, coming in.

Luis was right behind him. 'Everything's all clear at the moment. You ready?'

'Ready as we'll ever be.'

Heart racing, Tal walked quickly with Frank and Luis towards the lifts. On the floor above them, Rick was alone in his cell, with no idea that at this moment his rescue was underway. Perhaps it was good that Rick didn't have his hopes up, because there were so many things that could go wrong. Maybe Dr Unwin had suddenly decided to pay a call on his captive patient, or Cilla had swapped guard duty with Brad, or . . .

'Tal, come on!' One of the three lifts had arrived at their floor and stood invitingly open. To access the restricted upper floors, Luis's palm print was required. He slapped his right hand onto the reader. The lift started its smooth ascent.

Brad would be their first obstacle, as he was rostered to do his extra shift on the fourth floor. Tal said to Luis, 'How did it go with Brad?'

'You were right, he *is* a lazy bastard. "Go get a coffee, take it easy, I'll keep an eye on things," I said. He'd gone before I'd finished speaking.'

When the lift door hissed open, Luis peered out before motioning to Frank and Tal to follow him. A forlorn nameplate at the deserted reception desk announced that Gloria should be sitting there.

Two days earlier, when hacking into the centre's database to check who was authorised to enter the restricted fourth floor, George had discovered that Gloria had resigned. Luis confirmed this, saying, 'Gloria's one tough lady. She could put up with being hounded by reporters, but when she found one of those little air cams hiding under her kitchen bench, it was the final straw.'

Sorry, Gloria, we lost your job for you.

'Tal? You coming?'

They hurried down a luxuriously carpeted hallway to a heavy metal door. Luis stared into the iris reader and the lock disengaged. 'He's in cell one, at the very end of the corridor. There's a switch on the wall to unlock the door.'

As they ran down the corridor, Frank tugged a ski mask and a spray can from the back pocket of his voluminous pants. When they reached cell one, he pulled the mask on. After a test spray of the paint, Frank said, 'Okay, open it.'

Tal threw the switch and Frank leapt through the door. Locating the lens of the surveillance camera in the ceiling, he blinded it with a blast of black paint. Another blast choked the microphone beside it.

Following him into the cell, Tal found Rick curled in a foetal position on the bed. He didn't stir.

'I'll wake him up,' Tal said to Frank, who was stripping off his oversized jumper. 'You get his clothes ready.'

Under his jumper, Frank was wearing the T-shirt Petra had provided for Rick. The jeans were wound around his waist and the thongs were shoved into the side pockets of his tracksuit pants.

Tal shook Rick's shoulder. 'Hey, Rick, wake up. We're here to take you home.'

Slowly he opened bleary eyes, then slid them shut again. 'Go away.'

'Rick! Come on!' Tal hauled him into a sitting position. 'We haven't got much time.'

Rick squinted at him. 'Is it really you?'

'Yes, it's really me. And Frank. Can you stand up? We've got to get you changed.'

With Tal's assistance, Rick got to his feet and stood, swaying. 'I'm dizzy.'

Getting Rick into jeans, T-shirt and thongs was like dressing a sleepy child. He tried to cooperate, but he was clumsy and uncoordinated.

Attaching the fake ID, Frank said, 'Do you think he can walk?'

Rick had closed his eyes again. Tal took his arm, led him to the metal basin and splashed his face with cold water. 'We've got to get you out of here. Can you walk?'

Rick nodded. 'Sure.'

Frank put on his huge jumper again, shoved the sleeves up past his elbows, and grabbed Rick's other arm. 'Let's go!'

They half-dragged Rick down the corridor to the security door where Luis was waiting.

Luis got out of the lift at the third floor, leaving them to continue to the foyer.

'He's lost a thong,' said Frank, wrenching the remaining one off Rick's foot. 'You'll have to go barefoot, mate.'

The second floor held medical offices and examining rooms. It was always busy, so when the lift stopped a bunch of people got on, forcing them to move to the back. One guy in a white medical coat frowned at Rick. Tal checked his name tag. Felix. It meant nothing to him, but still Tal felt a shiver of alarm. The guy looked away. No one else seemed to notice that Rick was semi-conscious and would have fallen without Tal and Frank propping him up.

At the foyer level half the passengers got off, including Felix, who hurried away without a backward glance. The people still in the lift were continuing down to the underground parking, so Tal and Frank had to shuffle Rick through them. 'He's sick,' Tal told one woman who stared at Rick with concern.

He stood compliantly between them as Tal scanned the foyer, praying Cilla wouldn't be there. They could easily fool Scot, the guard on the scanner, but Cilla would know something was wrong immediately.

Tal's heart sank. There she was outside the entrance, arguing with reporters and cam operators. Beside her, Scot stood with his hands in his pockets, looking bored. Cilla gestured vehemently at a cluster of Cyclops-eyed air cams pressed against the glass wall, peering into the building.

With relief he saw Petra and Jennie with the Clear Minds contingent who were obviously preparing to stage a demonstration.

'Shit!' said Frank. 'Here comes trouble.'

A second lift was disgorging passengers. Roughly pushing his way through them was a furious Howard Unwin. As he got close to them, Tal saw that Rick's wild punch had left the doctor's lip painfully swollen. Behind Unwin came Carter Renfrew, looking ill.

'What the hell do you think you're doing with my patient?' Unwin snarled. Hearing his angry tone, several people stopped to watch.

'*Our* patient,' said Renfrew.

Unwin ignored him. 'You have no right to remove anyone under my care from the premises.' Rick shrank back as Unwin attempted to grab his shoulder. 'You're coming with me, young man.'

There was an interested murmur from the small but growing crowd.

'No, he isn't.' Tal put out his free hand and shoved Unwin hard in the chest. 'You and Dr Renfrew have been treating Rick like a lab rat, not a patient.'

Red with fury, Unwin raised his clenched fists. 'Keep your hands off me, boy!'

'If you're going to have a fight,' said Frank, 'there's quite an audience.' He pointed towards the entrance.

Not only was the cluster of air cams growing, the Clear Minds Forever members, most wearing masks, had collected at the sliding glass doors. Petra had disappeared, but Jennie was there beside Hugo Z, who was urging them on. Paying no attention to Cilla and Scot's efforts to move them away from the entrance, the group began to chant, 'Clear minds forever! And ever! And ever!'

'One last chance,' Unwin ground out. 'Leave Rick and get the hell out of here. If you do that, I won't press charges.'

'Rick's the one who'll be pressing charges against you,' Tal retorted.

'Who'd believe a word?' Unwin gestured disdainfully at Rick, who sagged between them. 'Take a look. He's obviously incapable of rational thought. Anything he says will be totally unreliable.'

'Howard, we went too far,' said Renfrew. 'Let him go.' Unwin ignored him.

A lift opened and Brad ambled out. Seeing the doctors, he made a half-hearted effort to tuck in his uniform shirt. 'Someone said there was an emergency.'

Unwin glared at him. 'Get the other guards in here – they're useless outside. They can deal with these fools while you take my patient back to his room.'

Tal saw Cilla look up as Brad spoke to her through a protected security link. She activated the entrance doors long enough to allow her and Scot to slip through.

'Look!' said Frank, fascinated. 'I haven't seen a Snooper until now.'

The guards hadn't entered the building alone. A swarm of miniature air cams whipped past them, and spread out across the foyer.

The clump of spectators who'd been watching the confrontation scattered as a formation of Snoopers zoomed towards them.

Unwin swiped at one that was diving to inspect his face. 'You!' he yelled at Cilla. 'Get rid of them!'

'Sir, I don't know how.'

'They're recording everything we say and do,' said Renfrew. He looked up at the little device hovering above his head. 'This is Dr Carter Renfrew of The Farront Centre. I'm making this official. We're sending Rick Lawrence home.'

'You stupid –' Unwin broke off and spun around to face Cilla and the other two guards. 'Escort my patient back to the fourth floor immediately.'

'No, don't,' said Renfrew. 'And that's an order.'

Unwin gave a contemptuous snort. 'And take Dr Renfrew with you. He's obviously suffered a breakdown.'

'That's absolute nonsense, and you know it!'

'I'm admitting Dr Renfrew to the psychiatric ward. Take him there at once.'

'The moment you lay a hand on me, you'll be fired!'

While the guards paused, irresolute, Tal whispered to Frank, 'Let's go.'

They hoisted Rick up and began an awkward run across the foyer to the sliding doors. They skidded to a stop at the scanning station. 'I think I can work the doors,' said Frank as he leaned over the scanner to eyeball the control panel.

Glancing back over his shoulder, Tal saw that none of the Snoopers had followed them. They were concentrated on the physical fight that had broken out between the two doctors. As Tal watched, Renfrew shoulder-charged Unwin and they both went down in an untidy tangle of arms and legs.

'You kids, stop!'

'Frank, it's Cilla. She's after us. Hurry up.'

The entrance doors slid fully open. Led by Hugo Z, Jennie and a wave of Clear Minds Forever supporters swept in, swamping Cilla. Although she struggled wildly, the momentum of the charge pushed her back across the lobby.

As soon as the way was clear, Tal and Frank dragged Rick out into a media pandemonium. Reporters raised their voices above the shrieking sirens of squad cars and the noise from a crowd of spectators, all of whom seemed greatly entertained by Grandeur Media's contribution – live images of the fight projected on the wall of the building.

Petra, who'd been waiting for them just outside the entrance, looked at Rick with horror. 'Oh, poor Rick. What've they done to you?'

'We've got to get moving,' said Tal urgently.

'Over there,' said Petra, pointing to David, who was signalling from the edge of the thickening crowd. 'Dr Stein's waiting in his car on the access road.'

'Awesome, dudes,' said David admiringly when they reached him. He looked at Rick with concern. 'He's totally out of it?'

'Pretty well. Frank and I will carry him, if you go ahead and make a way for us.'

'I've got two urgent messages for you,' said David, 'but they can wait until Rick's in Dr Stein's car.'

Petra and David forged through the crush, at times pushing and shoving to make a path. Petra flung herself into the task, yelling 'Medical emergency! Make way!' whenever anyone showed a reluctance to move.

They were in sight of Dr Stein's vehicle, an anonymous dark blue sedan, when Jennie caught up with them.

'Did you see what happened with the fight?' Tal asked.

She chuckled. 'The cops arrived and arrested them both. Clear Minds formed a cordon of dishonour, and applauded Unwin and Renfrew all the way to the squad car.'

Dr Stein was waiting impatiently. 'Put him in the back.' He gave Rick a quick examination. Grim-faced, he said, 'I'm taking him straight to my clinic. Could one of you travel with him?'

'I'll go,' said Jennie.

'What about Rick's grandmother?' Tal asked Dr Stein.

'I've spoken to her and explained why Rick's being moved to my clinic. She'll be meeting us there.'

'Omigod,' said Petra, 'if I saw my grandson's doctors rolling around on the floor fighting each other, I'd want Rick moved away from them quick as.'

Watching the car speed away, Tal said to David, 'You said I had two urgent messages?'

'One's from your mum. She called the centre and when they couldn't find you, she called around our parents. George told his dad he could get a message to you. He passed it on to me, so here it is: Go home immediately. Your mother says it's vital.'

'What's the second message?'

'It's from George,' said David, 'and it's the same – go home – except he wants to meet you outside first. George says he's got something sensational to do with Villabona. He wouldn't say what it was.'

THIRTY-ONE

Audrey's luxurious Mercedes was parked in front of the house. Rob steered around it and pulled into the driveway, stopping near Tal and George, who were in a huddle by the garage door.

Leaping out of his compact electric car, plastered with FinagleAlert logos, he said urgently, 'Tal, what are you doing out here? Didn't Grace get you? She's trying to cope with Audrey Farront and Joe Villabona by herself.' He changed gear to say, 'And by the way, congratulations on your activities this afternoon. It's all over the internet. Renfrew and Unwin's reputations are in tatters.'

'George has got hold of something that will nail Joe Villabona too.'

George was his usual dishevelled self. The many pockets on his frayed shorts bulged with mystery contents, and his grubby T-shirt had a coffee stain dribbled down the front.

Rob looked George up and down, his disapproval plain. 'I've done some research on you, George Everett. We'll talk later about hacking into FinagleAlert's database.'

'Don't blame me. Blame your security.'

'Forget the break-in,' said Tal, impatient with both of them. 'Rob, look at what we've got on Villabona. It hasn't been released yet, but George says it will be any moment.'

As he leafed through the pages Tal thrust at him, Rob's eyes widened. 'These are internal Interpol documents. Highly confidential documents. How did you get them?'

'I'm a cyber god,' said George with a smirk.

Tal's mother looked distraught when she opened the front door. 'Hello, George,' she said absently, too upset to wonder why he was there. 'Tal, what took you so long? Audrey and Joe arrived almost two hours ago. Audrey's taking legal action against you for initiating the cyber attack on Farront. And naming me, Rob and Victor as accomplices. I've said it isn't true, but Audrey and Joe claim to have irrefutable evidence.'

Looking past them, she spied Rob in the front seat of his car, talking on his comm. 'Isn't Rob coming in? I need him here.'

'He has to make a couple of calls.'

'At a time like this?' she said, near tears.

'It'll be okay, Mum.'

'It won't, you know! Audrey's just fired me. I don't have an income, and we'll need lawyers to defend the charges, and you know how much that will cost. And the fracas this morning at the centre . . .' She shook her head. 'I'm glad you rescued Rick, but you've just given Audrey another reason to sue.'

'Awesome, wasn't it?' said George, beaming. 'Tal and the others are heroes, don't you think?'

'Heroes who could find themselves locked in a cell,' she said bitterly.

'Mum, it really is okay.'

Rob got out of his car and hurried over to them. 'Grace, let's go in and slay the dragons.' He nodded to Tal and George. 'All set.'

Tal followed his mother and Rob into the living room, George tagging behind with the documents tucked under one arm. The wall screen, audio off, was showing images taken at The Farront Centre that morning. Caught by Snoopers, Tal saw himself and Frank supporting Rick as Carter Renfrew mouthed the words, 'We're sending Rick Lawrence home.' Footage of the undignified brawl between the two doctors followed.

Audrey got to her feet, her grey eyes steely. 'Well, young man,' she said to Tal, 'you're going to find the unconscionable cyber war you had the temerity to launch against me very costly. Very costly indeed. As for your disgraceful shenanigans today –' she threw up her hands – 'you've done your best to destroy the careers of two fine doctors.'

Joe Villabona, who had remained comfortably seated in a lounge chair, added, 'And you've also ruined your mother's career, I hope you realise that.'

'I rather think that was your work, Joe,' was Grace's acerbic response.

Audrey was inspecting George's appearance with obvious displeasure. 'And you are . . .?'

'My friend, George Everett,' said Tal.

'You can leave, Mr Everett. This has nothing to do with you.'

'You heard her,' said Villabona, when George didn't move. 'Get out, kid.'

'Last time I looked,' said Rob, 'this was Grace's house. It's her decision who stays or leaves.'

'You'll want George to stay,' Tal told Audrey. 'He has some interesting information for you.'

Villabona put his hands on the arms of the lounge chair, preparing to stand. Smiling arrogantly, he warned George, 'Don't make me get up and throw you out.'

'Mr Villabona, does the name Javier Jiminez sound familiar to you?' asked Tal.

'Or Miguel Cruz?' added George.

Villabona's face went blank. He got slowly to his feet, his dark eyes fixed on Tal.

'Who are these people, Joe?' Audrey asked. 'Do you recognise the names?'

'Complete strangers to me.'

Tal took the documents from George and gestured with them. 'That's odd, because right here Interpol lists those names as two of your aliases.'

Both Tal's mother and Audrey looked stunned. 'Interpol?' Audrey said.

'The International Criminal Police Organization,' George put in helpfully. 'Jiminez and Cruz are wanted in several countries for fraud and murder.'

Villabona was balanced on the balls of his feet, ready to move in any direction. 'A stupid case of mistaken identity.'

Even though he knew he was no match for Villabona physically, Tal moved to block the doorway.

'The internet's a wonderful thing,' said Rob. 'It flashed your face all over the globe, and even though I'm sure you've made changes to your appearance, it was only a matter of time before you were recognised.'

'This can't be true! Joe?'

'No, Audrey, of course it isn't true. There's not a shred of proof I've ever done anything criminal.'

'I'm betting the doctors will turn against you,' said Tal. 'And what about the Brownbolt executives and your deal to sell Farront's research data to them?'

Audrey looked ill. 'Joe?'

'These are vicious lies, Audrey.'

Joe checked his comm and nodded to Tal. 'They're here.'

Tal sprinted down the hall and opened the front door. 'Down there,' he said and gestured back to the living room. 'He's about to leave.'

Villabona shot out into the hallway, took one panicked look at the police officers, and turned to run in the other direction. Tal was faster than anyone. He brought Villabona down with a flying tackle outside the kitchen.

The officers hauled Villabona to his feet. 'Joseph Villabona, we have a warrant for your arrest.'

THIRTY-TWO

After Rick's rescue, Tal and Frank were web heroes for a few days, but then they were supplanted by the next sensational story.

After two weeks in Dr Stein's clinic, the doctor agreed that Rick was well enough to go home, although his therapy would continue for some time and he wouldn't be back at school until next term. Rick was still terribly shaken by the experience, but he was surprised by just how comforted he was to be back in his familiar home.

Three days after Rick's return, Thelma planned a quiet welcome home dinner for Saturday evening. The guest list was restricted to the Five plus George and Frank.

Meeting up with Tal outside Rick's place, Petra said, 'Omigod! How about Audrey Farront's big apology? Awesome! She was really crawling, promising all that money.'

'She had to,' said Tal. 'There are zillions of people threatening to sue the company.'

David and Jennie joined them. 'Don't tell me Audrey didn't know about Villabona,' said David. 'She's as guilty as he is.'

'I don't think so,' said Tal. 'Mum said Audrey was totally sucked in, like most people.'

Tal's mother had told him that Audrey had been shattered, both by Villabona's duplicity and by her own poor judgement. In an attempt to head off legal action against Farront, she had decided to make an abject public apology and to guarantee generous financial settlements to those who had been disconnected as part of Villabona's scheme. The Farront Centre would be shut down, although Audrey promised that the company would continue to fund research by supporting studies carried out by reputable organisations.

'What's happening with your mum?' Jennie asked Tal. 'Last week you weren't sure if she still had a job.'

'Audrey's promoted her to the new position she was angling for, but I don't think Mum will stay with Farront. She says she doesn't feel she can ever trust Audrey again.'

'After all this,' said David, 'who *can* you trust? Even Rick's grandmother let him down.'

'He doesn't blame her,' said Petra. 'Dr Stein helped him understand how it happened.'

David gave her a sceptical look. 'You're telling me Rick confided in you? I can't see it.'

Petra glared at him. 'I asked Rick how he felt about Thelma and he told me. Is that so hard to believe?'

'Are you lot coming in?' Rick asked from the front door. 'George and Frank have been here for ages.'

David bounded up the steps and slapped him on the shoulder. 'Dude, looking good.'

'You sure are,' said Tal, thinking that two weeks in Dr Stein's care had made a huge difference. Rick was still too thin, but his eyes were clear and he was relaxed and smiling.

Jennie gave him a hug and Petra planted a big kiss on his cheek. 'David doesn't believe you told me you didn't blame Thelma for anything,' she said.

'Petra beat it out of me,' said Rick with a grin. 'It was useless to resist.'

Inside they were met by Rick's grandfather, Les, who looked almost his old self. He shook hands with each of them. 'I haven't had the chance to thank you properly for all you did for Rick. Thelma and I are so grateful he has true friends like you and the other two boys.'

They trooped down the hall to the kitchen to say hello to Thelma, who was busy cooking, while George and Frank sat at the table scoffing down miniature sausage rolls.

'Just in time for the show,' said George. 'Frank and I have compiled highlights of Villabona, Renfrew and Unwin.'

Jennie sent a doubtful look in Rick's direction. 'Are you sure this is a good idea?'

'No worries,' said Frank, popping another sausage roll into his mouth. He added indistinctly, 'Rick cleared it with Dr Stein. He says it's okay.'

'Dinner will be a while yet,' said Thelma, 'so we can see it now.'

Tal said to George, 'I've got a message for you from Rob Anderson.'

George looked apprehensive. 'It's about hacking into the FinagleAlert system, isn't it?'

'Rob says that since it was to help Rick, he's going to act like it never happened. But don't do it again.'

George gave a relieved grin. 'I reckon Anderson's in a good mood because of the wedding. When is it? Next weekend?'

'Don't ask.'

Out of habit, Tal sounded unenthusiastic, but he wasn't really. After the events of the last weeks, Rob marrying his mother didn't seem such a bad idea after all.

George and Frank's video was going to be shown on the living room screen. On the way there, Jennie whispered to Tal, 'I wonder how Thelma's going to feel, watching the guys who fooled her into having Rick locked away.'

'Angry, I guess. And maybe a bit embarrassed.'

'Talk about embarrassed,' said Petra, 'have you heard about Dodder's mother? Was her face red! She had to resign from the cyber bullying committee when she found out Maryann was behind half the attacks.'

'Dodder's going around calling herself a cyber goddess and saying she saved Rick,' said David with disgust. 'I told you we should never have let her into the group.'

'It was good we did,' said Frank. 'Maryann worked really hard.'

'Oh, *please*!' said David. 'It's always about *her* – she wasn't there to help Rick.'

'But she did help Rick,' said Jennie, 'so it doesn't matter why.'

'Sit anywhere,' said Les as they entered the room. He added with a chuckle, 'Except for my chair.'

When everyone was seated, George said to Thelma and Les, 'No offence, but this setup of yours is pretty primitive. I'd be glad to help you upgrade.'

'That won't be necessary, dear,' said Thelma. 'We're quite happy with what we've got.' Rick rolled his eyes.

'Okay, guys,' said George, 'you're not seeing this at its best, but it'll have to do.'

The screen announced it was a George Everett production. 'What happened to my name?' Frank asked. 'We're co-producers, remember?'

'It's cool. I'll fix it later.'

'There's a word for you, George,' said Frank, scowling.

'And the word is megalomaniac,' said Petra.

Villabona appeared on the screen. Most of the footage dated from his arrest. Before that, except for

Uncle Ian's close-ups at the barbecue, Villabona had avoided being photographed.

Tal was sure the others shared his feeling of satisfaction at seeing the images of Villabona in custody. When being hustled in and out of cars for his court appearances, he maintained a blank expression, ignoring questions shouted by reporters and jeers from the crowd. In front of the judge, Villabona was stone-faced and silent, leaving his high-powered lawyers to speak for him.

Villabona was facing multiple charges, including the attempted murder of Victor O'Dell. The driver of the ute had been arrested for another offence, and when his fingerprints matched those found in the abandoned vehicle, he had implicated the small-time criminal who had contacted him to arrange the hit. This second man led the police to Villabona.

No matter how skilled Villabona's lawyers might be, it seemed highly unlikely that he would ever be a free man again. The web of secrecy he had woven about himself had been destroyed. Almost every day further damning evidence came to light. And even if Villabona served his prison time and was eventually released, there were other countries waiting in line to bring him to trial for crimes he'd committed within their borders.

There was much more material available on the two doctors, particularly for Carter Renfrew, who'd had a higher profile career than the psychiatrist.

Seeing the two doctors on the screen, Thelma

exclaimed, 'How could I have let them pull the wool over my eyes? Rick, I'm so sorry!'

'You don't have to keep saying that,' Rick mumbled, obviously uncomfortable.

After showing Renfrew and Unwin at the height of their success, the most recent footage provided a stark contrast. Now the two men were utterly discredited professionally, and this catastrophic fall was reflected in their grim, unsmiling expressions.

'I like this next bit,' said George, 'where they try to convince everyone they're good guys.'

'Not everyone,' said David. 'They'll be aiming to influence potential jurors.'

Dr Unwin, facing the prospect of serious prison time for Rick's unlawful detention and treatment, announced that he'd found God. He supported this assertion with several tearful appearances on popular evangelists' shows.

'What a hypocrite,' said Petra. No one contradicted her.

For his part, Renfrew claimed to have discovered the importance of good works. He undertook to devote himself to the care of the underprivileged. As proof of this, he was shown working in a homeless shelter, serving hot meals to the poor, and assisting in a free clinic for sick children.

'Another total hypocrite,' Petra announced.

'I'm not so sure,' said Tal. 'At the end, he wanted to let Rick go.'

ater, after dinner, Les and Thelma settled down to watch television, while Rick and the others went up to his room.

'I see you and Allyx are back together again,' said David from his position on the floor. 'How's that working out?'

'Fine,' said Tal.

That wasn't altogether true. Things weren't quite the same between them. It was as if being a disconnect had subtly changed Tal. He asked more questions and thought more deeply. Allyx had been driven to ask, 'Can't you just relax and enjoy things?'

'I'm trying,' was all Tal could say.

Sprawled on the bed, Rick said, 'The other day Dr Stein asked me what I'd learned from the experience I'd gone through.'

'And?' said Jennie.

'I'll tell you in a minute. Right now I'd like to know what everyone else thinks.'

'Well,' said Petra, 'one thing I know for sure – not having a comm is foul.'

'Running a cyber war's a blast,' said George.

Frank shook his head. 'That's nothing next to taking a huge risk and getting away with it, like when Tal and I got Rick out of the centre. That was a *real* blast.'

'Jennie?' said Rick.

She frowned. 'I'm not sure. Belonging, maybe. Like when we were together at David's house and the cops were outside. Or even when I was with the Clear Minds people and we pushed our way into the foyer.'

She shrugged. 'I can't explain it.'

Tal said, 'If there's one thing I've learned, it's what Rob meant when he warned me that there's a law of unintended consequences. We never meant to, but we did change people's lives. And usually not in good ways. Like all the staff at The Farront Centre losing their jobs because it's closing.'

'Heavy,' said David. He added with a grin, 'What I've learned is you've got to be connected. Ask Rick. You're nothing if you aren't connected.'

'Okay, Rick,' said Petra. 'Your turn.'

'After I was disconnected, I remember telling Thelma that once I was connected again, I'd be fine. Now I know that being connected is important, but it's not everything.'

'So what is?' Petra asked.

'Being part of the Five. Having friends like you. Knowing that whatever happens, none of us will let the others down.'

'Watch it, dude,' said David, 'or you'll have me in tears.'

Petra stared at him. 'Omigod,' she said, 'David really means it!'

ACKNOWLEDGEMENTS

With appreciation for their valuable contributions to *Gotta B*, my deep thanks to my agent and dear friend, Margaret Connolly and to my charmingly indefatigable editor, Kimberley Bennett. Thanks also to Rachelle Matherne and Jeanie Kim for their advice.

Ads R Us
Claire Carmichael

Ads R Us is set in a modern industrialised city in the near future, where advertising is a constant stream of inescapable noise and information, and corporations sponsor everything from music to schools.

Barrett Trent has been raised in total isolation from mainstream society in an eco-cult called Simplicity. After the death of his uncle, he goes to live in the city with his rich and powerful Aunt Cara and Uncle Adrian, and spoiled cousin, Taylor.

But his aunt and uncle have a hidden agenda – there is a lot to gain from uncovering the effects of advertising on an untouched mind. Barrett is the perfect guinea pig for their experiments.

But Barrett may prove harder to crack than they think – and Taylor is certainly not the cousin he expected …

**Notable Book for Older Readers
in 2007 CBCA Awards**